Out of the Shadow

By J. K. Winn

Dear
Ave :
May you always
live life Out of
the Shadows.
Thank you for your
love + support.

with love,
Jamie

Chapter One

She had been dreaming … perhaps was dreaming still. But the moment David crawled into bed beside her, the dream slipped away. Becca stretched, glanced at the clock, which read 3:02, and snuggled up to the warm body next to hers. Then she caught a whiff of scent that was strangely disorienting. His hand came down over her mouth.

Surprised, she made a muted appeal, tried to squirm out from under him. Was he being playful in the middle of the night? She couldn't imagine it.

The hand pressed down harder. "Don't move or scream, or I'll kill you," said a muffled voice through what appeared to be a ski mask.

Becca reacted with the horror of a dreamer unable to run from her assailant. Wild with fear, she made an effort to cry out, but it was useless with the hand covering her mouth. She jerked her head to the side to loosen his grip, but he held on firmly. She was at his mercy.

Was this actually happening to her, or was it all part of a horrific nightmare? She pounded palms into the intruder's chest, but with his superior strength, he managed to roll on top of her, pinning her beneath him. Barely able to breathe under him, she pressed her legs together in a desperate attempt to keep him out. But he jerked up her nightgown, tore off her panties as if they were paper, pried open her legs. And violently forced himself into her.

Becca screamed, fought back, tried to dislodge him, but he clamped down on her arms with his. Another scream escaped her lips.

"Shut up," he said, "or you're dead."

She swallowed the cry that rose to her throat, stifling the desire to kick and flail. Her brain raced, her muscles tensed. "Please God, please God, please God," raced through her mind with the insistence of a demanding child. A loud buzzing sound filled her head.

He groaned and moved harder against her. Her insides felt as if they were being torched. Pain followed every thrust. The more she struggled, the more it hurt, but she couldn't lie still for long. He continued to hump steadily, ignoring her efforts to dislodge him, until she managed to free a hand long enough to smash her palm against his jaw and, with all of her might, shove him away. He reached up and slapped her across the face with such force, tears sprang into her eyes. It was over for her, there was no winning this war. She shut down her mind, felt her awareness leave her body; became numb to his ongoing assault. After what seemed like an eternity, he grunted and collapsed onto her, his body slick with sweat and sickening to the touch.

The clock showed 3:15 a.m. when he finally lifted off her.

"Be quiet," he snapped. "Don't move or call out, if you know what's good for you."

Becca watched, stunned, while he hurriedly

pulled up his pants. Even in the dark with his back to her and a ski mask obliterating his face, something seemed eerily familiar about him. But what was it? Did she know her attacker?

Before she could consider, he turned back to her and said, "You haven't seen the last of me." Then he was gone.

Becca lay paralyzed for a few agonizing minutes. She rolled onto her side in a fetal position, wrapping her arms around her knees, clutching herself. Every cell in her body quivered, every muscle quaked. Bile rose, sickening and sour, at the thought of the rape. Horror gripped her; nausea followed. She felt defiled. Disgusted. With slow, deep breaths, she tried to calm the churning inside.

Minutes passed before she could lever herself up and lower her legs over the edge of the bed. A burning sensation flamed in her crotch, causing tears of fear and fury to run down her face, dampening her nightgown.

She listened closely, reassured by the silence around her, then stumbled from bed on legs that shook like jelly, tripping over bedclothes tossed carelessly to the floor. She had to steady herself with a hand on the footboard before she could tiptoe toward the living room.

All at once, she remembered David. What had happened to him? Why hadn't he been there to protect her? Another wave of terror gripped her and she wrapped her arms around herself. Something was terribly wrong. David might not be the most attentive husband on the planet, but he would have reacted to the break-in. He would have done something.

Becca hesitated at the entrance to the living room before working up the nerve to switch on the overhead light. She immediately spotted David sprawled across the sofa in a pool of blood.

In a panic, she rushed to his side and tried to take a pulse. Although faint, his heart still beat. Relieved, she tore open his blood-soaked shirt and pants. The extent of the wounds on his chest and stomach could not be determined because of the blood, which covered his body and dribbled onto the carpet.

She rushed into the kitchen and wet down a towel, returning to soak up a profusion of blood. With the towel pressed against a deep gash on his belly, she hoped to arrest further blood loss.

Still maintaining her pressure on the towel, she scooped David's cell off the coffee table with her free hand and dialed 911.

"Please help me," she wailed into the receiver. "I've been raped and my husband's been stabbed."

When the police and two paramedics thundered into the apartment through the door she had left unlocked, Becca was busy performing CPR on David. A policewoman had to tear her away from his side to prevent her from interfering with the paramedics' efforts. Huddled in the corner with the cop by her side, she again glanced at the clock on the mantle: 3:42 a.m. So much had happened in such a short time, it seemed surreal. It stuck her as strange that she could measure such a monumental life change in mere minutes.

The paramedics immediately went to work, attempting to revive David. After vain attempts at cardiac resuscitation with shots of adrenaline and epinephrine, and shocks from a defibrillator, one of the paramedics turned to her.

His flat eyes told her everything.

Chapter Two

A hand rose above the heads of my attentive audience. I stopped my lecture mid-sentence and glanced out over the rows of well-groomed professionals. I'm tickled that more than fifty of my peers saw fit to attend my seminar on Repressed Memory Syndrome at this swanky Hilton Hotel on City Avenue in suburban Philadelphia. Using Rachel Robbin, a.k.a. Rebecca Rosen, as an example of the disorder might have been the attraction. All eyes are on me, their curiosity obvious.

"Do you have a question? Please stand. I'm having trouble seeing you."

A powerfully built man stood up. He wore a charcoal gray pinstriped suit with a white shirt and a yellow tie.

"Dr. Abrams, I find Rebecca Rosen's case quite interesting. I think it's a clever way to present Repressed Memory Syndrome without a dry factual lecture, but it would be helpful to know your definition of this condition and how it applies to Becca."

This stranger exuded a certain quiet confidence.

"Your name please?" I asked him.

"Farley. Dr. Adrian Farley."

"Dr. Farley, may I call you Adrian?"

"Certainly."

"Feel free to call me Sarah." I took a sip of water to soothe my parched throat. "As I'm sure you must be aware, in Repressed Memory Syndrome, a child unconsciously suppresses traumatic memories of a crisis or an event, because it was too brutal or frightening to integrate into their developing sense of self. Often these memories don't surface again until much later, when another equally dramatic set of circumstances triggers a reaction that can bring them gradually back into consciousness. Becca's case was straight out of the textbook on Repressed Memory Syndrome. If you give me a chance, I'm sure by the conclusion of the seminar you'll appreciate the power of it."

He nodded. "Your lecture is so detailed. How were you able to glean this much information?"

I smiled inwardly, thinking about Rachel-how open she had been under the circumstances, and how trusting. Of course, she didn't reveal everything to me immediately. But in due course she was more than willing to share what she was going through. The risks she had taken taught me so much about accessing my own inner strength and resourcefulness.

"Rebecca was an excellent and thorough reporter. She remembered much of what happened to her in detail."

Adrian offered me a cock-eyed smile. "Aren't you embellishing her story at all?"

"Perhaps a little. But I have little need for hyperbole in describing Becca's situation, and I never alter facts. I took copious notes and recorded our therapy sessions with her permission. I had a great deal of material to work with. Any other questions?"

Adrian Farley shook his head and retook his seat behind the heavy-set social workers I had spoken with before my two-day seminar began. One of the Bobbsey twins, I couldn't remember whether it was Arlene or Darlene, raised a hand. Not only are these two women nearly identical, but they dressed in the same dowdy fashion, with floral print dresses and cordovan loafers. "Sarah, you seem quite comfortable using the patient's name. Is that ethical?"

Exposing Rachel to danger was the last thing I'd do. The frightened child in her touched a deep nerve within me. I would never openly share one of my clients' identities, especially not Rachel's. She was still at risk, as far as I knew. "Naturally it would break my code of confidentiality to use my patient's real name. Rebecca Rosen is a pseudonym. I have disguised all but the guilty in my cast of characters."

An anorexic-looking younger woman stood up. "You failed to mention anything about Becca's appearance."

"You're right. She's a petite and an exceptionally attractive woman with shoulder-length, red hair, and expressive green eyes."

"And when exactly did this rape and murder occur?"

"Four years ago this coming July."

I glanced about the room. "Any further questions?" No one addressed me, so I resumed my lecture.

The ambulance skidded to the curb at the Thomas Jefferson Hospital Emergency Room. Inside, a doctor pronounced David dead, sending him off in the direction of the morgue. The gurney had barely disappeared from view when Becca was escorted to an examination room for a painful gynecological exam. Her head still spinning, she had only enough time to zip up her jeans before a couple of police officers showed up to question her about the rape and murder. Then she waited. And waited. And waited. What a relief when her friend and co-worker, Angela Petrocelli, rushed in to give her a hug and take her home.

Fortunately for Becca, Angela's strong arms supported her as she hobbled to the car and did most of the heavy lifting when they stopped by her apartment, now a taped-off crime scene, to pick up personal items. Angela took charge of rounding up the suitcases and filling them with needed belongings, but it was up to Becca to coax her cat, Cecil, out from under the bed. She had to tempt him with a treat before she could place him in a carrier.

After one last stop, at Walgreen's to pick up a tranquilizer prescribed by the ER doctor, they drove past run-down row houses next to stately columned post-Colonial buildings to arrive at the redevelopment area of large brick townhouses where Angela lived. Once inside Angela's upstairs apartment, Becca released Cecil in the guest room, where he bolted from the cage and dove behind the burnt orange futon. Lacking the strength to lure him from his lair, she meandered into the living room and took a seat on an overstuffed, beige corduroy couch, with her feet up on the slightly scratched but serviceable mahogany coffee table.

"I'd like a drink," Becca said, settling in.

Angela stared at her through wary brown eyes with dark circles beneath. Although the same age as Becca, Angela bore the appearance of someone more mature. Perhaps it was the lines etching parentheses around her mouth, or the sprinkling of gray in her ebony hair. Whatever it was, it always made Becca feel she was with a much wiser woman.

"Do you think that's a good idea with the Lorazepam the doctor prescribed?"

No fooling Angela. As a nurse, she would know. "Probably not, but I could sure use a glass of wine."

"Okay, you're the boss." Angela poured her a glass of rich red merlot.

Becca downed the alcoholic elixir with the urgency of someone lost in the dessert. Then she washed down the medication with a second glass. The mixture proved potent. Angela helped her into bed minutes before she fell into a deep sleep.

She awoke shortly after noon with a viral-like ache throughout her system. Before she could remember what had happened the night before, she found herself in a state of full-blown despair and sobbed her anguish into a pillow to stifle the sound. Angela appeared next to her nonetheless, enclosing her in strong, protective arms. Against the soft warmth of Angela's chest she released a torrent of tears; until finally, depleted and exhausted, she collapsed back on the bed for the remainder of the day.

For the next three days, Becca rarely left the room, but on the fourth morning, Angela poked her head through the door to notify Becca the police had arrived.

Becca rubbed her eyes. "I thought I'd told the cops everything already. I don't know what more I can add."

Angela made a face. "Sorry, kiddo. I hate to see you forced to go over and over this thing, but you know what it's like when the cops are insistent."

Good to have Angela on her side. "Don't worry. Talking to the police may be the full extent of my social life for the time being."

"Tell them I'll be right out." Becca rose, slipped into black leggings, a long, black tee-shirt, and a pair of flip-flops. She went to the bureau to brush her hair for the first time in three days, struggling through matted knots. A stale odor rose from her skin and informed her the time had come to rouse herself enough to take a shower. She dabbed a dash of Angela's *L'air du Temps* behind her ears.

By the time she made her way into the living room, two impatient officers waited for her. The man stood to the side, watching her through narrow eyes. He was big, burly, and looked like a stereotypical cop. His partner, a slender woman with long, blond hair and manicured fingernails, introduced herself as Detective

Sally Mills. She dressed in a brown suit with a yellow blouse, instead of the blues worn by her partner.

What attracted Mills to that line of work? Becca wondered.

Becca took a seat on the beige sofa adjacent to the detective. "We have a few more questions we'd like answered," Mills said. The detective glanced down at her notes. "According to Officer Wright, you told him you thought the intruder awoke you at around three a.m."

"Uh huh."

"And he wore a mask over his face?"

She nodded.

"But you thought there was something familiar about him."

"That's right."

"Can you tell us what it was?"

Something about the detective's demeanor made Becca uneasy. Her dewy complexion and pale blue eyes didn't diminish her tough and unyielding manner. "I wish I could."

The heavy-set cop stepped closer. "You're not giving us much to go on."

"I just don't know... Is there a reason for all these questions?"

"Just routine." Mills raised a hand and the other cop backed off. "You said you were raped. Is that correct?"

Becca's skin crawled. She had established this fact earlier. Why was the cop asking her again? "They checked me out at the hospital. There should be evidence on file."

"The evidence has been tested for DNA," the detective responded. "It seems the only match is your husband's."

Becca sat back, stunned. How could that be? Maybe the rape had been a bad dream. A nightmare. "Are you sure? That doesn't make sense."

The detective shrugged. "That's all they found. Is there anything else you can tell us that would help your case?"

Her case? What was the detective talking about? "I was raped. I found my husband stabbed to death. There's nothing else to tell."

"What do you know about a missing knife? We found one missing from the knife set on your kitchen counter. Was it gone before the murder?" the cop inquired.

"No. I had a full set…" Becca stared at him, mouth agape. "It was there when I went to bed."

"It's not there now. We think it might be the murder weapon. What I don't understand is how you slept through the stabbing."

A tremor ran through her, but she tried her best to control it. She didn't want her interrogators to spot any weakness they might pounce on quicker than Cecil could corner a mouse. "David used to say a truck could drive through the room if I was asleep."

"Yeah...sure," he said, sounding unsure.

"Look, I'm not the murderer and I'm certainly not the rapist. There's a lunatic out there. Do you have any idea at all who did this?"

Detective Mills shrugged. "Nothing more than we've already told you. We've questioned your husband's partner, the other people in his office, your neighbors, your friends, his parents, but we still have no clear-cut lead. Anything more you can tell us? Friends? Enemies? Anything?" Mills jotted a note on her pad.

"Not anyone I haven't mentioned before." She could swear the walls were closing in on her. The room seemed smaller, stiller, stifling. She sensed the twitch under her eye and hoped it didn't make her look guilty. "Did you figure out how the killer broke into the apartment?"

"Good question," the blue-clad cop replied. "No broken windows or obvious entry point. You have any idea?"

"All I know is David planned to fix the security latch on the dining room window this weekend. Did you notice if the window had been tampered with?"

Detective Mills looked up from her scribbling. "It was unlocked, but it wasn't open. Someone could have crawled through it, but there's no evidence they did."

"Oh..." Becca swallowed the curse that came to mind.

The woman stared at her. "Anything else you want to tell us?"

Becca didn't like the detective's accusatory tone. "No. Nothing." She wished away the quiver in her voice, took a deep breath of courage before asking, "Am I a suspect in David's murder?"

"Not yet," the woman said, but her cocked brow and piercing eyes told Becca a different story. "Just one more thing. In the initial report, it mentions you didn't act like a woman who had lost her husband only moments before."

"I was in shock. How was I supposed to act?" The detective didn't answer. Becca's mind whirled. "Listen, I'm tired. Is that all for now?"

"We're done removing evidence. You can do what you want with the apartment. Since I'm the detective assigned to the case, contact me if you think of anyone or anything else. Here's my card." Mills handed the small, white card with blue lettering to Becca, stood, and started toward the door. She glanced over her shoulder with a hand on the knob. "And stay where we can find you if we need you."

"Don't worry. I'll be here."

The moment the cops left, Becca rushed into Angela's guest room, lunged into bed, and tugged the covers over her head. Moments later she heard Angela enter the room, smelled the faint hint of stale tobacco, and felt her take a seat on the end of the bed.

"What was that about?" Angela asked.

Becca lowered the covers just enough to meet Angela's worried gaze. "From what I gather, the police think I might have killed David. The only semen sample was his. How can that be?"

Angela frowned. "Shit. I wish I knew. A condom?"

"That's possible." She had to bite back the tears that welled in her throat. "One of my kitchen knives might be the murder weapon. If I read them right, everything points to me."

"You have to be kidding! Don't they have eyes? There's no way you could have pulled that one off. You're hardly strong enough to turn Browning in 222 when you have to change the dressing on his butt. They can't possibly think—"

Becca nibbled her bottom lip. "Yes, they can. And they do."

The day following the police visit, her cell rang repeatedly. A couple of the calls were from her frantic mother, Julie, worried to death about her. But a number she didn't recognize flashed on the display more than once. Assuming it must be the police or other official business, she finally answered it...to total silence. No one responded to her 'hellos,' and after a couple attempts to elicit a reply, she hung up. She assumed it was a wrong number, and promptly forgot about it.

A second silent call came in a couple of days later. When no one answered her this time, she raised her voice. "Who are you? What is it you want from me?

Why won't you answer me?"

She heard a click and the phone went dead.

Days slipped by with no drama and little variation. Besides an occasional call from the police with a question about the crime, time dragged on, affording Becca the opportunity to ruminate about the incident. Memories kept her awake at night and overshadowed her days. And there was something more. Obsessive thoughts of the intruder's returning preoccupied her every waking minute. She couldn't stand being alone much longer.

Six weeks after moving in with Angela, Becca's paid leave and sick time ran out. So, on a typical hot and humid Philadelphia summer morning, she put on her brightly colored dress to make herself feel alive, and took the El on her way to St. John's Convalescent Hospital. At Macy's, Becca caught a bus that wobbled past towering cement and stone giants that lined the city streets and dropped her off a block from the hospital.

It took every ounce of Becca's resolve to enter through the automatic jaws that fed her into the asylum for the suffering and the senile, known as Saint John's Convalescent Hospital. Blazing fluorescent lights, the shrill of the intercom and a subtle scent of decay met her at the door. When she locked her purse in a staff locker and pinned her name-tag to her starched shirt, resistance moved inside her like a fetus about to be born.

At the nurses' station she was greeted by two nursing assistants, who looked at her with drawn, serious expressions and peppered her with questions about what she'd been through. She answered them circumspectly, putting them off with as few details as possible. She didn't want to dredge up the entire painful experience before beginning her day.

Taking leave of them, Becca made her way from one patient's room to another; checking temperatures and blood pressure, then entering notes in charts.

First stop, Beverly Samson in 204. Beverly had a reputation around the hospital for being cranky and difficult, taking every opportunity she could to complain about her son's infrequent visits, which was a far cry from the truth. Robert Samson made the obligatory trek to the hospital once each week on his day off, even though he looked exhausted and beaten-down after every visit. When Becca reminded Beverly of his routine, she was met with outrage and a raised voice; called insensitive and unprofessional. Normally, this wouldn't have fazed Becca in the least, but she wasn't in her normal state of mind.

Next she entered George Lowry's room, to discover he had lapsed into a coma while she had been away. George had always been one of her most good-natured patients. Even in the face of his progressive neurological illness, he had maintained his sense of humor. Now he lay flat on his back with eyes closed. Drool drained from his mouth, and snot from his nose. She took a cloth and cleaned him off, but he failed to stir. Her heart hurt seeing him this way.

In the adjoining room, the stripped down bed took her by surprise. She marched down to the nurses' station to inquire about Barbara Cranfield. One of the nursing assistants informed her Barbara had passed away the day before. While not totally unexpected, she hadn't known it would happen this soon.

All this added up to greater disappointment and sadness than Becca could handle. She had always taken pride in her work, but any enthusiasm she possessed before the rape and murder had dissipated among the bedpans, the moans of misery, and the odors of illness emanating from the patients she attended. She had functioned quite proficiently when treating the diseased and the dying, had learned years ago to turn down the flow of sympathy as she would an IV. But today, every sight, every sound, every ailment, every infirmity, cut through her with tiny invisible blades. After only two hours on the ward, she could no longer bear to witness another suffering patient. She had to speak to the head nurse.

Becca tried her best to hide her agitation with the head nurse, but she must have been more obvious than she intended, because Rosemary offered her another month unpaid sick leave without much persuasion. Becca decided to use the opportunity to facilitate her recovery from what she now realized was a profound and prolonged case of post-traumatic stress.

While she still resented sitting around the house day after day, she knew it was better to stay put instead of trying to resume her life again, and failing. Thank goodness Angela had offered her this opportunity.

Chapter Three

Becca had known the time would come when she would have to move on from Angela's, she just didn't know how soon. Angela had lived up to her name and been the most tolerant of angels, but two weeks after Becca's failed attempt to return to work, she began to drop hints about her new boyfriend Elliot spending the night.

So, on a crisp, early autumn afternoon, nearly two months after the rape and murder, Becca answered Angela's halfhearted protestations with reassurances she'd be all right, gave Angela a big hug for agreeing to take care of Cecil until she settled back into her apartment, and waited for her father with her suitcases on the row home's front steps. Before moving home, she would spend a couple of weeks with her parents while her apartment was properly secured and the blood-stained carpet and sofa were replaced.

The pearl-white Buick pulled to the curb in front of Angela's building, where she exchanged pleasantries with her dad while they loaded her suitcases into the trunk. Once strapped inside the car, they threaded their way through city traffic and took the Schuylkill Expressway toward Lower Merion. To pass the time, she tried to make small talk with her father, but he seemed reluctant to make eye contact, and answered her questions in a cursory fashion.

Finally, at a stop light, without so much as a glance over at her, Irv mumbled. "How are you doing...you know...after what happened?"

Since he addressed the rape in such a tangential fashion, it became instantly clear how awkward the subject was for him. "I'm okay, Dad, but to be honest, it's a bit of a struggle."

His jaw clenched in a stony expression. "I'm sorry to hear that. I wish it hadn't happened..."

"You and me both."

He nodded. "We've been worried about you. I don't have to tell you how much your mother is looking forward to your visit."

"She's mentioned it once or twice."

"I'm surprised it was only a time or two. I've heard the refrain a couple hundred times lately."

Becca grinned. "No doubt."

"Bec, I hope you'll be patient with her. She's been a wreck since...since your troubles. You know how easily upset she is. I know she can be irritating, but she loves you more than you can even imagine."

Becca glanced over at her father and noticed the deep pockets under his eyes. His thinning and fading brown hair was brushed sideways to cover a bald spot. A warm feeling washed over her. She had always adored her dad, but while Irv had been her quiet champion for as long as she could remember, he also acted as referee between mother and daughter when they were all together. He wanted peace at all costs, even if it meant convincing her to squelch her reactions to Julie's intrusive over-protectiveness. He excelled at that.

Becca sighed. "I'll do my best, Dad." But she knew it wouldn't be easy.

At their knock, Julie flung open the front door of the two-story, suburban Philadelphia home and embraced Becca in a brusque hug, then pulled back with her hands on her daughter's shoulders and a distressed stare at her face. Worry lines dug deeply into the soft flesh around Julie's eyes and mouth. "I'm glad you're home! You look like the hell you've been through. Come."

She took Becca by the hand and led her upstairs to her childhood room, a well-preserved museum of her early years. Nothing had been altered or removed since she had married David and moved into his apartment eight years earlier. Red and white checkered comforters on the twin beds matched the gingham window treatments. A plush red throw lay at the foot of the bed. Posters of Dave Matthews and Mariah Carey hung over her white melamine computer desk. Everything a frozen testimony to adolescent hopes and dreams. Hopes and dreams long gone. As dead and buried as David.

Julie watched while Irv brought in the last of the suitcases, then orchestrated where he should place them. Nothing had changed-not her room, not her parents, not their power struggle. Julie still told Irv what to do, and Irv still silently did what he was told. Then he withdrew from his wife to punish her for the crime of controlling behavior. And on and on and on. Over the years, under all circumstances, and obvious to everyone.

What would it be like living with Julie and Irv at this juncture in her life? How long could she tolerate it?

As soon as Irv finished carrying in her things, Becca gently shooed her parents from the room. As expected, Julie put up a fight, emphasizing how much help she could be with the unpacking. To Becca's surprise, Irv took Julie by the hand and escorted her from the room, glancing back at Becca with a knowing nod behind his wife's back.

Finally alone in the stuffy room, Becca drifted over to the dormer window and pried it open. She glanced out at the massive oak in the middle of the manicured lawn, the elm trees clustered beyond. As a child, how many times had she hidden in a copse of maple or elm to avoid Julie's demands? As much as she needed her parents right now, she didn't want to take advantage of their largesse for long.

The sun shimmered across rust-colored and yellowed leaves which blanketed the trees and speckled the ground. The sight of dying leaves stirred up her inner conflict. It had been months since David's death and she remained stuck in suspended animation, her life on hold. She dreaded being back in this house. She no longer belonged here, yet she had nowhere else to go.

Restless, with a sense of unease, she knew she still hadn't recovered from her trauma. Would she ever feel peaceful and safe again?

She no sooner began to unpack when she heard Julie's raised voice from below. "Becca, come down! I've made your favorite strawberry lemonade!"

"Sounds great, Mom," she called down from the banister. "Give me ten minutes."

She returned to place her clothes in closet and

drawers. Upon completion she would join her parents downstairs and make the most of a difficult situation.

But not for long.

She knew she had to move on before Julie discovered a way to take advantage of her predicament and indefinitely extend her stay. Her mother had never trusted that she could survive in the world on her own. Now with David gone, there was no doubt Julie would want her 'home.' She had to find the courage to move back to her apartment alone, and jump-start her new life. She couldn't rely on the kindness of others forever.

But where was the spark that would ignite her?

Two days later, the police made their first visit to the Goldstein house. At the sound of the doorbell, Becca came out of her room to the railing over the foyer and watched Julie answer the door, with Irv trailing closely behind.

The officers explained they were here to speak with Becca, but had a couple of questions for them first.

"What can you possibly want with us this time?" Julie asked. "We've been interrogated twice before."

"Just a couple of quick inquiries," she heard Detective Mills say. "We learned your daughter was in a mental hospital at the age of 12. We've requested the records, but we want to know what you can tell us about that time."

Becca cringed. They had more ammunition to use against her.

"Rebecca was having panic attacks and wouldn't go to school. We didn't know what to do for her. Our physician suggested we get her some psychiatric help," Julie answered.

"What was the nature of these 'attacks'?" Mills asked.

"How do you explain panic attacks? She was going through early adolescence. She was having problems adjusting. That's all there was to it." Even from a distance Julie appeared strained.

Becca nibbled her bottom lip. This line of questioning made her nervous. It seemed they couldn't overturn a stone without exposing a fault on her part. What if they were right and she was crazier than she knew? The doctors certainly thought so. If they hadn't, they wouldn't have locked her up and given her those pills which made a zombie out of her.

"And did they put her on medication?" Mills asked.

"Don't they always?" Julie shook her head. "If you're implying my daughter is mentally ill, you're way off base. She had some adolescent issues. That's all."

Mills made a face. "I don't think they hospitalize teenagers on a regular basis for having issues." There were other things going on with Rebecca and we need to know what they were. Can you tell me how long she was in the hospital and what she was like after she returned home? Did she continue treatment? And for how long?"

Julie threw up her hands. "She was hospitalized for a few short weeks and was fine after she returned home. I'm sure she had appointments with her doctor afterwards for a time, but they were outpatient. I still don't understand this line of questioning. I hope you don't think her bout in a mental hospital over fifteen years ago has anything to do with your investigation!"

"It's all relevant to our investigation," Mills said, consulting her notes. "When was the last time you saw your daughter and her husband together before the murder?"

"A week before," Julie replied. "They came over for dinner regularly."

"Did you notice anything unusual about them?"

"No."

"How did they get along?"

Julie had turned her head away, but Becca could only imagine her mother's expression. A long silence ensued, then Julie said, "They had a good relationship as far as I knew. Why do you ask?"

"Just a mere formality. Were you aware of any tension between them?"

"No, nothing noticeable."

"Did you ever see them argue or fight?" Mills asked.

"Not more than Irv and I argue and fight. I still don't see your reasoning."

"We're just trying to gauge the nature of your daughter's relationship with her husband..."

Suddenly, to her surprise, she heard Irv's voice rise above the rest. "Are you suggesting our daughter had anything to do with her husband's death? Because if you are, you're barking up the wrong tree. My daughter's the victim here! Don't try to frame her for this crime. It's time you start looking for the real perpetrator!" Irv moved Julie aside and stepped up to Mills, squaring his shoulders as though he was ready for a fight. "I think we've had enough of this line of questioning. Either you stop right here or you're leaving right now."

Stunned, Becca listened closely; the anger in Irv's voice apparent even from above. It was uncharacteristic of him to be so forceful with anyone, especially the authorities. What had gotten into him? Was he more upset about the entire situation than he had let on to her?

Not nearly as shocking, Julie took over where Irv left off. "I don't understand why you won't leave Becca out of this. She's not the guilty party. Why do you keep pestering her?"

"Look," Mills' burly partner answered, "we have our job to do and the job entails questioning your daughter. It's not your place to interfere."

Becca smiled to herself, wondering when her mother didn't interfere.

Then she heard Sally Mills say, "We're not here to bother your daughter. We just want to clarify a few points."

Again Irv jumped in. "You're aggravating her, whether you intend to or not. She's been through one hell of a time. I wish you'd let her be."

"We will, right after we speak with her," the uniformed cop said. "Now will you let her know we're here?"

Becca descended the steps in time to see Julie glare at him. "You don't seem to understand..."

Grateful for her parents' defense of her, Becca wanted to spare them more trouble. She raised her voice. "It's okay, Mom and Dad. I'll take over from here."

"Are you sure you feel up to this, Rebecca?" her mother asked, still staring darts at the officers.

Becca patted her mother on the arm. "I can handle this, Mom. You and Dad go on back to the kitchen and brew up some coffee. I'll be in for a cup when I'm through."

"Come on, Jul," Irv said, taking her arm. "Becca's a big girl. She obviously wants to handle this on her own."

Julie shook her head. "I don't like this harassment," she mumbled to herself before following Irv to the back of the house.

Sally Mills' shoulders drooped the moment they disappeared from view. "Your parents certainly care about you."

Sometimes a little too much. "Do you want to have a seat in the family room?"

Before the officers could answer, she led the way in. The police took two chairs on one side of the coffee table, Becca sat on the loveseat across from them.

After everyone was seated, Mills looked over at her. "We still have a few things we need to clear up. You told the officers at the hospital David was still alive when you found him. What happened after that?"

Now what were they getting at? "I tried to staunch the blood and called 911."

Mills frowned at her. "Anything else?"

Becca squirmed at the implication of the question. Did they actually believe she wanted him dead? "I tried performing CPR, but I wasn't successful."

Mills stared at her with a fixed expression.

All at once, rage soared up inside of Becca with the force of a fire hose. "I don't understand why you keep questioning me as though I'm the bad guy! I didn't murder David and I certainly didn't rape myself! It's time for you to begin looking for the real killer and stop focusing all your attention on me."

The burly cop leaned forward. "We've been looking, but so far the evidence hasn't led us anywhere else."

"What have you been doing to find the real perpetrator, besides badgering me?"

Mills shrugged. "You're not the only one we're questioning. We've interviewed quite a few people."

Becca stood. "Well, maybe you better do more.

Keep looking, because you're not going to find anything here. Is there anything else today? I need to go."

Mills and her partner rose. "Nothing more for now, but we'll let you know when there is."

"I'm sure you will." Shaken, Becca watched them leave the room. Their questions made her question herself. She had been diagnosed with a mental illness and hospitalized once. Was she going down the same path again? Maybe she was crazier than she cared to admit. Was she in denial, or even delusional?

Could she have carried out something as heinous as murdering her husband, convincing herself she hadn't done it? The violence had certainly exposed a tightly-woven web of tangled feelings within her; a web she tried desperately to hold together. even though her relationship with her parents, and the police scrutiny, kept threatening to rip it apart. One small tear at a time.

The police visit had stirred up so many emotions in Becca, she found it hard the following day to do anything except skulk around the house in sweats and slippers. It didn't take long for Julie to take notice, and complain. To remedy the situation, Julie suggested a spirit-lifting outing to the mall. Busy emptying the dishwasher, Julie sent Becca into the master bedroom to retrieve her purse.

The moment Becca stepped inside the room, a

spasm radiated through her solar plexus, leaving in its wake an eerie, detestable sensation. She shook it off as quickly as she could, located the purse, and joined Julie downstairs, but the sense of impending doom lingered for the remainder of the day. She had trouble shutting off her mind that night, and it took longer than usual to fall asleep.

In the middle of the night, Becca awoke from a deep sleep when a shadow passed over her eyes. Before she could turn on the light, she heard muffled footsteps. With a creak, the doorknob turned. She could swear she glimpsed the silhouette of a man standing in the doorway.

Startled, she bolted upright, switched on the bedside lamp and glanced around, but everything was exactly as she had left it the night before-the door closed and the curtains drawn. The room empty. It took several inspections of the bedroom before she could return to bed. An hour passed before her heart slowed enough for her to go back to sleep.

Five days later work had been completed on deadbolts, window latches, and a new alarm system. Becca lugged the last of her suitcases from Irv's Buick into her Queen's Village apartment in a gentrified area at the edge of Center City Philadelphia. Back at the car, she reassured Irv she'd be all right and sent him on his way. She surveyed the tree-lined street with lovely older townhouses, before entering the building and traveling the few steps to her apartment.

Exhausted by the hell raised after she broke the news to Julie that she was moving out - but hadn't she established that fact upfront - she slouched onto an overstuffed alabaster armchair against the far wall, glancing around the apartment at the familiar expanse of brass and glass. She stared across the brand new carpet at a sofa Julie had picked out to replace the one stained with David's blood. How many times had she sat in this chair across from David and discussed the possibility of starting a family? At the time his refusal to even consider the idea had upset her. But as much as she had wanted a child, she now wondered how the white-on-white living room would have fared under the onslaught of chocolate pudding and Crayolas.

A noise in the hallway outside the apartment distracted her from her ruminations, and she tensed. Only after the building door had closed with a decided swoosh did she release her breath. Minutes passed before she could calm herself, but the shivers remained.

She pried herself from the comfort of her chair, went over to the thermostat and raised the temperature ten degrees. Warm air and a stale odor gushed through vents into the room. Since she was up, there was no reason to put off unpacking any longer. In the bedroom, she splayed open a suitcase on the bed and carried a handful of folded slacks to the dresser, placing a stack on top, and another in a drawer below.

The jangle of the phone snagged her attention and she jogged into the dining room to answer it, but before she had a chance to lift the receiver, Julie's number flashed on the display. Not quite ready to deal with her mom, Becca let the answering machine pick up the message. She'd call back later when she felt more in control.

But she couldn't miss the words spilling out of the machine, sounding apologetic with a hint of blame. Becca could decipher the subtext. She knew how much Julie fretted about her, and how little she believed in Becca's ability to manage her own life, especially now. That's why she always wanted to control—

A shattering sound made Becca jump. She placed a hand over her racing heart, as if the pressure would quiet its wild rhythm, and cautiously made her way back toward the bedroom.

The overwhelming scent of perfume assaulted her senses before she spotted the broken bottle on the bedroom floor. She must have created the disaster herself when she moved bottles aside to place her pants on the dresser top. She bent over to pick up a large remnant with a label that read *Raffinée*.

Her disappointment at demolishing her favorite fragrance did little to diminish her relief the noise was nothing more than a broken bottle. She tossed the glass shards in the trash, swept up any remains, and soaked up the perfume with a towel.

Afterwards, she put the rest of her clothes away and reclaimed her seat in the living room. She tried to concentrate on a *Glamour* magazine she'd brought along, primarily for the purpose of distracting herself, but discovered she couldn't. Still jittery, she had to escape the oppressive apartment. Breathe some fresh air.

Becca made a bee-line for the front door,

stopping only long enough to shrug her way into a black fiber-filled jacket. Outside, she took a seat on the front steps. A glance at her watch told her the time, 5:30 p.m. Only two hours had passed since her dad had dropped her off, and already she was a nervous wreck. How could she possibly stay the night by herself?

She lowered her chin into her hands, staring down at the cement pavement, when a pair of white Nike running shoes came into view. She raised her eyes past long legs in denims, a beige vest over a navy-blue wool shirt, and into the deep chocolate-brown eyes of her next door neighbor. His chestnut-colored hair had been combed away from his face, which was creased with a warm and sincere smile.

"Where have you been? I've been looking for you," he said. "I'm so sorry about what happened."

"Thanks for your concern."

He pointed to the step. "Mind if I sit?"

"Of course not." She moved over to make room for him.

"What are you doing out here all by yourself? It's awfully cold this evening."

Right. She had been so preoccupied she had hardly noticed the plummeting temperature until now. She wrapped her arms around herself. "I moved back in today, but I'm having trouble being in my apartment alone."

"Oh, I see." His knowing look put her at ease. "Too many ghosts?"

She nodded.

"I understand."

"I'm embarrassed to admit this, but I don't know your name."

"Evan," he said, holding out a hand to shake. "Frankin. And yours is Rebecca Rosen, am I right?"

Surprised, she studied him. His slightly receding hairline informed her he was probably in his mid-thirties, but he had the physique of a younger man. Then she remembered his passing the window on one of his morning jogs. She had made small talk with him on a handful of occasions when their mailbox schedules coincided, and she had always thought of him as kind and courteous, and attractive in a way; but her marital status prevented her from ever considering him more than just a friendly neighbor. Even though she wouldn't have thought of him as handsome in the traditional sense, there was something especially appealing about him. "How do you know—"

"Besides seeing it in all the papers, I had a visit from the police a couple days after the tragedy. They wanted to know what my relationship was with you and your husband. You know, the usual questions."

"Yeah, they've asked me one or two as well."

"I bet they have, Rebecca."

"Please call me Becca. Everyone else does. So what do you do with your time, Evan Frankin? I see you leave every morning and come back in the evening. You must be up to something in between."

He chuckled. "I guess you could say that. I'm a student at the Philadelphia College of Osteopathic Medicine."

"What's the difference between Osteopathic Medicine and Allopathic Medicine?" she asked.

"Osteopathic Medicine focuses on the whole person, not just body parts and symptoms."

"Interesting," she said. "I'd sure like to hear more about it sometime."

"Tell you what. I was about to go inside and toss together a pasta dish. I'd love company. After we eat, I can join you at your apartment if you want to watch TV. Being there with a neighbor might help. What do you say?"

Becca's first impulse was to agree to his terms, but she paused to consider. What did she know about him? She had watched him rescue a cat from a tree across the street, and knew he sponsored a kid through Big Brother, because she had spoken with the boy while he waited on the stoop one afternoon, but was that resumé enough to reassure her he was safe?

She gazed into Evan's eyes for a long moment and his remained steady, not blinking or flinching. The way he looked at her told her he was honest and trustworthy. She needed a friend right now. She would have to rely on her instincts. "Okay," she said, shrugging. "That sure beats the mental breakdown I was planning this evening."

"Good." He stood, took her hand, and pulled her to her feet. "This way to Chef Wolfgang Suck's kitchen."

She laughed for the first time in weeks.

Chapter Four

From the front row of the conference room, a professional-looking woman dressed in a gray cotton suit with a tailored white blouse, raised her hand.

"Yes?" I asked.

She lifted her eyeglasses from her face and used them as one would use a pointer while speaking. "Sarah, I can't help but wonder about this neighbor of Becca's. Obviously she knew him casually before the rape, but now he seems so interested and available. Is it possible he might have something to do with it?"

I shrugged, thinking again of Rachel and all she had gone through. While I don't typically reveal too much information at this point in the lecture, because I could lose my audience's interest later on, tossing them a scrap to chew on wouldn't hurt. "I'm glad you noticed this and said something. Certainly he appears eager to help Becca out, but we don't know yet if it's because he's a true knight in shining armor, or a cad in cool clothing. I don't want to say too much just yet, but keep your eye on him as the story progresses."

Another hand went up in the back row and a wide-eyed younger woman in jeans and jacket spoke. "How long after the rape did you start meeting with Becca?"

"Not long after," I said, recalling the first time we met. "Once back at her apartment, Becca's terrifying dreams didn't end, but magnified and multiplied. It didn't take long before she couldn't stomach suffering in silence, and sought out the services of a psychotherapist. Not knowing where to turn, she approached Angela, who had occasionally been in to see me with relationship problems. Only a few hours later she called for an appointment.

Upon entering the waiting room for our first session, I saw a striking redhead with high cheek bones and large, incandescent green eyes. When she stood to follow me into the office, I noticed she wore a floral print dress with a flouncy skirt and high heels. While on the short side, she possessed an appealing pixy-ish quality. Later, I attributed this to her mischievous grin, and the way she wove her words with her hands.

"She took a seat on the couch and launched into an explanation of why she had come, beginning with the rape and the murder. She described in detail what had taken place in her apartment in the early hours of that August morning, and what had followed with the hospital, the police, and her family. Although I listened intently and took extensive notes, a part of me stood back, refusing to leap to any judgments.

The psyche can be a trickster, camouflaging and twisting the truth to protect itself from what it sees as bad behavior. Even though Becca professed her innocence more than once, this hadn't appeased the police; and it wasn't totally persuasive to me. I never allow myself to draw conclusions about a client until I have had a chance to work with them. After getting to know them, I can begin to sort out truth from delusion.

As a psychotherapist, I'm part scientist, part archeologist, and part detective. I take the puzzles my patients present as problems, and help them put the pieces together in the right configuration to uncover the truth. While they dig deep for artifacts long buried, around which they have built elaborate and often impregnable defenses, I help them chisel away at the bedrock with my bag of tools and tricks. My job is to assist my clients in the difficult, painstaking work of uncovering the haunting and hurtful past traumas in order to diminish their power. It's only by recognizing what happened to them, and how it has shaped their perception of reality, that they can begin to heal.

I began by asking Becca questions about her early life leading up to the rape and murder. She shared with me about Julie and Irv, and what it was like growing up an only child in an overprotective Jewish family. In colorful language she recreated her early school years, her awkward adolescence, and her blossoming interest in boys and sex. Before we wrapped up our first session, she told me about her marriage to David, which she described as a 'marriage of convenience.' She explained how disloyal it made her feel to say anything negative about him, now that he was gone, but she had never loved him the way a woman should love her husband. That fact did not prevent her from grieving his death, and she was only beginning to recover from it.

The hour ended with my giving her an assignment to keep a journal of both her waking and sleeping life. I asked her to keep pen and paper by her bed, and to write down her dreams immediately upon waking. During the day I told her to note any thoughts, feelings, experiences, or fantasies she sensed might be of significance—even those she didn't take too seriously. I wanted her to pay attention to everything *going on in her inner and outer life.*

I could see my attentive audience mulling over my explanation. I hadn't shared with them my personal reaction to Rachel because the more I listened to her story, the more I related to her. I've never had this type of visceral reaction to a new client, but Rebecca's history so closely mimicked my own, it was difficult not to feel an immediate connection to her. Something beyond the typical therapist-client bond. I had also been raised in an overprotective Jewish family, and had made poor choices about men and marriage. My most recent disaster had cycled, months earlier, through divorce court.

But what made her all the more relatable was a wounded and vulnerable quality, a quality I had often felt in myself. She seemed ripe for the advances of those who would use and abuse her. While I actively worked on this character defect in myself, it occasionally reared its ugly little head, especially in my relationships with the opposite sex, and made me want to protect and defend Becca, even while I had my doubts about her innocence.

An older man with long hair in a ponytail stood and snatched my attention. "Did you think Becca had it in her to murder her own husband? From what you described, it's hard to believe."

I smiled. "Anything is possible. Remember Karla Faye Tucker and Susan Smith. If you had run into either of them on the street, you wouldn't have thought they could murder anyone. But they did. As a therapist, you must be open to all possibilities and not let appearances deceive you. Any other questions? I glanced around. "Okay, if there are none, let's continue."

After a long second day back at St. John's, exhaustion flowed like an intravenous sedative through Becca's veins. By the time the double doors of the convalescent hospital disgorged her into the mass of humanity scurrying home for the night, the sun had hidden behind tall buildings, its light filtering through the grime-laden air. In the murky haze, buildings faded one into another. Sights that had looked luminous earlier, now seemed as pallid as one of her elderly patients.

She caught the bus 31 that rambled down traffic-packed streets past shops and restaurants to the Broad Street line. Overjoyed to be on her way home from work, she was equally grateful to Angela for asking her to cover the extra shift. Not only did it postpone the moment when she would have to return home alone, but it had also sapped the strength she'd require to fret about it. A tinge of fear rippled through her at the thought.

To take her mind off her own troubles, she replayed Angela's earlier plaintive plea on the phone. Angela had complained bitterly about not seeing her boyfriend for two whole days, and had intimated she wanted time off to spend with him. But all Becca could detect beneath the appeal for shift cover was the lilt of love in her friend's husky voice. She had given Angela a bit of a hard time for fun, holding out for a few minutes before agreeing to do it. But after all Angela had done for her, helping her out was a no-brainer.

Funny, she had first learned about Angela's new beau the day her life changed forever. How mundane the day now seemed...how routine. How could such an ordinary day have turned out to be so horrific?

She remembered the day before David's death so clearly. Her only break had come just after noon, when she managed to maneuver away from Mrs. Bluestone in room 208. Poor Mrs. Bluestone clung to the nurses as though their presence would spare her further suffering. Becca only wished it would. The woman's Alzheimer's disease seemed to progress daily. When Becca finally loosened the waif-like woman's surprisingly strong grip on her arm, she made her way to the cafeteria. Angela waved to her from a table in the rear of the room. She picked out a wilted-looking salad and joined her friend.

"Can you believe this beautiful day?" Angela had asked after Becca took a seat across the table from her. "What the hell are we doing in this den of depression?"

"Yeah, and to think I almost left the bus at Independence Square," Becca mused.

"And leave me all alone here with all these fun things to do? What are friends for?" Angela chided her.

"Like you didn't stick us last weekend to run off to the shore." Becca gave her friend a knowing glance and noted how well she looked. Angela considered herself too plump, but Becca had always admired her dark Mediterranean looks. The last couple of times they were together, Angela had looked especially attractive.

"I'm sure you've heard about the great things I came back to, like—" she eyed Becca— "complaints from Harriet Wilson about your nursing care."

"So I've joined the legions."

"What do you plan to do about her?"

Becca sent her friend a sneaky smile. "Give her an extra dessert."

"You're too kind to that nasty witch."

Passive was more like it. "That's because I never say 'no' to anyone."

"Don't underestimate yourself. I don't know how I'd get along without you. Nothing would ever get done around here."

"I wish that were true elsewhere in my life." Becca took a closer look at Angela's beaming face. Even when describing her problems at work, she never lost her luster. "You don't look at all like your old miserable self. What are you so happy about?"

"Promise you won't ride me on this one?" Angela asked.

"What's the big deal?"

She watched Angela scope out the room. Her gaze fixed on Sylvia Haas at the next table. Angela lowered her voice. "Sylvia's such a gossip." She pushed her thick hair out of her eyes and whispered, "I met a man. A doctor. He's handsome, brilliant, attentive...not like most jerks I meet. What more can I tell you? He's a hunk." Angela took a sip of coffee. "Yuk! Mississippi Mud."

Becca picked at the romaine on her plate. "Lucky you."

Angela eyed her. "Come on, Becca, you have nothing to complain about. You have a stable relationship, which is more than I can say."

"I guess that's true, it's just that David and I haven't been getting along again." She spoke a little too loudly and glanced over to see Sylvia staring at her.

Angela scooped a spoonful of yogurt out of a container. "What's the problem now?

"Same old, same old," she said in a low voice. "I brought up the idea of having a child again, but he nixed it." Becca put her fork down and wiped the corners of her mouth. "He says we have to wait to start a family until he's more established in his law practice. But I have the sense he'd have to be as successful as F. Lee Bailey before he'd feel ready. I'm not sure what we're waiting for."

"It will happen." Angela flapped her hand in a gesture of reassurance. "Just give it some time and, before you know it, you'll be overrun with rug rats. Then you'll be complaining to me about them."

Becca had chuckled. "You're right. I do have a little teeny bit of an impatient streak."

"Then I'm sure you're dying to go back to work."

The honk of a car horn drew Becca's attention back to the office buildings lined up beyond her window on the Broad Street line. A pang of guilt over her feelings toward David stabbed Becca, but she shook it off.

The idea she'd soon be back at her empty apartment...alone...disturbed her. Evan had willingly slept on her sofa bed the last couple of nights, so she wouldn't have to stay by herself, even though it wasn't the most comfortable arrangement for him. She hated to be what Julie called a 'scardy cat', but when she was alone, every sound seemed amplified, every shadow alarming. If she didn't get over this soon, she'd have to begin looking in the paper for other living arrangements.

Before Evan left for school that morning, he had informed her that his plans for the evening made it impossible for him to stop by. Too bad. She had begun to rely upon him to make her feel safe, even if she had to ignore the tender look which sometimes filled his spectacular eyes. As attractive as he was, it seemed way too soon after losing David to consider anything but a friendship. She had made that clear from the start.

At Third she exited the El and sprinted the two blocks to her red-brick four-story building. The streets were well lit, but she still had to be alert for anything unusual. Even in the best of neighborhoods, a woman alone had to be on guard at night. Whoever had raped her and murdered David was still out there; maybe waiting for her now. She regularly spoke with the police. but they never had satisfactory answers to her inquiries about the investigation, or a clue as to who might have done it. They were always more focused on her actions and whereabouts, and not on other leads. No matter how many times she asked them about their progress, the answers all led back to her.

She let herself into the dimly lit hallway of her building. Distracted by what was going on around her, she fumbled with the key in the apartment lock, as awkward as a toddler with a new toy. It took several tries before she could open the door. She finally heard the deadbolt bar slide into the lock and rushed inside, thrusting the deadbolt into place behind her.

Once inside, the darkness closed in on her like a thick wool cloak. She searched for the overhead light switch, flicking it on to illuminate the living room and banish the threatening images that had managed, in mere seconds, to spring into her mind. She double-checked behind doors and curtains, reassuring herself nothing menacing was skulking about. Finally convinced, Becca stepped into the kitchen and brewed herself a cup of soothing chamomile tea, which she carried back into the living room. Without Cecil—who had remained at Angela's because of Julie's allergy to cats—the apartment seemed uncompromisingly empty. She'd pick him up on her day off. To fill the void, she flicked on the television, channel-surfing her favorite shows, and settled on Lost. A feeling Becca knew all too well.

She had trouble paying attention, even with the crescendo of background music and the dramatic events unfolding on the screen in front of her. Frustrated, she flicked off the TV, but while the sound had done little to aid her comfort, the ensuing silence scared the hell out of her. She sat sipping her tea, hoping the herb would soon soothe her shattered nerves, but even her usual panacea did nothing to calm her. At wits end, she scribbled a note for Evan to come by when he returned, and left the apartment to tape it to his door.

Home again, she ran a tub while heating water for another cup of tea. Perhaps adding a bath to her routine would improve the results. In the tub, she leaned her head back and pictured Evan. He had been so giving and supportive the last couple of nights, his absence had created an aching longing. His interesting anecdotes and slightly off-beat sense of humor had kept her occupied enough so she rarely thought about her troubles, and made him indispensable to her. They had played cards, watched The Daily Show, eaten together, and talked and talked and talked. She'd no idea a man could be so open and revealing, nor how much she would enjoy the repartee. His absence left a palpable hole in her soul. Was she becoming too attached to him?

She leaned her head back and allowed the steam to rise up and surround her in a warm fog of silence and safety. Suddenly a loud sound in the outer hallway disrupted the silence. She jumped up, wrapped herself in a towel, and dribbled her way to the door. Through the peephole, she spied one of her neighbors climbing the bottom flight of stairs. She drooped back against the door, relieved.

After towel-drying herself, she climbed into bed in her sweats, in case Evan came by, and tried to sleep, but a disturbing feeling of being watched prevented her from dozing off. She rose to make certain all the shades were drawn and the front door locked. While she hated to be so fragile, nothing she did seemed to vanquish her sense of vulnerability. She placed a chair at an angle against the door for further protection, but it only helped a little.

Back in bed, her exhaustion must have been greater than her fright, because she awoke with a start from a terrorizing dream at 2:15 in the morning. In the nightmare, a faceless man attempted to crawl through the bedroom window of her parents' home. Why her parents' house? Why did these anxiety dreams always take her there?

Immediately she rolled over toward David's side of the bed, only to be reminded he was no longer there. As much as she still felt the sting of David's refusal to have children, and his sometimes stated, often implied, criticism of her, she couldn't help missing him on nights like this. They did have fun together at the beginning, and she could look back fondly on their movie dates and picnics in the park. While often irritated by the pressure of building his legal practice, and intolerance of her those last couple of years, he had offered her an out from living under Julie's constant vigil, and for that she would be forever grateful. But how often would she have to turn to him before accepting the fact he was gone for good?

She flicked on the light, wishing Evan were nearby, but aware he would never come by this late. She undressed and tried to go back to sleep, surprised by the extent of her disappointment at his absence. He owed her nothing and had been more than generous with her, but she couldn't deny her feelings. Why hadn't he bothered to check in? Had he begun to tire of her neediness?

And where could he be at this late hour?

The next morning, Becca had to drag herself from her bed. After waiting up for Evan, she could barely keep her eyes open. While waiting on the platform for the El, she swayed from one foot to the other, trying to keep herself alert, hoping for once it would be on time. All she could think about was Evan's failure to appear the night before. She barely noticed people crowding in around her.

She heard the screech of the train as it rounded the bend and barreled toward the station, glancing up the track to watch as it arrived. All at once a sharp object pressed against her back and a surge of adrenaline pulsed through her. She sprang forward to the edge of the platform, almost overshooting the cement and landing on the track. When she turned her head to see who had poked her, she immediately noticed the back of a man frantically weaving his way through the crowd to board the train. Unfortunately, all she could see of him before he exited the platform was his black trench coat and a hat covering his hair, but he did look tall and burly. While she could have been overreacting, she couldn't deny a feeling the trench coat covered her rapist. Her heartbeat surged, far outpacing the mechanical rhythm of the oncoming train.

A hand grabbed her arm at the same moment the train pulled up alongside her. "You're awful close to the train," a man's voice rumbled in her ear. "You could have hurt yourself."

Still shaken, she turned, half expecting to see her tormentor, only to stare into the kind eyes of an elderly Asian man. "Thank you. I'll be fine."

"Be careful there," he said, and left her to board the train.

But she stood glued to the spot, and missed her train. It took many minutes before she recovered enough to make her way back to the now-empty bench. With a shake of her head, she considered her predicament. If it had been her stalker, how much danger was she actually in? If it hadn't been him, how sensitive was she to the slightest provocation? How traumatized was she still, and how much longer would it take for the emotional scars to heal...if they ever did.

Angela placed her tray on their customary lunch table and took the seat across from Becca. The pink tinge on Angela's cheeks, the sparkle in her eyes, gave away her elation before she even uttered a word. Her excitement might have been contagious, if Becca wasn't worried about Evan. He hadn't called once the day before and, when she stopped by his condo on the way to work, he wasn't there. She hoped nothing was wrong.

"What's new with you?" Angela asked with a mischievous grin, looking more eager to talk about herself than listen to anything Becca had to say. Under the circumstances, that was a relief.

Angela had one of the most expressive faces Becca had ever seen. While it absolutely radiated love at the moment, it could just as quickly transform into unbearable dejection with the swiftness of one of her elderly patients' deteriorating conditions. Becca had seen it happen in too many instances, and prayed it would be different for Angela this time around.

"I slept alone in my apartment for the last two nights and let me tell you, that was a major medical breakthrough."

Angela arched a brow. "I didn't sleep alone last night and that was a breakthrough, too. Believe me."

No surprise to her. "Don't tell me the independent 'I don't need a man' Angela P has met her match! This sounds serious. It might require surgery."

"If it does, I'm with the best operator in town."

"Tell me more." Becca scooped out a spoonful of strawberry yogurt from its container and listened while Angela gave her the run-down on Dr. Elliot, enumerating his many good qualities. The list went on and on and included such diverse things as his thriving medical practice and his love of gardening.

Becca was tickled by Angela's good fortune, but couldn't deny a tiny twinge of regret. She had never felt the type of love Angela described, and had settled for David as a way to pacify her mother and to escape from the suffocating nest. If she had tried to move out on her own without a husband, Julie would have put up a protracted battle. She hadn't been up to the fight.

Of course, she could have done far worse than David. To get away from troubled families, a couple of girls in her class had married too young, made questionable choices. But Becca had skipped past the blush of first love, and continued to yearn for it.

"… and he asked me about you."

That grabbed Becca's attention. "Why me?"

"Aren't we a little bit paranoid?" Angela giggled. "I told him about you and he wanted to know more. You're my closet friend, aren't you?"

Becca took another mouthful. What was she thinking? Naturally, Angela's new beau would be interested in every facet of her life—how silly of her to be suspicious. "It sounds like you hit the jackpot with this roll. You're one lucky winner."

"Bingo. The lottery has finally paid off big. It's about time, after all those years of lousy first-and-only dates." Angela paused and stared at her. "Jesus, Becca, what planet am I on? I'm so euphoric right now, I forgot how you must be feeling. You're the last person who needs to hear me raving about Elliot."

Was she that obvious? She forced a smile. "Don't be silly. You said I'm your closest confidante. I expect a bent ear."

Angela lowered her gaze. "I'm being totally insensitive. I'm sorry, Becca."

Becca wagged her index finger. "Stop right now. I'm not the walking wounded. It's been over two months since David's death and I'm healing. I don't want you to pussy foot around me." Should she say more? "Besides, my sexy neighbor has been helping me out."

Angela cocked a knowing brow and opened her mouth to say something, but Becca stopped her with a raised hand.

"Don't go there. It's not what you think—at

least not yet. I'm not ready for anything as hot and heavy as you're describing, but it's been lovely having him around."

Angela's face lit up. "I'd love to meet him. I have an idea. Why don't you and..."

"Evan."

"Yeah. Why don't you two join Elliot and me on a double date one of these nights?"

"Because we aren't dating." Becca could tell by the look Angela sent her she wasn't buying the answer. "Maybe we can meet for a drink one evening after work. I'll run it by Evan." *If I ever see him again.*

"I know it's been hard losing David, but it's time you came out of hiding. Who knows, a male friend might be the ticket right now."

Was that true? Maybe so, maybe not. A man hadn't been the answer to her problems in the past, but this was different. She'd have to wait and see how it played out.

The first sound Becca heard after letting herself into the apartment after work, was the beep of the answering machine signal. After greeting the recently retrieved Cecil with pets and pats, she approached the machine, eager to hear if Evan had called back. She crossed her fingers and tapped the button, but instead of Evan's seductive baritone, Julie's voice filled the room.

"Hello, darlin'. I know you told me not to call

you every day, but I couldn't resist. I won't talk long. I just want to know how you're doing. You know I worry about you. Call me this evening." Click.

She waited for the second message, filled with anticipation, but all she heard was a long, disquieting silence. It wasn't the first time since the rape she'd received one of these calls. Shaken, she immediately erased it and had to take a minute to quiet the pounding pulse in her head before she could listen to the third message.

"This is Detective Sally Mills of the Philadelphia Police Department. Something has come up and we need to speak with you. Call me at 555-0199 when you get this message."

Becca stared at the machine, wondering what Mills could possibly want with her this time. Four months had passed since the rape and the police had made very little progress; she continued to be the only one on their radar screen. Frustrated, she had to take a deep breath before she could lift the receiver, dial the police department, and ask for Detective Mills.

Mills answered with a cursory greeting.

"I'm returning your call. You mentioned you had something new to talk to me about."

She heard the ruffling of paper before Mills said, "One of our units was out looking through the landfill on another homicide, and they came across a butcher knife wrapped in a kitchen towel. We have reason to believe it's your missing knife. We'd like you to come down and identify it."

This might be a chance at redemption. She pulled the receiver closer to her ear. "Did you find anything on the knife?"

"We've sent it to a lab to see if there's anything we can lift off of it."

"I'll be right down."

For a full minute after hanging up the phone, she stood frowning down at it. Would this discovery clear her or convict her? If the killer was careful, her fingerprints might have been the last ones on the knife. She might have even nicked herself when chopping the salad, as she often did, and her blood could show up on the towel. Suddenly shaken, she lowered herself into a dining room chair and massaged her temple with a trembling hand.

No use putting her visit off any longer than necessary. Postponing it wouldn't affect the outcome in her favor. With resolve, she grabbed her purse and headed out the door.

Chapter Five

"Before we take a morning break, I'd like to speak with you about Repressed Memory Syndrome. As you all know, RMS has become controversial over the years, and there are questions in the professional community about its validity as a diagnosis. Dr. Elizabeth Loftus, in an article in Scientific American, 1997, wrote that 'a growing number of investigations demonstrate that under the right circumstances, false memories can be instilled rather easily in some people...'

"While I'm certain this is true, we must remember the ability to retain and assimilate memory is not fully formed until a child reaches adolescence or beyond. That's why many of our early childhood memories are sketchy or nonexistent. Add to this the effect of trauma on the developing mind, which can either bring an event into sharper focus, or obfuscate it, rendering it difficult, if not impossible, to integrate. Therefore, I believe children can imprint memories which are not conscious or easily accessible."

I drew a deep breath and surveyed the wood-paneled conference room to make sure I hadn't lost everyone. "What we, as therapists, must remember is to never, ever plant thoughts or ideas in our clients' minds. Our job is to give them the latitude to explore and discover the truth for themselves.

"One more thing. While Becca was having a tough time accepting her fragility, it is not unusual to take a year or more to heal from the type of trauma she experienced."

I took in the rapt faces of my appreciative

audience. I knew I had them exactly where I wanted them. Taking a breather now would only increase their curiosity. "I think I've said enough about this. Let's take that fifteen minute break. Be back here at 10:45 to continue."

I waited temporarily at the podium, sorting through my notes, while people rose and shuffled toward the back of the room. A handful of participants formed a line at the coffee urn against the far wall, others stood by the bathroom door to my right. I decided to stay put with the afternoon's lecture notes, refreshing my memory until the lines diminished.

At a sound, I looked up and into the startlingly blue eyes of Dr. Adrian Farley. "Sarah, I have a question for you."

"What is it?"

A clump of thick, dark wavy hair fell over his forehead and he raked fingers through it, away from his face. "I want to know more about Becca. What did you think was going on with her?"

"Could you be more specific? I'm not sure what you are alluding to."

"It's just that she seems naive in so many ways. Why do you think that is?"

I nodded. "Becca was emotionally stunted and much younger than her twenty-nine years."

I pictured Rachel as she was when I first met her. 'I don't know what to do, Sarah,' I remember her saying often in those first couple of meetings. 'I'm being stalked by this madman and the police are sitting on their hands.'

She had just finished describing to me her close encounter at the El station, and the intimidating phone calls that kept her on edge. Her hand shook when she raised it to massage her forehead, her anguish clearly visible. I initially had doubts about her veracity, but my meetings with her, and the evidence I had already gathered, suggested she was telling the truth. Either way, I had to act cautiously. Unless she had fabricated the stalker and his calls, she was in serious danger.

"What can you do to protect yourself if the police won't?" I had asked her.

"I guess I could move back into my parents' house, but that doesn't seem like much of a solution. I don't know how to answer the question."

I studied her. In her navy blue capris with a pale blue knit top and her hair pulled back in a ponytail, she looked like the dictionary definition of ingenue. While there are limits to my relationships with my clients, and I am typically conscientious in maintaining my professional boundaries, I knew in this case I had to do more. Since the authorities were unwilling to do anything, there wasn't much leeway for timidity on my part: I had to act decisively to defend her.

"From what I hear you're at terrible risk. You have to do something now. If you're not able to, then I'm going to have to step in and help you out."

She glanced up at me in puzzlement. "What can you do?"

Good question! I had to think fast. "I can call

the police, with your permission."

She made a dismissive sound. "Good luck with that. They seem certain I'm making this whole thing up to cover my tracks. What good will that do?"

"I'm a professional, which offers me a little more clout. If you'd like, I'd be willing to try to convince them to do something. Or, if all else fails, shame them into action."

She shrugged. "Okay, but I hope you have more success than I've had."

I rose to find a permission slip for her to sign.

Adrian rubbed his square jaw seductively, and caught my eye. "You don't look any older than twenty-nine yourself."

I had to remind myself he was referring to Rachel's age. A tremor ran through me. Is he flirting with me? No doubt this man's a hunk, but I can't believe my reaction. As a professional, I've always prided myself on my self-control. This is ridiculous, I tell myself, which did nothing to keep the quiver from my voice. "Actually, I'm thirty-eight."

He whistled through straight, white teeth. "You don't look it. I didn't realize we were close in age. I thought you were much younger."

Self-conscious, I said, "How kind of you, but back to Becca. Because of events in her life I have yet to reveal, and the fact she'd been sheltered by her parents, she had a developmental lag and was functioning at an age younger than her chronological years."

"And you...you seem to have taken a personal interest in this case. You must be a caring person." He caught my eye again, but I turned away, flustered.

How did he figure me out this soon? Did he suspect how much I identified with Becca, or am I reading too much into what he said? "You're being too kind. It's my job to be caring, but..." I looked back at him pointedly, "I have my boundaries."

"I see." He smiled as though he knew something I didn't. "You must be a good psychotherapist."

"I certainly hope so."

"I'd like to find out more. Perhaps at lunch?"

I looked at my watch, relieved it was time to resume my lecture. It gave me an excuse to end our conversation and to spend a minute regaining my composure. I had to admit Adrian was exactly my type, with a deep throaty voice that could heat the room on a winter day. To maintain my professional distance and integrity, I'd better watch myself around him. "I have to refill my coffee before curtain call. I'll speak with you later."

He smiled again. "I look forward to it."

I watched him saunter off as I wiped perspiration from my brow, wondering if anyone had tampered with the thermostat without my permission.

Meeting Adrian might be the most interesting thing that's happened to me in recent memory, but it's at such a bad time. I have barely recovered from Ken's betrayal and the messy divorce. I couldn't even consider in my wildest imagination—okay I could consider, but it doesn't mean I'd start a relationship with anyone new. What advice would I give myself if I were my own client? 'The timing's not right. Don't go there. Use your head, not your heart.'

Sure, I had all the answers, but would I follow my own advice? Typically yes, but Adrian's obvious interest made him more appealing than any ordinary man. And I was in no ordinary mood.

Back at the podium I cleared my throat and waited for the room to quiet. Then I began.

That night the jangle of the phone woke Becca from a deep sleep. Thinking it might be Evan, she reached across the nightstand, knocking over a glass of water. Flustered, she picked up the call before the answering machine did. Her heart sank on hearing Julie's raspy voice.

"I've been trying to reach you for days. Where have you been?"

"Sitting by the phone anxiously awaiting your call."

"Why do you always have to be so rude to me?"

Because you woke me out of the best sleep I've had in months, to berate me for not being available to you. Perhaps Julie was right, she should be more tolerant, but sometimes it was damn difficult. "Sorry, Mom. I've been busy at work."

"Too busy to call your mother? You know I

worry about you."

"That's the problem, Mom. I don't need you to worry about me. I'd let you know if I needed anything. I can take care of myself."

Julie gave a derisive laugh. Becca heard the reprimand coming before her mother spoke. "I'm not so sure about that. Why, your dad and I were shocked at the condition of your apartment last week!"

She tried not to sound defensive. "You do remember I just moved back in? A few weeks before, the police were picking the place clean."

Silence for a second. Perhaps Julie was reconsidering. "I'm your mother and I worry about you. Is that a crime?"

No, but it was the crux of the problem. No use arguing with her. "So, besides my daily check-up, to what can I attribute this early morning wake-up call?"

"I have good news. My baby brother, your Uncle Paulie, has returned to town from California. I'm having a small get-together at the house next weekend. Plan on being here Saturday night for the gathering."

No way ready to face new people—or even old relatives for that matter—in a social situation, Becca cringed. "I don't remember Paulie well."

"Of course you don't. He moved away when you were only twelve, but you were quite close before he left. He adored you. I know he's eager to see how you've turned out."

Not so well at the moment. She rubbed her

irritated eyes. "I don't know, Mom."

"I won't take no for an answer. We expect you next Saturday no matter what. Bring your friend from work if you like, but be here one way or the other."

Julie sure had a way of putting things. She needed time to consider. "Angela has a new boyfriend and I doubt she'll be available."

"Bring another friend. Just come."

She heard a click on the line. *Saved by call forwarding*. "Hold on a sec. I have another call coming in."

She compressed the button. "Hello?"

"Where have you been hiding?"

Evan's melodic voice immediately acted like an elixir and wove a spell over her. She had to remind herself of her upset with him.

"I could ask you the same thing! Let me give you a call back when I'm done with my mother. I'll only be a couple of minutes."

She put Julie off on the dinner without making a firm commitment, and took a moment to soak up water with a tissue before getting back to Evan. Her mom was driving her crazy. She couldn't have Julie calling all the time, making her feel guilty for something she hadn't done, or had yet to do. If she didn't think of an excuse, she'd be at the dinner party. Who knows? Maybe showing her face would get Julie off her back. But first, Evan.

She pushed the recall button on the receiver.

"So, where have you been?" Was she beginning to sound like her mom? She hoped not, but she wouldn't be surprised after all the years of rigorous training. "You've been missing in action the last couple of days. Let me guess. You were captured by a band of terrorists and held for ransom. You barely escaped to call me."

"Must be the same organization that seized you. I stopped by your place a couple of times, but you weren't home."

"Oh, you haven't heard about my stimulating night life. I've been on a double-shift at St. John's. Just living it up."

He laughed. "I don't know if I could handle that much excitement. But," his voice dipped lower, "I could sure handle seeing you."

Against her will the last of her resistance and resentment melted away. "Your timing's impeccable. I have a dilemma I wanted to run by someone, and you're it. But," she glanced at the clock, "I have to go to work. What are you doing for dinner?"

"Bringing wine and dessert?"

"And a willing ear. Come by around seven."

She hung up and started the shower, luxuriating in the sensation of frothy water sluicing down her stomach and over her thighs. She found herself humming one of her favorite tunes, but in the middle of U2's Beautiful Day she stopped, annoyed. Even though she had no claim on Evan or his time, he had never answered her question about his whereabouts. Why was he being so secretive if he had nothing to hide?

"Do you want anything else?" Becca asked, glancing over at Evan, who looked spectacular in jeans, tooled boots, and a forest-green flannel shirt. He certainly carried clothes well on his lean- but-muscular frame.

He put down his fork and pushed back his chair. "I'm stuffed, what a great meal. You're quite the cook."

She wouldn't know about the meal. She'd been so enthralled with Evan she had hardly touched her fish. Between bites of salmon with hollandaise sauce and steamed asparagus, he had answered her questions about the use of medicinal herbs in the treatment of rheumatoid arthritis, and explained the application of acupuncture needles for mitigating pain. While telling her about his first successful patient, he absolutely glowed in the candlelight. She could hardly take her eyes off him.

He took a sip of wine. "What else do you want to know?"

"Since I don't know a thing, it's an open-ended question. Are you sure you want to go there?"

He smiled. "Can we limit the scope just a little tonight? I do have to catch a few hours sleep."

She smiled. "Okay. But I'm dying to know how you became involved in all this."

"Hum..." He stared thoughtfully away, which gave her a chance to study his strong profile and cleft chin. "Let's see...I've been interested in metaphysics for many years. Started reading writers like Marianne Williamson and Eckhart Tolle when I was an undergrad, and immediately felt the calling. Are you familiar with them?"

She shook her head.

"Sorry."

"No reason to apologize. You're not alone. They opened up a whole new world for me. I'd never considered myself a spiritual person, and actually thought of myself as an empiricist. I figured if something couldn't be weighed or measured, it most likely didn't exist. But metaphysics makes sense. It gives me a whole new perspective."

She leaned forward. "Explain it to me."

"Tell you what," he said. "If I help you with the dishes and brew a pot of Evan's extraordinary coffee, we can talk over dessert."

He came around the table to help her to her feet. When his fingers touched her arm, a tingle of fear shot up her spine. She involuntarily pulled away, but his hurt expression made her wish she could undo her reaction. What was it about a sexy man touching her, even in such a non-threatening way, that frightened her so much? Was this another symptom of her rape?

"Sorry."

He studied her face. "No problem. I should be more careful with you, after all you've been through. It's no big deal," he said, but his expression told her otherwise. "I need you to come by my place to pick up the fixings."

Relieved to be distracted by the chore, she followed him to his condo in the next building over. Once there, he remembered he had left his key at her apartment and fished around for a hidden one above the door jamb. He let her into a room that looked much as she had expected: with dark wood shelves along one wall full of books in every size and shape, a large Buddha statue on the floor alongside the bookcase, and an intricately patterned charcoal-gray oriental rug underfoot. Black and white yin/yang posters hung from adjacent walls. He immediately strode off to the kitchen, which gave her a chance to peruse his unusual book collection. She glanced over every now and then to watch him fill a bag with whipped cream and tart shells, gather up a container of chopped fruit, and add a jar of honey.

Back at her apartment, she scraped dishes and placed them in the dishwasher while he ground coffee. Soon the aroma of fresh brewed java filled the room. With two heaping plates of rainbow-colored fruit tart topped with a frothy cloud of whipped cream in hand, he led the way back to the table.

With only one sip of the coffee, she knew she was hooked. A man who could brew a perfect cup of coffee, while extrapolating easily on the use of acupuncture needles to anesthetize arthritis pain, was a man worth getting to know. But what impressed her most was his gracious nature and generosity of spirit. It had made quite an impression on her. She took a taste of the fresh fruit and whipped cream over white cake. "Um. This is heavenly."

He smiled. "Almost as heavenly as being with

you."

Self-conscious, she glanced away, even though she secretly enjoyed the attention. "Go on now. Tell your story."

He sipped his coffee. "Where were we? Metaphysics, right?"

"Uh huh."

"Metaphysics is the study of why things exist. What their purpose is. The way it explains our existence makes sense to me, much more than my religious training. I was raised as a Protestant. Even though my father was nominally Jewish, he was agnostic, so my Episcopalian mother took over my religious upbringing. I never fully accepted what the Bishops preached. To me, metaphysics is more real."

"Do you believe in God? I've always had a problem accepting the concept someone's looking out for us, but more so since David's death."

He looked pensive. "I know what you're going through, I've been there myself, but recently I've come to believe in a higher consciousness, which you can call God or Higher Power or Spirit. I like to think of it as Spirit, because it takes away all the old connotations. My concept of Spirit is nothing like the Judeo-Christian one of a bearded man on a throne. To me, Spirit isn't separate from us. It's more like a unifying force existing in all of us, on something similar to a subatomic level."

The fire that filled his eyes ignited a flame in her. Here sat a thoughtful man of conviction. A far cry from where she was at, and she had to admire him for it. "How did you go from atomic man to alternative medicine?"

He chuckled. "One thing led to another. I was pre-law at Temple University when I decided to follow my heart and switch to alternative medicine. Since much of modern metaphysics is based on Buddhism and other eastern traditions more than western religious practices, it was a natural transition from metaphysics to oriental medicine."

She took a bite of the tart, grateful to be getting to know him.

"But enough of me. You said you had something to talk about."

"Nothing as inspiring as yours, I'm afraid." She looked up and met his patient gaze. "My mother's throwing a party next weekend for my uncle, who recently returned from California after seventeen years. She's insistent I attend, but I'm not sure I'm ready to be social just yet. I thought about skipping it, but she'd throw a fit. I thought I might go if I don't have to do it alone." She held her breath, not sure she was prepared for a "no."

"I wish I could help you out, but I have a major project due the following week. I'll have to stay close to home and library all weekend."

Too bad. Or maybe it wasn't. She couldn't predict what would happen if she introduced him to Julie. "Any other ideas?"

"Why don't you be honest? That's usually best."

"Not with my mom it isn't. She'd never understand. I need an excuse."

"I'm not good at making excuses," he said, but she wasn't convinced of that yet. He took their cups and returned with fresh coffee. "Since I can't go with you, I'd love to make it up with a dinner date the following weekend."

How could she say no, when she wanted so much to say yes? Besides, he'd been more than generous with his companionship. She owed him one. Where else could she have turned with Angela in love and unavailable? And even if she had the chance, would she want to go anywhere else? "I'd like that, but..."

"What?"

"There's one thing bugging me, and I'd like to clear it up before we go anywhere. You never told me where you went the other night."

He shrugged. "I had a lecture. You knew about it."

"And it didn't end until the middle of the morning? Must have been a good one. Metaphysics for the insomniac."

He furrowed his brow. "Are you checking up on me?"

"Of course not. I couldn't sleep. I wanted company. So I looked for you."

"I know you're in a vulnerable place, but I have no reason to report in to you." He rose and carried their plates to the sink, rinsed them off and stacked them in the dishwasher. After drying hands on a towel, he approached the table. "Okay, I'll tell you where I went, but not because I have to. I was out drinking with a friend after the lecture. I spotted your note when I came home, but it was too late to disturb you. And that's that."

"Sure," she said and offered him a weak smile, kicking herself mentally for being suspicious of such a kind man. Just one more piece of evidence she had a long way to go before she recovered from her trauma.

At the police station, Becca watched Sally Mills make a note in a chart, her long, blond hair obscuring her face. "So you're saying I might be a suspect in David's death?"

Mills brushed her hair back, exposing a slight scar by her right ear. "I didn't say suspect. I said a person of interest. Right now we're looking at everyone, including you. You don't have any corroborating witness to what happened, and you have a motive."

Stunned, Becca scrunched up her face. "Motive? What type of motive do I have?"

Mills shrugged. "Someone at work overheard you griping about your husband the day of the murder. Seems like you were unhappy with him. What can you tell me about it?"

Damn, Sylvia must have overheard her conversation with Angela after all. Unnerved, the walls of the interview room seemed to be closing in around her. "We had a few marital problems, but nothing that would drive me to murder him. You're way off base."

"Perhaps, but we have to follow every lead."

Even if they always led back to her. "Do you have any real leads? Because you're barking up the wrong tree with me."

"None yet, but we're working on it," Mills said.

"I'd like to see you work harder. Some lunatic is out there telling me he'll be back, and all you ever do is question me and my motives. I'm at risk and I need your protection." She swallowed the frustration that rose like bile into her throat. "I'd like to know if you've been able to trace those strange phone calls I mentioned."

"It seems someone has called your number a few times from different phone booths on Market Street. Do you have any idea who the someone could be?"

She shook her head.

"We'll put a tag on one of the phones; see if we can find out anything." Sally stood. "Okay, that's it for today. Stay where we can get hold of you if we need to. It might be a good idea to get yourself a lawyer. Your call, but it can't hurt."

Becca cringed. Every shred of evidence the police uncovered seemed to point in her direction. Eerie. As though fate, like the manipulative chess-playing personification of death in an Ingmar Bergman film, had stepped in to rearrange the crime scene.

She returned to her car, wondering again whether she'd be the one to take the rap. The police had her in their sights and didn't seem to be actively seeking out another suspect. At this thought, her head throbbed with a ringing in her ears that sounded more and more like an emergency alarm.

Becca smoothed down the skirt of her sapphire-blue dress with painted nails, and adjusted the faux fur wrap that had shifted down her upper arm. Already reluctant to join the party on the other side of the stately carved, oak double-doors leading into her parents' house, an uproarious guffaw, followed by giddy voices, only magnified her resistance. She had failed to come up with a plausible excuse for not attending her parents' soirée, which obligated her to make an appearance, but was considering bowing out anyway when a couple started up the steps behind her. Concerned they might recognize her and report her defection to Julie - which she would never hear the end of - she opened the door as inconspicuously as possible and slipped into the foyer.

No matter how invisible she tried to make herself, Julie still spotted her in the entranceway, and rushed over to wrap her in an unexpectedly warm hug after the recent tension between them.

"You're here at last! I've been waiting for you."

Breaking free of the embrace, she placed her cape on an ornately carved bench.

Julie appraised her. "You look lovely! Come. I'd like to show you off to my guests." With a hand under Becca's elbow, Julie guided her through the family room, stopping every few feet to make small talk with a relative or an old friend.

The reactions Becca encountered failed to surprise her, but still made her feel uncomfortable. Neither Bea nor Jay Schecter would make eye contact with her when inquiring about how she was doing. Jay shuffled from one foot to the other, while Bea mumbled a couple of questions. Equally awkward was Barney Samuels' attempt to put her at ease, giving her a half-hug at arm's length. He must have figured she was too fragile for the real thing.

After another one of these bungling exchanges with her elderly Aunt Sadie, Becca was beside herself with a desire to flee. With Julie engrossed in a conversation nearby, she prepared herself to make an excuse and head for the exit, only to spot her favorite cousin approaching.

Janet flung her arms around Becca and whispered in her ear, "I'm glad you're here. Save me from this maddening crowd."

Finally, someone who treated her like a real person and not like one of her mother's expensive and irreplaceable china plates! "You're the one who better rescue me. I can't stand another moment of this."

Janet glanced over at Julie, still chatting up Gail Samuels. "Think you can break free from your Siamese twin?"

Becca shook her head. "Not for long. But while

I have a moment, tell me how you're doing."

"You're the one who's been through it lately. You go first. I'm all ears," Janet said.

"And more hugs, I hope."

As though to prove her availability, Janet embraced her again. "I'm here for you, kiddo, and don't you ever forget it."

Thank goodness for Janet. She single-handedly made it possible to remain a little longer. Becca gladly shared her recent experiences with Janet, with only minor editing to minimize the gore and unpleasantness. She didn't want to put a damper on the festive mood. She then encouraged Janet to do the same. They were in the midst of catching up when Julie broke away from Gail and joined them.

After greeting Janet, Julie took Becca by the arm. "I don't mean to interrupt you two, but Becca hasn't had a thing to eat—I would guess the entire day. I hope you'll excuse us while I do the motherly thing, and make sure she doesn't fade from famine."

Becca rolled her eyes at Janet, who smiled back at her. "Of course," Janet said. "But only if Becca promises to call me."

Having gladly sealed the deal, Becca trailed after Julie, with a couple of short detours to say hello to a group of neighbors and a distant relative, to the buffet table, where Julie insisted they fill up their plates. Becca didn't have much of an appetite after meeting with the police, but halfheartedly spooned food onto her plate to appease her mother.

When she reached for a bagel smeared with lox, her hand grazed another. She looked up into the deep-set turquoise eyes of a stranger. "Excuse me."

He grinned and shrugged, shaking his full head of sable-brown hair. "No problem. Why don't you go first."

Becca politely consented, noting his rugged good looks. Why hadn't she met him at her parents' house before?

Julie stepped forward. "I bet you two don't remember one another, do you? It's been so many years." Before either could reply, she went on. "Drew, this is my daughter Becca. Drew is Sam and Lisa's son. He left for college when you were still fairly young."

"Drew?" Becca held out her hand, trying to remember this handsome stranger. "I can't place the face, but your name sounds familiar."

Julie beamed at Drew. "I'm glad you were able to come tonight! I can't tell you how much it's meant to your folks when you moved back into town. I don't know if Lisa could have survived Sam's diagnosis without you around. You're a good son."

"Only doing what any son should do for his parents."

Julie sent Becca a smirk. "Not all children are as concerned about their parents as you are."

Becca did her best not to react to Julie. She shook the hand Drew held out to her, which was as warm as his smile; but a mild feeling of revulsion passed through her. She couldn't wait to withdraw her hand. Since the rape, every attractive man she met generated a similar reaction. She hoped she would get over it soon. "Where were you living before?"

"In Washington. I was working as a Congressional Clerk. I just moved back here a couple of months ago to start my own law practice."

"What type of practice do you have?" Becca asked.

"I specialize in environmental issues."

She should have guessed, noting his obvious counter-culture jeans and tweed jacket. "That's a noble cause. How's it going?"

"I've only been in practice here a little over a month, and I already have two cases. It looks like I'll be busy. But enough about me. I'd love to discover more about you. Let's finish filling our plates and see if we can locate a couple of free seats."

She turned back to the buffet and forked a slice of lox onto her plate. He handed her the salad spoon. When they were done piling it on, they excused themselves from Julie and made their way to the side of the room, where they cornered two black leather club chairs being vacated.

"Whew, that was a close one," Drew joked as a couple glided by and eyed the chairs. "Where did we leave off?"

"We were finding out about one another."

"Right. Go on."

In between bites of lox and bagel, she shared

with him a retrospective of her career. She kept it light and frothy, but he seemed more interested than her description warranted, and peppered her with questions. Then he glanced down at her ring finger with the tan line and his expression changed.

"I heard about what happened from my folks. I'm sorry to hear about your trauma. It's quite a thing to go through."

She followed his gaze to her naked finger and felt immediately overwhelmed with a powerful sense of sorrow. Remembering how she had carefully locked David's ring away after the funeral, she swallowed the knot of misery forming in her throat. "Thanks. I appreciate your sentiment, but I'd rather not speak about it right now."

A stricken look formed in his eyes. "I shouldn't have brought it up."

She could see his embarrassment. "I'm the one who should be sorry. You were only trying to be helpful."

"Tell you what," he said. "To make up for my blunder, how about if I take you out for coffee sometime. I'd like to get to know you better."

Before she had a chance to answer, Julie appeared at her side, with an expression Becca knew only too well. Her mother's pleasure because she had hit it off with Drew dampened her enthusiasm for him a little.

"I have someone I'd like you to see." Julie held onto the hand of Becca's cousin Andy who, according to the set of his jaw, had been dragged over against his will. She smiled up at him, noting how much he looked as she remembered him, skinny and shy, with disheveled, mousey-brown hair and a wrinkled shirt. Andy might have graduated from college by now, but he had quite obviously never advanced much past nerd.

She rose to give Andy a hug. When she asked him a simple question, he immediately lunged into a long diatribe about his stamp collection, offering Julie the opportunity to pull Drew aside and bend his ear.

Always polite, Becca listened absent-mindedly to Andy, although what he called philately, or stamp collecting, didn't interest her in the least. She soon found herself distracted by her cousin Freddie, who stood a few feet behind Andy and performed a card trick to the amazement of a couple of kids. Out of the corner of her eye, she caught sight of Barbara Murray piling her plate high with caviar-covered crackers.

As Andy droned on about his discovery of a rare 1860 Brown Jefferson Mint, all Becca could think about were the many parties she had attended at this house over the years. Card club parties, birthday parties, anniversary parties, graduation parties. Even her wedding had been held in a tent in the backyard.

Parties provided opportunities to come together in camaraderie and joviality - to celebrate life - but she couldn't relate to those emotions at all. Instead, the animation of others only amplified her sense of alienation, until she was on the verge of tears.

Julie sidled up alongside her and, with an excuse to Andy, nudged her aside. "Your uncle has arrived. I want you to come with me to welcome him."

Grateful for her mother's intrusion, she didn't put up a fight when Julie grasped her by the arm and piloted her over to a large man with his back to her. When Julie tapped him on the shoulder, he turned toward her.

"Oh my God," he said to Julie. "It's Becca. My little Becca. My, how you've grown."

He scooped her up into a comforting bear hug, until a familiar scent made Becca's stomach lurch. She pulled back, but much to her surprise, the room had begun to spin as if she'd had too much to drink. She seized the back of a chair to steady herself. Everything around her had taken on an unreal quality, as though she'd accidentally stepped out of the present dimension into a cartoon world.

What had happened? This was her dear Uncle Paulie. Her mother's brother, who bore a close resemblance to the photo on Julie's mantel; except for a couple of extra pounds, the shaved head, and the wire-rimmed glasses. Why the strange reaction?

He wrapped an arm around her shoulder and the room spun faster.

Although she tried to smile, her lips refused to cooperate. "It's good to see you, Uncle Paulie."

He turned toward Julie, offering Becca a second to compose herself, but she couldn't quite calm the shivers inside.

"She's a beauty, sis. A real beauty."

To be social, she answered his questions about her as briefly as possible. But when she made a simple inquiry into his life in California, intending to finish off the conversation, he launched into a colorful description of Napa Valley, depicting the verdant rolling hills of vineyards, and quaint communities.

Finally, Cousin Freddie sauntered up behind him and slapped Paulie on the back. To her relief, Paulie rotated around to shake Freddie's hand, exclaiming how it had been years, and they immediately detoured into an extended game of "catch up." She used this opportunity to excuse herself, located her jacket, and headed straight for the front door.

Drew stopped her on her way out. "Where are you going?"

"I'm sorry. I have to leave."

He turned up his hands in a gesture of exasperation. "I don't understand. I was hoping we could get to know each other a little better."

"I can't explain." She lowered her voice. "I have to go now."

"Is something wrong? Did I do anything to upset you?"

She shook her head. "Please don't take this personally. It's not you. It was wonderful meeting you—again." Before he could stop her, she slipped out the door and sped down the road away from Uncle Paulie and all the ugly feelings.

By the time her head had cleared enough for her to think things through, she knew something from her past had been unearthed at the sight of Paulie. A buried shard had poked its ugly head out of the wreckage of her childhood. Even though she had only caught a glimpse of it, she could no longer turn her eyes away from the sight.

The following evening at Evan's condo, Becca faced his curious stare. "My reaction to Paulie was definitely one of the weirdest experiences I've ever had. I've racked my brains since leaving the party, trying to figure it out, but I can't." She rubbed her throbbing head. "It's even hard to describe, but I suddenly felt as if I had stepped into another time/space continuum; had entered the Twilight Zone. I know it sounds crazy, but something about him scared the bejesus out of me."

Evan shot her a sideways glance. "Are you sure this wasn't a trick on the part of your psyche, to give you an excuse to leave the party?"

He had her there. She had intended to slip out immediately after meeting her uncle, and perhaps her imagination had helped her along. "I guess it's possible. It's no secret I'm having trouble being with those people right now. They look at me with pity. Besides, I can't be too much fun to be around."

"I don't know about that. The most fun I've had lately is with you."

"Then you can't be having much of a life."

"Au contraire."

Their eyes met for a long, sizzling moment. Not ready to take this further, she stood and wandered over to the wall of walnut bookshelves, turning down the disc of Native American drumming he had wanted her to hear. "I've taken up enough of your time tonight. I should be going."

"All right," he said, looking disappointed.

"I'm sure this isn't the last you'll hear about Uncle Paulie. I can guarantee I'll be trying to wrap my mind around this one for some time to come." She took his hand and helped him to his feet. "Walk me to the door."

At the door, he put his hands on her shoulders and turned her to him. "Why don't you give this thing a rest for tonight and we'll talk about it again tomorrow. Whatever it is, more will be revealed to you."

She stood close enough to feel the heat rising off his body, to inhale the subtle scent of aftershave. "Sure."

"I'll give you a holler during the day to see how you're doing."

He held her eyes for a moment with a look of such love and tenderness it frightened her. A part of her was tempted to kiss him, but it seemed too soon after her rape and her husband's murder for this level of intimacy. She reached for the doorknob. "I'd appreciate it. You're a good friend, making time for me."

"Is that all I am to you—a friend?"

She hadn't expected him to be so blunt, but it called for honesty. "For now. You know I'm still healing. I hope you understand."

"Of course I do."

He gave her a hug, but held onto her a moment longer than necessary. She couldn't say she minded.

"You're worth waiting for," he whispered into her hair, but before he could say or do anything more, she scurried out the door and was gone.

Chapter Six

A glance at my sleek, black Movado watch— the one Ken bought me mere days before I found out he was sleeping with the blond— told me it was time for lunch. Since I had come to a natural break in the story and the audience had begun to squirm, I announced the lunch break to a smattering of applause.

People took their time rising from their seats and, with the well-rehearsed behavior of a herd, headed out the door. Only one person remained behind: Adrian Farley. I gathered up my things and began to descend from the stage. He watched my every move with the hint of a smile.

"Aren't you hungry?" I inquired.

The smile widened. "I'm waiting to carry your books, Dr. Abrams."

"Sarah, remember? That won't be necessary, but you're welcome to join me at the table."

"That's what I was hoping, *Sarah*."

He deliberately emphasized my name, for effect. I fell into step beside him and we marched together down the corridor. I entered first into a long, narrow dining room packed with tables. A huge crystal chandelier hung perilously over a table on the near side of the room, making it clear the area had been partitioned off for our group. Adrian and I seated ourselves at a two-person table across from the entrance and made small talk until our chef salads were served.

He took a couple of bites, then lowered his fork. "Tell me more about your practice."

I haven't had a man express curiosity in me or what I'm doing in eons and I'm flattered by his attention. "I'm not sure what you're asking. I have a decent practice. Your typical depressives, marital conflicts, out-of-control teens. Nothing too esoteric. Must be similar to yours."

He nodded.

"The only difference between my practice and the practice of other therapists I know, is the two cases of Repressed Memory Syndrome I've seen in the past couple of years."

"Interesting. Please pass the salt." He waited until I did.

"What about you? Where do you practice and what do you specialize in?"

"I'm Chief of Psychology at a small local hospital, and have a general private practice in Pittsburgh. But a local friend, Dr. James Mayor, recommended this seminar to me. I recently picked up a tough case of Repressed Memory Syndrome and he thought I'd get something out of this weekend."

"Are you?"

He sprinkled his food and took a bite. "Becca's an intriguing case."

I pictured Rachel. "That's an understatement. Her case became more engrossing as the therapy progressed."

"Do you still see her in treatment?"

"Not any longer, but she keeps in contact."

With a head tilted to the side in rapt contemplation, his eyes never left my face. All I could feel, except excitement, was terror. I knew what he was looking at. I was about as average as they come. Average looks, average height, average weight. Nothing about me was exciting enough to deserve this much attention. And I was still a basket case after Ken's deception. I swallowed hard, hoping he wouldn't notice my discomfort.

"Did you place her on medication?"

I lowered my fork. "I'm not a psychiatrist, but even if I were, I'd be wary of referring my patients for psychotropic medication for every little thing. I know therapists who do that, but I'm not one of them. I guess I'm old school, but I believe you can change both perception and emotions without having to tinker with brain chemistry."

"You don't look 'old school' at all."

I ignored his awkward attempt at flirtation. "I was blessed with terrific teachers at the University of Pennsylvania and the Philadelphia Child Guidance Clinic, who thought medication wasn't the answer for every condition. They believed, as I do, our moods and thought patterns are often symptoms of an underlying emotional problem, and to medicate them might mask the real problem rather than treat it. Psychotropics are appropriate in certain situations, but not all. How about you? Do you often have patients placed on psychotropics?"

"I assume more often than you do. I find the serotonin re-uptake inhibitors particularly helpful with depressed patients like Becca. I had one man recently who attempted suicide multiple times, until I recommended him for Paxil. He hasn't had a suicidal episode since."

"That's good. I'm not saying I wouldn't medicate a patient who was suicidal or vegetative, but I didn't treat Becca with psychotropics, only hypnotherapy and behavior management, and it worked well."

"What do you do when it doesn't?"

"I try to encourage them to take a look at their life-style choices before I send them to a psychiatrist. Many of them eat fast-food on a regular basis, never exercise, and are under a tremendous amount of internal distress. Add to this alcohol and cigarettes, and you have the perfect storm." I took a bite of my salad. "I ask them to cut out the drinking and smoking, look at their dietary choices and exercise. I also suggest they look into vitamins and minerals, as well as a couple of herbs I find useful for treating mental health problems: St. John's Wort for depression and Obsessive/Compulsive Disorder, and Kava Kava for anxiety and insomnia. This often does the trick without any other medication. Have you tried any of these?"

"Can't say I have. I guess I'm more traditional than you are."

"I'm not saying alternative methods always work, but when they do, it's much easier on the patient and there's no possibility of dependency, which is there with anti-anxiety and, to a lesser degree, anti-depressant drugs. Perhaps medication would have worked just as well for Becca as anything else we did, but she would have run the risk of common side-effects such as weight gain and suicidal ideation. And, as you know, medicated and feeling better, she might not have been motivated to do the hard work necessary to explore her underlying conflict. It's easier to avoid dealing with trauma when you're not in pain."

"And in her case the conflict was?"

I wagged a finger at him. "That's why you're being attentive to me. Well, forget it. I'm not about to give away the punch-line before its time. You'll have to wait like everyone else."

"You're wrong." Adrian leaned forward. "That's not my attraction at all."

His smooth voice and sensual manner proved magnetic. I could sense myself being drawn to him.

"Then what is it?" I asked. My voice sounded husky to my ears.

"I find you fascinating."

He held my gaze until, ruffled, I looked away. I decided to change the subject. "Have you seen many Repressed Memory patients?"

"The one I mentioned is the first I've ever treated, but I'm glad I came today. It's been both informative and pleasant getting to know you."

Again he caught my eye. A part of me wanted to break eye contact, but another, more powerful part, could have gone on looking into his baby blues forever.

But it wasn't to be. The clock showed 1:45 and I had notes to go over before my lecture began again at 2. I rose. "I have to go. I'll meet you back in the conference room."

I reached for my tray, but before I could raise it, his hand covered mine. "I'll see you at break."

I tingled from head to toe. *How can I put him off when I want so much to turn him on?* "I'll look for you."

A smile lit his eyes. "You won't have to look far."

I turned away, slightly shaken. I felt something deep and dark and powerful take hold of me— something I could only compare to black magic or voodoo. It might only be lust, but my attraction to Adrian felt more mysterious and alive. My feelings tumbled over each other, trying to grab my attention. They were both wonderful and terrifying. I had avoided any man I found attractive or interesting over the past year, but this might be my opportunity to turn things around and stop behaving like a wounded animal. The time had arrived to begin moving on after my divorce, I decided. I can't hibernate forever!

I looked forward to the next break as another opportunity to get to know Adrian better, while I still had the nerve.

Fifteen minutes later, I was back at the podium and ready to begin the afternoon's lecture.

"Welcome back," I said over the din of the audience. I waited for the chatter to die down.

A woman in the front row raised her hand. "Sarah, before we move on, would you remind us of where we left off this morning?"

"Of course. I was planning on it. As you may recall, I stopped the story right after Becca met her Uncle Paulie for the first time in seventeen years, and had what she described as a dreadful reaction. That night she had another of her recurrent nightmares, in which an unidentified man had her trapped in her parents' bedroom, and she couldn't break away. She awoke in sheer terror, knowing he would be back for her.

"Becca arrived for her session a couple of days later, ready to do the work. She told me about a couple of disturbing dreams she had the previous week, and a memory that had resurfaced. But when she shared her curious reaction to her uncle, she seemed at a loss. To help her with this, I asked her permission to use hypnotherapy. She agreed—not yet fully aware of what she was getting herself into."

The next fifty minutes with Becca turned out to be a critical juncture in our treatment; and the beginning of our real work together.

Becca unfolded herself onto the sofa as

instructed. At my suggestion, she closed her eyes and used the deep breathing and progressive relaxation technique of muscle contraction I had taught her in our earlier therapy sessions to release tension. The moment she appeared more relaxed, I encouraged her to picture herself right before her encounter with her Uncle Paulie, to envision herself walking up to him, and to observe her response when he turned toward her.

It took only a minute before she shook her head. "I feel dizzy. Slightly nauseous. But everything has gone blank. I don't know if I can do this."

"Try to stay with it," I gently persuaded her, knowing I needed to be persistent in my approach. "Please describe to me what you're experiencing."

Becca clutched at the side of the sofa as though it were a life preserver, her knuckles white. "All I feel is fear. Pure unadulterated fear."

"Can you tell me more?"

"I feel...I don't know...strangely disoriented. As if Paulie has a sort of power over me...like I am at his mercy."

"Stay with the feeling and see if you can tell me what might be causing it."

She sniffed at the air, making a face. "An odor. A bittersweet scent. A sexy scent. A repugnant scent. I don't know what it is, but it's making me nervous. May I open my eyes now?'

"Try to stick with it a little longer and tell me what it is about the smell that's bothering you."

"There's a reason I'm reacting to it this way, but I can't put my finger on it...it's too uncomfortable."

"Does the odor awaken any memory in you?" I asked.

"I can't tell...I just lost it..."

"Can you take this any further?"

"No...I can't..." she said, a single tear making its way down her cheek.

"All right," I said, sensing her intense agitation. "That's enough for today. What I want you to do—"

Before I could continue, Becca flung open her eyes and levered herself upright on the sofa. She thrust her legs over the side. "Damn! Whatever the smell was, it's hard to believe Paulie wasn't in the room with us." She shivered and rubbed her arms for comfort.

"Don't worry. You're safe here," I reassured her. "Do you think you can identify the odor?"

Becca stared out the window, looking as though she'd rather be anywhere but here. "I don't know...it seems like some type of aftershave or cologne. I adore men's cologne. I can't imagine why it's affecting me this way."

"Neither can I just yet," I said, "but at least you're beginning to pinpoint what triggered your reaction the other night. The next step will be to figure out what caused you to react the way you did."

"I'm not sure I like this at all," she countered. "It feels ominous, like I'm stirring up something I shouldn't."

"I can sympathize with what you're going through," I assured her. "Whatever happened to you all those many years ago must have been objectionable enough for you to lock it away, deep inside. You're bound to feel a tremendous amount of dread when it resurfaces."

"And if I've been able to hide a truth this big from myself, what else am I denying?"

Becca rose abruptly as though to leave, but before she could, I stepped in front of her. "Before you go, I have a little something for you."

"What is it?"

"You know I had about as much success with the police as you did, and I'm not certain they'll do anything more to protect you than they've already been doing—"

"Which is nothing."

I drew a deep breath, knowing I was about to step outside my comfort zone as a therapist. "I've decided to take the matter into my own hands." I pressed a key into her palm.

She stared down at it. "What is this?"

"It's the key to my friend's apartment. She only lives in Philadelphia part-time and I care-take her apartment when she's out of town. She's given me permission to let you use it as a sanctuary anytime you feel threatened. I know you won't abuse this privilege."

Becca looked up at me with tears in her eyes. "Oh my God, Sarah, I can't believe you're doing this for me. After all that's happened lately, when even the police won't protect me, I was losing my trust in humanity. It's funny. I was just thinking of dropping out of therapy because it has stirred up too much, but this gesture makes me realize how much I need you right now. You're the only one I can trust to be there for me, who doesn't have another agenda. That means the world to me."

I squeezed Becca's hand closed around the key. While I felt a little uneasy about transgressing a professional boundary, I knew deep down I had done the right thing. Becca might never need to use the key, but with everything she faced, we both felt better knowing she had it.

A grid of downtown Philadelphia made it look like any other large eastern city, but from Rittenhouse Square, all Becca could see was the lovely old park, surrounded by stately eighteenth and nineteenth century buildings. Certain areas of the city bore a closer resemblance to a bombed-out Beirut, but the downtown had a generous sprinkling of high rises scattered among older, low-slung townhouses, elaborately carved fountains, and a well-preserved historical district. On Market Street, a statue of William Penn prominently rose above City Hall. For years no one had been allowed to build higher than the statue's hat, but all that had changed with the times. Now, tall, modern office buildings clustered nearby. Becca had always loved her native city and her love affair didn't suffer because of her view from Rouge Restaurant on Eighteenth.

Julie tattooed painted nails against the table top. "Julie to Becca, where are you? A minute ago I asked you a question, but you're too busy orbiting earth to respond."

Becca looked back at her mother. "Don't you think the park looks lovely in the afternoon light?"

Julie frowned. "You're such a dreamer! When are you going to come back to reality?"

"Better a dreamer than a schemer, I always say." Becca secretly enjoyed turning the tables on Julie. Then her attention was drawn to the sidewalk, where a stylish young mother pushed a stroller. Her mood quickly shifted to longing and envy.

"Finish your salad if you want to go shopping, I don't have all day. I have plans for this evening. Paulie's joining your father and me for dinner after six."

At the mention of Paulie's name, Becca flinched.

"Since I'm making a big meal, why don't you join us? Paulie would be thrilled to see you again, and I'll invite Drew if you want me to."

Although she had found Drew appealing at the party, the idea of Julie's matchmaking turned her off. Besides, she wasn't sure where she stood with Evan and she didn't want to lead Drew on. "Funny running into him after all those years."

"Not as funny as you might think. He's been nagging Lisa about seeing you ever since he moved back to town."

"Isn't it unusual I don't remember him, if he recalls me so well?"

"You were still young when he moved away to attend college. I always marveled at how tolerant he was of you when he was around. Not many teenage boys have that type of nature." Julie reached across the table and placed a hand on Becca's arm. "Please join us tonight."

"I can't, Mom. I made plans for this evening already," she said, stalling. She had to think fast. The last thing she wanted was to spend an entire evening with her parents. She had enough to cope with already.

"What plans can't be modified to spend time with us?"

"It's a visiting lecturer in my friend Evan's department, and she won't be in town again for a while. I've been planning to attend since I heard she was coming, and I don't want to miss out on it." She crossed her fingers under the table for telling a half-truth. Evan had mentioned Byron Katie would be speaking in Philadelphia this evening, but she hadn't planned on going along.

Julie folded her napkin and sat back. "Can't you change your plans? It would make Paulie happy."

Who would it please, Paulie or Julie? She knew the answer. "I made a commitment to him."

"How about your commitment to your family? That's never stopped you from doing what you wanted."

The words stung like a slap on the face. "How

can you say that? I always did what you and Dad wanted me to. I wanted to go to George Washington University, but you didn't want me to be far from home, so I attended Temple University—"

"A good school—"

"That's beside the point. And I married David even though I wasn't quite ready to settle down, because you didn't want me to move out on my own. I designer-made my life to suit you, and now all I want to do is a little something for myself and you make a problem out of it."

"Ha!" Julie slapped her open palm on the table, startling Becca. "You can't pin your choice of a husband on me. I liked David, but you're the one who brought him home. I didn't make you go out with him."

Technically true. Even though he was the son of a family acquaintance, she had met David on her own. Of course, Julie had made sure they would both be there and told her they should meet, but she and David had taken it from there.

Perhaps Julie was right and she couldn't totally blame her mom for the choice she had made. Sure, Julie approved of David, because she perceived him to be a strong, solid man who would take care of her daughter. While Julie might have played a part in her decision to marry him, Becca had ultimately picked him over her other suitors - a man for whom she had no real passion. Could there have been a connection between her choice of David, and what she now realized was her knee-jerk reaction to other, more attractive men? And did it mean there was something more insidious behind her choice?

She glanced over at Julie who, although still a handsome woman, seemed to be aging of late. Lines had etched their way into the soft skin around her lips and eyes, and a bulge had formed under her chin. The longer Becca looked at her mother, the less she wanted to argue with her. "I promised Evan I'd go with him this evening, but I'll definitely make arrangements to do something with all of you another time."

Julie leaned her head forward in a conspiratorial manner. "What's with you and this Evan fellow?"

"Nothing, Mom. How could there be? I just buried my husband. I'm not about to start anything new."

"But you told me you only married David to make me happy. Obviously he wasn't the love of your life."

"I cared deeply for David. Maybe not always as a wife should, but unwaveringly as a friend. Anyway, thrilled or not, he was my husband, Mom, and I owe him my loyalty. I'm surprised to hear this coming from you. I thought you were the authority on family allegiance." The words were out before she heard the inflection in her own voice. Too late. Julie heard it, too.

Hurt filled her eyes. "It's impossible to have a decent conversation with you. I hope someday you can accept me for who I am. We'd better get going."

In the same way you accept me? Becca thought about adding. But there was no use prolonging the pain. "Sorry, Mom. I didn't mean to upset you." Becca reapplied her lipstick and placed her compact back in her purse. She wanted to be more patient with her mom, but she had a lot to learn. When the hell would she ever learn it? And what type of lesson would it take?

Back at her apartment, Becca tried on the low-cut dress she had purchased at *Ross*, in an attempt to lift her mood at the end of the tense afternoon with Julie. As if being with Julie wasn't enough stress, she had come home to another of those unsettling silent messages on the answering machine.

With Cecil by her side, giving her legs a grateful rub, she modeled the dress in the full-length mirror on her closet door, then hung it up. In the kitchen, she fixed herself a glass of iced tea and Cecil a bowl of kibble. She was about to carry the tea into the living room when the phone rang. It was Drew.

"I've been meaning to call you for days because of the way you left the party the other night. How are you? Is everything all right?"

After an afternoon with Julie, that was a tough question to answer honestly. "I'm fine. How are you?"

"Busy, but I had to call and let you know how much I enjoyed meeting you at your parents' house the other night. I've been thinking about my promise all week. Since I owe you a coffee, I was wondering if we could get together downtown one afternoon after work. What do you say?"

What could she say? Not sure she should start anything new with all she had on her plate, she couldn't think of an excuse. "I say okay—as long as we keep it casual."

"Sure. Sure. No problem. Since I'll be in court this week, how about if I give you a holler early next week and we make plans?"

After agreeing to this, she carried her tea to the window seat, curled her legs beneath her, and sipped the spicy chai brew. Glancing out over the sugar maple in front of her apartment, she suddenly felt sad. Its vibrant red and orange leaves had turned brown, littering the pavement and the street, reminding her of how long it had been since David's death.

She watched as the wind kicked up leaves and sent them tumbling into the gutter. As though sensing her mood, Cecil leaped into her lap and purred. She petted him absently, and thought about her mother. No matter how hard Becca tried, she had trouble being patient with Julie. She knew her mother only wanted the best for her, and wished with all her heart she could control her tongue better. But Julie would only have to open her mouth, and Becca would find herself on the defensive again.

The last thing she wanted to do was hurt Julie. Her mother had enough to deal with, married to a man who hardly ever acknowledged her. Even during Becca's earliest years, Julie had turned to her to fill the void in her empty marriage. And for a long time, Becca had done her best to make her mother happy. Somewhere around her early teens, she had stopped trying. She had to be her own woman, but being strong always set up a battle of wills with Julie.

A knock on the door roused her from her

reverie. She opened it to Evan's beaming face.

"Where have you been? I came by earlier."

She ushered him into the apartment and offered him an iced tea and a seat on the couch. "Didn't I mention I had a lunch date with my mom?"

"No, I missed that one. How did it go?"

Becca made a face. "Hunky-dory. She insisted I come by for dinner, but I refused. Naturally that set off fireworks. A fun time was had by all."

"Did you tell her how you felt about needing more space for yourself?"

"You have to be kidding. It's impossible to tell my mom anything she doesn't want to hear."

He raised a brow.

"Okay." She stuck out her hand. "Slap me now. I know I've been bad, but how do you tell your mom you have trouble being around her? If you think of a polite way of saying it, let me know."

"You can't put this off indefinitely."

"Watch me. I excel at keeping Julie in the dark about my life. If I open the door even a crack, she's rummaging around inside, rearranging my mental furniture. Where do you think she'll put the surround sound?"

"You don't trust her, right?"

"Elementary, my dear Frankin."

"Did you ever figure out what bothered you about your uncle the other night?"

She topped off their drinks and placed the pitcher down on the coffee table. "I think it was his cologne or aftershave. That's as close as I've been able to come."

"You don't know the type by chance, just in case I wear it. I wouldn't want to offend you."

"How could you?" She poked him playfully. "Can you stay long? I'll make dinner."

"I have to go back to school for an acupuncture class, but I actually stopped by to see if you're free tomorrow. I've been thinking about a hike over to Independence Square. I haven't done anything but study for weeks, and I thought it would be fun to spend the afternoon with you. I'll even take you out for a bite afterwards."

The possibility of being with him pleased her. Even though she'd considered punishing him for his recent lack of availability, the idea instantly vaporized at his proposal. Why was it so damn hard to stay angry at him? "Sounds like an offer I don't want to refuse."

"Good. I'll come by around noon."

He stood. "And don't worry about your mom. Everything will work out the way it's supposed to."

"Metaphysical mush, but sweet nonetheless. May I escort you to the door?"

At the door he turned toward her. "Out with you," she said, and gave him a playful shove forward before she had a chance to take him up on what his eyes offered. "Go back to work. I'll see you tomorrow."

The thought alone would get her through the night. She quickly closed the door behind him and leaned back against it. The idea of spending time with Evan sent a warm wash over her. Then she considered his unexplained absences of late, and the warm feeling turned into a cold splash of reality.

Again she reminded herself she had better take her time with him. She didn't want to lose her heart before she found her head.

Two days later, Angela caught up with Becca on her way out of Mrs. Wilson's hospital room. In a thoughtful mood after her date with Evan, Becca just wanted to finish her work and find her way back to a quiet place. Not that Evan hadn't been the prefect gentleman. They'd had a super afternoon visiting the historic district, admiring the renovated houses of historical figures like Benjamin Franklin and Betsy Ross, as well as Independence National Historical Park. But the kiss he had given her at the end of the evening had set off so many conflicting emotions, she needed time to process through them all. The moment she spied Angela, she realized that wasn't about to happen.

Angela's cheeks glowed with uncharacteristic elation. "You have a minute? It's important."

Sensing her need, Becca melted. Angela was worth the temporary deferment of her own desire. "Two for you. Come with me to the nurses' station."

They found facing seats in the back of the

station.

"I have a big favor to ask of you," Angela said. "I hope you don't mind."

"You want me to empty Bergman's bedpan. Right?"

Angela made a face. "That's beyond big; that's criminal! No, it's more of a personal favor."

Becca narrowed her eyes. "Doesn't have anything to do with handsome and smart, does it?"

Angela blushed. It was the first time Becca had ever seen her react that way. Angela looked as shy as a new student in the school cafeteria, and it amused her.

"I'm in love."

"Nah, I never would have guessed."

"It's written all over me, isn't it? I've never been good at camouflaging my feelings. That's why I've avoided getting involved with anyone before this." Angela giggled. "Too late now. It's the most amazing thing. I can't believe it's happening to me."

Becca studied her friend. "I can see your problem, since you're five hundred pounds overweight and have killer body odor. Other than that, you're quite a catch."

Angela laughed. "I know. I know. You always said I underestimate myself."

"Underestimate yourself? Weren't you coroneted the Duchess of Self-Doubt? I'm glad a guy has finally come along who can break through your roadblocks. Maybe he'll help you to see yourself for who you truly are."

"Sure...sure," Angela continued, obviously embarrassed. "I need someone to cover my Saturday shift. Handsome is taking me to Atlantic City; we'll stay at the Trump Casino overnight. Not bad, eh?"

Wonderful for Angela, Becca thought, as her heart suddenly began to hurt. When was the last time a man escorted her out of town on a romantic holiday? She couldn't remember. "If I were a gambling woman, I'd say it sounds like a winner. That is, as long as you don't bet your week's pay."

"Don't worry about it. I doubt we'll spend a great deal of time in the casino, if you know what I mean." Angela winked at her. "What are you doing this weekend?"

The hurt deepened. "Nothing exciting. Evan mentioned he's going to a herbology conference in the Poconos. I guess I'm doing what I often do—mental masturbation and mindless television watching. And don't forget marathon binge eating. Ben and Jerry's here I come."

Angela patted her hand and tried to look concerned, but unsuppressed joy lit up her eyes. "It's not all that bad. At least you have Julie and me."

"Shoot me! Just kidding, but don't ruin my fun. I get off on self-pity."

"Can you do it?" Angela asked.

"I don't know. Covering for you might take my mind off my misery for too long. How can I be a martyr if I'm not miserable?" Becca smiled. "Sure. At least it'll get me out of the house for a few hours."

Angela threw her arms around Becca's neck, nearly knocking her out of her chair.

"Whoa there, lover girl; curb your enthusiasm. I don't know if I can stand that much affection. It's the most I've had in months."

Angela imitated a small violin being played with her fingers. "You're a serious nut—but I love you. I don't know what I'd do without you, dear friend."

Becca had the same thought. Who would be there for better or worse if not Angela? She couldn't for a second consider going through this tough time without her dearest friend.

Chapter Seven

Little Becca clenched her pillow to her chest, certain a man waited just outside her bedroom door, ready to force his way in. Alone and afraid, she ducked her head under the covers much as her pet turtle did with his shell, and curled up as small as she could. Perhaps this time he wouldn't detect her. But she knew better.

After a moment, she peered out from under the covers and noticed his shoes were casting shadows in the crack beneath the door. She could hide in the closet behind her dresses, but he'd know where to find her because he'd found her there before. Under the bed? Behind the chair? There was nowhere to hide where he wouldn't discover her. All she wanted was to disappear. Like on Star Trek, into thin air. The door creaked open and she screamed—but as hard as she tried, the only sound that escaped her lips was a loud ringing...

She awoke with a start to the jingle of the phone, and shook her head to clear away the disturbing scene before lifting the receiver. "Hello..."

"Becca?" Julie asked with hesitation.

"Yes, Mom?"

"You okay? You don't sound like yourself."

She glanced at the clock. Seven-thirty. She had set her clock for eight. "I'm not awake yet."

"I didn't mean to disturb you this early, but I thought you'd be getting ready for work."

"I covered for Angela yesterday and arranged to

go in a little late today. What's up, Mom?"

"Good news!" Her mother's enthusiasm might have been contagious—later in the day. "Uncle Paul dropped off a little something for you last night. Since tomorrow's your day off, and your birthday, I'd love you to stop by for coffee. Please don't say no. I'd like to see you on your birthday."

Hearing how much it meant to Julie softened her initial reaction. "Of course, Mom. I'll be there after ten."

"Mom? Dad? Anyone home?" Becca called from the foyer of her parents' home.

A moment later she heard Julie holler, "Pour yourself a cup of coffee! I'll be down in a minute."

Becca made her way into the recently renovated high-tech kitchen, replete with gleaming stainless steel appliances and every possible gadget one could imagine, only stopping once to drape her coat over the arm of a black leather chair. She retrieved a red enamel mug and poured herself a cup of steaming, ebony coffee from the coffee maker, bolstering herself up onto a stool, while careful not to burn herself with the hot liquid. To be safe, she blew on it first before taking a sip.

Ever since the call from Julie the day before, mild anxiety had plagued her. Not enough to ruin her day, but enough to distract her from her work, as well as her nagging preoccupation with Evan. And the worst part: she couldn't, in a million years, figure out what unsettled her so much. She was sure it had been the provocation behind another one of her hellish nightmares that night.

"Hello, darlin'," Julie said, sweeping into the kitchen in a cloud of fuchsia silk robe. "I'm glad you could come by." She held out a sealed envelope. "I didn't want to misplace this before I had a chance to give it to you. It was sweet of your Uncle Paulie to remember your birthday."

Becca hesitated before taking the envelope from Julie's soft-skinned, perfectly manicured hand. She turned the envelope over, studying the large block letters of her name.

Julie watched her with the eagerness of a child on Christmas morning. "What are you waiting for? Open it and see what it says."

She pried open the card and read it out loud.

"To my favorite niece. You're as beautiful as always. I hope you have a wonderful birthday and we can celebrate together soon. Love, Uncle Paul."

Her throat constricted at the thought, and she quickly put the card back in its envelope.

"Wasn't it sweet of Paulie to remember your birthday? Now I have a little something for you." Julie pulled a black velvet jewelry box out of an oversized pocket and handed it to her. "Open it." Her eyes danced in anticipation.

Distracted by her reaction to Paulie's card, Becca absent-mindedly flipped open the box. Inside, cushioned in more black velvet, was a pair of shiny fourteen karat gold hoop earrings from Italy—the same earrings she had coveted for months in the window of *Zales* on Market Street. She reached over, giving Julie a big hug. "Mom, they're beautiful!"

Julie's thoughtfulness surprised her, and caused her to question her typical attitude toward her mom. Her sensitivity to everything Julie said and did protected her from the shackles of their smothering bond, but it also kept her from appreciating her mother's kindness and affection. At the moment, she regretted the loss.

"How did you know I wanted them?"

"David told me. He would have given them to you himself if he'd been here."

Without warning, love and tenderness nudged aside her reservations. She drew Julie closer. "I'm touched."

Julie patted her on the back. "After all you said to me about David, you did care for him, didn't you?"

"And I care for you, too, Mom. You and Dad."

"I don't know if I can take all this affection coming from you!" Julie remarked, laughing nervously. "Now if you'll only join us on occasion, my joy would be complete."

Not surprised Julie would suggest more family reunions in exchange for her consideration, but feeling as fragile as she did now, Becca knew she'd have to find a way to postpone them.

Julie broke the embrace with a small, playful shove, allowing Becca to retake her seat and another sip of coffee. Of course she still had a place in her heart for David—and the earrings only served to remind her of this, and of how much she had lost.

The silence of the lecture hall permitted my voice to carry easily to the back row. "Talk therapy can be as mundane as active listening and advice-giving, or it can rise to the level of the mystical. At those rare moments when it does, the therapist becomes one with the patient, and both experience a profound transformation of mind, body, and spirit.

"You can liken this to the experience philosopher Martin Buber describes in his book, *I and Thou.* Buber believes all relationships are potentially spiritual in nature. It is only through our affiliation with other human beings that we can connect with the sublime. When we experience these fleeting but miraculous moments of kinship, our consciousness is elevated to the level of the sacred. In that instance, we touch the face of God.

"This coalescing of the therapeutic and the spiritual remains one of the deepest, darkest mysteries of psychotherapy, and the ultimate goal of every conscientious psychotherapist. No one can teach you how to create this phenomenon. Distrust anyone who tells you they can. But every once in awhile you will strike the right chord in your practice, and the music will flow. I wish you all many of these transcendent moments."

I continued my lecture with what had transpired in early November.

Becca had called my office the day before her scheduled appointment and, since I had only minutes before ended a session, and was going over my notes, I answered the phone.

"Sarah, I need to see you today," she said in a plaintive tone.

Fortunately I had a cancellation later in the afternoon, and was able to fit her in. I could hear her barely restrained gratitude. As the saying goes, 'When the student is ready, the teacher appears', and Becca sounded eager to enroll in my class.

She arrived at my office wearing tailored black slacks and a red and black checkered sweater, a change from her usual short skirt and heels, and an obvious concession to the colder weather. She found a seat and immediately plunged into a description of her reaction at receiving the birthday card from her Uncle Paulie.

I advised her to lie back on the sofa, close her eyes, and take a couple of deep breaths. Then I urged her to go back to the moment of opening the card, and to re-experience her reaction to it. She lay silent for a couple of minutes and I gave her the space she needed before I asked, "How are you feeling?"

She shook her head. "Nervous. Confused. I don't know what's the matter with me."

"There's nothing wrong with you," I reassured her. "But stay with your feelings and allow them to lead you back to an earlier time when you felt the same way. When you arrive there, describe to me what you see."

For another minute, she lay perfectly still, then her features took on a strained appearance. "I can't tell you... I can't tell anyone."

"Don't be afraid," I said to her in encouragement. "I'll never judge you."

She hesitated for what seemed an awfully long time. I was about to offer my help, when she sighed.

"Okay...all right..." Another silence followed. "I...I see myself in my parents' bedroom."

"How old are you?"

"I don't know. Seven or eight."

"And what are you doing?"

"I'm looking at a book my parents have hidden away from me. There are nude pictures in the book and I'm not supposed to be looking at them, but I do."

She stopped again. "This is so awkward. Do I have to go on?"

"Try. It's important."

She wrapped her arms around herself, and a tear trickled down her cheek. "I hear the doorknob turn and someone enters the room. I quickly try to hide the book under the bed, but he catches me. He takes the book from my hands, looks at it and scolds me for being sneaky. 'I'm sorry,' I say, 'I'll put the book back where I found it. Please don't tell my mom I looked at it.'"

"Who are you talking to?" I asked.

"I don't know. It's a man, but I can't... I can't see his face...only a shadow..."

"Is there anything you notice about him?"

"He smells nice. Sweet and spicy. Like...Paulie." Her chest heaves and she places a hand over her heart.

"What does the man say to you?"

"He says he won't tell on me if I let him see the pictures. He sits down beside me and flips through the book. I can hear his breathing grow louder, which scares me. There's something not right about this, but I'm not sure what it is."

"What's frightening you?"

"He's looking at me funny. He asks me if I want to see the real thing. A naked man. I tell him no, but he starts to unbutton his shirt. Oh my God, he's removing it... Stop that! Don't do it!"

"What's happening?

"I'm trying to get up, but he won't let me. We must be alone in the house. I want to cry out, but I can't."

"What happens next?"

"He kisses me. A wet, sloppy kiss turns my stomach. I push him away, but he pulls me back. He tells me how beautiful I am. How I'm his little sweetheart. How he loves me. He holds me against him, but I squirm and try to break free."

"And?"

"I start to weep. He stops, tells me not to be

upset. He won't hurt me. He loves me too much. I tell him I want to go watch TV, but he says we can have more fun here. He says he wants to play a game with me, but I tell him I have homework to do. He laughs and kisses me again. Then he takes my hand and starts to move it down..."

Becca covered her mouth, rolled onto her side and curled in on herself. "That's all. I can't see anything else. It's all gone blank."

I could hear the distress in her voice. "I understand." And I did. These types of memories were painful; you had to take them in small doses. "You did a fine job today," I said, my heart going out to her. "You should be proud of yourself."

Becca remained fetal-style on her side for about five minutes, finally recovering her composure enough to slowly rise. She had taken a big risk by allowing herself to be led back to a time and place she never wanted to visit again. But she was the only one holding a ticket for the return trip to that time and place. In spite of her reluctance and fear, she would one day inevitably cash that ticket in, and wind up back in that bedroom.

Angela reluctantly sniffed from a sample bottle of cologne. "Explain to me again what we're doing here?"

"We're spending our precious lunch hour at Macy's, snorting up men's cologne instead of slurping on something scrumptious and fattening. This is your pre-holiday diet. Haven't you read about the cologne diet in *Cosmo*?" Becca picked up another bottle, inhaled, and recapped it. "Strike three."

"How about this one?" Angela asked.

Becca took a whiff of the open bottle, disappointed. "Nope. Wrong again. I don't know if I'm ever going to figure out which one Paulie wore."

"Then we can go to lunch, right? I'm starving."

"Let me try a couple more." Two turned into four and still Becca hadn't discovered the right fragrance. She was about to give into Angela's impatience when Angela stuck another bottle under her nose. "Smell this."

Becca drew a deep breath and all at once, the ground shifted beneath her feet. Angela had found it all right. The one that drove her blood pressure up and her spirits down. She grasped the counter to steady herself. "What is it?"

Angela turned the bottle around so she could see the label. "*Aramis*, or as I call it, heaven in a bottle."

Becca pushed the offending bottle aside. "Pleeease. Give me a second to recover. I can barely handle the stuff."

Angela looked bewildered. "What's the problem? Don't you like it?" She sniffed the cologne. "It's the cologne Elliot used to wear. He said he hasn't worn it in years, but he tried it on when we were shopping last week, and I almost lost my mind."

"Believe me, it's not that I don't like it. It's

something else. We don't have much time left, let's go for a quick bite and I'll try to explain."

"Wait. Would you mind if I bought some for one of Elliot's Christmas gifts? I'd like to keep a bottle on hand at my apartment when he comes by."

"Of course not, as long as I don't have to get wind of it again."

Angela made her purchase and they left the store for the lunch counter two doors down. After they were seated and had ordered, Becca turned to Angela. "I know this is quite a coincidence, but Elliot's favorite fragrance might also be my Uncle Paulie's poison. I swear the cologne you just bought was the same one he wore the night of my parents' party; the one that threw me into such a tizzy."

"It might not be a coincidence. According to the package, *Aramis* is one of the most popular men's colognes. I'll certainly be doing my part to promote it. I'll buy it for all my men from now on. It will keep me in a state of constant arousal."

"Just don't bring them around me or I'll be in a state of constant craziness."

"What's new?" Angela flashed her a big grin. "I hope it didn't bother you that I bought a bottle."

Becca shook her head.

"It drives me crazy, too. Crazy for Elliot. We had so much fun when we vacationed out of town. I don't mean to bore you with the details, but I'm beginning to think he's the one, Becca."

Becca sipped the coffee, but it didn't agree with her churning stomach. "Do I hear wedding bells?"

Angela shook her head. "Not yet, but I'm working on it. It's hard to pin Elliot down with his practice and all, but when I do, it's definitely bells and whistles."

"Should be quite an affair. Bells, whistles, cologne and crazies. I'm looking forward to it."

"Me too." Angela looked down. When she looked back up, a small smile creased the corners of her eyes. "Can I tell you a small secret? Elliot asked me not to say anything to anyone, but I can't keep a secret from you."

Becca nodded.

"He knows how tired I am of my job at the hospital. Yesterday he mentioned when we move in together, I wouldn't have to work there any longer. Actually, he said I wouldn't have to work at all and could do what I wanted with my time. It's like a dream come true."

"Almost sounds too good to be true. Before you tie the knot with Doctor Elliot, how much do you know about him?"

Angela tilted her chin upwards in a defiant poise. "Enough." Then she narrowed her eyes. "Why?"

"He sounds...wonderful."

"Believe me." Angela laughed. "He's a find."

"Where did you say you met him?"

"In the scuba I took at the YMCA. How's that

for luck? I've taken a dozen *Learning Annex* and other classes and never met a soul. Then, I put on my scuba gear and look like the monster from Mars, and meet Elliot. We both love scuba diving. We've been talking about a dive trip to Cancun sometime next year."

"Lucky you."

Angela laughed a husky, phlegmy smokers' laugh. "You have that right. I chose the class because I thought I might meet an interesting man, but I never expected to meet anyone like Elliot."

"Yeah, it's hard to meet men who are willing to dive into something this fast," Becca joked. "But before you decide to marry the dude, perhaps you should make sure he's everything he's cracked up to be. Has he introduced you to his family and friends?"

"Not yet. But we've only known each other a short time."

"And how about the double date we were supposed to be planning? Whatever happened to it?"

"I mentioned it to him, but...well, he's busy with his practice..."

"I don't mean to sound suspicious, but isn't he the one who kept asking you about me? Don't you think he'd be curious enough to want to meet me? Maybe I'm being paranoid after everything that's happened to me this past year, but I'd be careful before I committed to anyone whose behavior was inconsistent."

"You are being paranoid. Elliot's the most terrific man I've ever met! He's loving and generous and supportive. I couldn't ask for anything more."

Angela gulped down her coffee. "Maybe you're a tad envious, too. I know you've been lonely and unhappy these last few months, but that's no reason to rain on my parade. Believe me, even if I were to marry Elliot, you'd still be my closest friend. Nothing would ever change that."

Becca cringed at Angela's reaction. While their friendship had always meant a great deal to her, it had been her lifeline these last few months. If Angela had decided this was the man for her, who was Becca to question her choice? She would support Angela in every way possible. Becca held up her hands. "I'm sorry. I didn't mean to upset you. My mind's still reeling from the *Aramis*. Please forgive me."

Angela pouted. "I'll think about it." Then she smiled.

Relieved, Becca returned the smile, but her stomach still churned with a sense of unease.

Perhaps Angela was right; she was being overly suspicious. She certainly hoped so for Angela's sake, and for the sake of their friendship.

But why did she harbor such doubt?

As planned, Becca met Drew the following day after work at a coffee shop near city hall. She was already seated at a table, reading a Tony Hillerman mystery, when he rushed in. The shadow of a beard failed to cover the scarlet glow of his cheeks on such a bitter December afternoon. His thick black hair, ruffled from the wind, looked sexy yet sophisticated, and fit in nicely with his red jacket and black jeans.

"Sorry I'm late," he said. "I had a last minute consultation. I left you a message on your cell."

"I got it. Don't worry, I only stumbled in here a few minutes ago." She failed to mention it was because she had stopped by *Macy's* to look at their late fall sale.

"What will you have?" he asked. "A mocha? Cappuccino?"

"Make that a seasonal eggnog Cappuccino, and you're on."

He made his way to the counter and she waited until he returned, carrying their drinks. She sipped the warm, rich coffee mixed with the sugar-flavored syrup and steamed milk. "How are the new cases going?"

He looked up with the cutest mocha mustache, before wiping it away with a napkin. "Not bad. I have a tough one going to court in a couple of weeks. Big corporate polluter. They have the money to pay the big guns to represent them. Should be a real challenge."

"Who are you representing?"

"A poor community down-wind from their plant. Industry often locates its most toxic plants in poorer neighborhoods, hoping poor people won't be able to fight back. That's the case here. But these people are determined to do the best they can for their families and their community. I've taken the case *pro bono*, even though I shouldn't take on any freebies just yet. At least not until I'm more established and making a real living at this."

"That's really noble of you. Do you mind if I ask what you're living on?" She sipped her drink, feeling more than a little guilty for allowing him to buy. Perhaps she should offer to pay for her order.

"I'm all right. I have money socked away from my last job. But let's not talk about me. I want to hear more about you."

"What's there to tell? I live a fairly mundane existence. All work and no play. Nothing much more than I told you at the party." She toyed with a napkin.

"I'd believe it if I hadn't seen your grand exit the other night. Mind telling me what was going on?"

She didn't know how honest to be, especially since their parents were such good friends. "I'm still raw from my trauma and not terribly comfortable in social situations. I can only take so much."

He ran his finger over the rim of his cup. "Does that mean you're not ready to go out with me?"

She looked over at his strong profile, his wavy ebony hair and violet blue eyes. A ruggedly handsome man, he must not be used to women turning him down. "I'm not ready to go out with anyone, but I sure could use a friend right now. Are you up to the job?"

"I don't know if your mom would approve, but I think I could take it on."

"It's a deal then." She reached across the table and grabbed the hand he offered her, letting him squeeze and release hers. "By the way, you should be sainted for your handling of Julie the other night. I'll put a word in with the Pope for you."

He laughed. "You don't have to. Your mom's been good to my folks."

Becca grinned to herself. She wished Julie treated her family as well as she treated his. She glanced over at Drew, and knew what she had to do. She rose. "It's my turn to buy us a couple of refills."

The moment Becca exited St. John's the following afternoon, a refrigerated burst of late autumn air smacked her in the face. She drew her coat closer around her, and hurried down the steps to the street. The sky, streaked with ominous grey and plum-colored clouds, shrouded everything in an eerie half-light. Leafless trees reminded her of scarecrows. Newspaper pages and empty Styrofoam cups tumbled against the curb. The wind blew the last of the autumn leaves around her. Chilled to the bone, she darted off in the direction of her bus stop, hoping she'd catch the 4:15 and wouldn't be forced to wait for the next bus. Lately she had the unsettling sensation someone watched her every time she left work. She didn't want to wait around to find out who.

The bus hadn't arrived when she reached the corner of 22nd and Cherry. She squeezed into a partially glassed-in bench between an old woman in a tattered wool coat and a young kid in a light jacket that appeared too flimsy for such a cold afternoon. She glanced up the street to see if the bus trundled in her direction, and spied a man in a black trench coat standing on the adjacent corner. A wool cap pulled down over his eyes and a scarf covering his mouth kept his identity secret, but she had a strange yet overwhelming sense she was in his sights.

Just to be safe, she decided to move to the next bus stop. She rushed off in the opposite direction of her usual route with the hope that by hustling up Cherry Street, she'd throw off anyone following her trail. When she glanced back, she could see the man in the trench coat pacing not more than fifty feet behind her. Shivers rushed through her.

To elude him, she made her first left at 21st and headed in the direction of Market Street, planning to lose him in the crowd. As the throng thickened, she wove her way between them, too frightened to look back and see if she was still being followed. At the corner of 15th and Market, she stopped to take a breath, glancing around. No sign of her stalker. Perhaps she had been imagining things. Julie always said she had a vivid imagination. She breathed a sigh of relief.

A flash of black nearby sent her racing again toward *Macy's* Department Store. Imagination aside, she better not take any chances. During the Christmas season, *Macy's* was thronged with shoppers at all hours of the day. If she had been followed, she could certainly lose her pursuer in the store.

She darted into the crowded grand salon of Macy's with its three story, high-columned courtyard, and found herself surrounded by Christmas lights, ornaments, and a pipe-organ rendition of Deck the Halls. The gaiety made her fear seem silly and misplaced, and she slowed her pace. This might be an overreaction on her part! No one chased her down; she shouldn't let fanciful thoughts get the best of her.

She maneuvered her way over to the Santa throne in the middle of the lobby and stood close enough to observe the parents with their kids. Armed with *Nikons* and *Canons*, they waited for their children to take a seat on Santa's lap. The joy in their eyes and the flush on their cheeks sparked the unfulfilled maternal longing in Becca. Squeals of delight and anticipation only deepened her desire to have a child of her own, a desire not lost with David's death.

Suddenly a hand grabbed at her crotch and a shock-wave of terror and anger surged through her. Furious, she spun around to confront her attacker, but all she could discern was a blur of anonymous faces surrounding her. Desperately scanning the crowd for the man in the black trench coat, she couldn't distinguish a soul.

Shaken, Becca fled against the swell as fast as the swarm would allow, to the escalator that descended to the subway trains. She waited impatiently on the subway platform for the Market Street line, constantly looking around for her stalker. At last the train pulled up, but she stood back until the majority of commuters were on board. At the last possible second, she hopped on the train, hoping to confound anyone who might be watching her. At that moment she saw a streak of black enter a car down-track.

The train lurched and she stumbled into another passenger, but refused to move away from the subway doors. She prayed she could exit the train without incident. At the next stop, she shouldered her way out of the train the minute the doors opened, and bolted toward the stairs. Before she entered the stairwell ,she glanced up-track. Surrounded by black, she was unable to spot her stalker. Afraid to move, she scanned the area in a panic. Out of the corner of her eye, she spotted a black trench coat steal into an exit staircase down-track from hers.

She could barely breathe from sheer fright. Swallowing hard, she dashed toward a different exit, surfacing on 18th Street.

She jogged down the street in her high-heeled boots at an unheard-of clip and, after a furtive glance up and down 18th, stole into a boutique, slipping out the back onto Chestnut Street. On the move, she maneuvered in and out of stores until, breathless, she skirted a doorway into a bookstore mid-block. From the vantage point of the picture glass window she observed her surroundings. Reassured she hadn't been followed, she sidled behind a row of books, flipped open her cell phone, and called Evan.

The phone rang four times and she prayed aloud he'd pick up on the fifth ring. He did. "Evan, I need your help! I'm being stalked," she gasped into the receiver.

"Are you okay? Where are you?"

"I'm in *Borders'* books. At Eighteenth and Walnut Streets."

"Sit tight," he said. "I'm not far from you. I have my bike. I hope you don't mind."

By bike, he meant his motorcycle. She gulped. "I've never ridden on one."

"Don't worry. It's not far and I'll take it slow."

"What about a helmet?"

He laughed. "Don't you worry your pretty head about it. I'll lend you mine. Hang tough."

She waited, shaken, hidden behind rows of paperbacks and books on tape. She peered out regularly, keeping a lookout for the stranger in the black trench coat, but failed to see anyone fitting the description. Men passing the bay window seemed menacing, even when they smiled at her. She wanted to hide herself in the ladies room, but she might miss Evan. All she could do was pray Evan would arrive soon.

And he'd be there first.

Forty-five minutes later Evan pulled his Ducati to the curb in front of Becca's building and cut the engine. She hopped off the bike, relieved to be home. "What a wild ride! I'm frozen solid."

"Come on up to my place for a hot drink and cold comfort," he suggested.

"Better mine. I'd like to change into sweats and thaw out."

In her apartment, he waited while she changed, heated water for tea and joined him on the couch with a tray of gingerbread cookies.

"Are you sure you're all right? You had quite a scare."

"Couldn't be better," she quipped. "I even had an aerobic workout without going to the gym. What more can I ask?"

He frowned. "All kidding aside, I don't like hearing you were followed. It must have frightened the hell out of you."

She had only quit trembling after they pulled up to the building. "More than you can imagine. It's not everyday I have a man chase me. And today I didn't even want him to."

"You're absolutely sure you were being followed?"

She shrugged. "It certainly seemed like it, but I guess I could have conjured the whole thing up out of apprehension."

He gathered her into his arms before she could protest. "I'm grateful you're in one piece, but what are we going to do to keep you that way?"

She liked his use of the word 'we.' To let him know she trailed her fingertips over his lips. "You have any ideas?"

"I can pick you up from work when I don't have class. Maybe you can ask your dad to drive you home on my busy days."

"No way," she said, shaking her head. The last thing she wanted was to alert Julie to her troubles. She'd be shanghaied back to the Goldstein home under twenty-four hour surveillance before she could say 'illegal rendition.' "I can ask one of the other nurses to give me a lift to the bus stop. I'll figure something out."

"I know you will, but I'm here if you need me." He sat back, but kept his hands on her shoulders. "Before I chicken out, I owe you an apology."

"What for? Making me risk my life and limb on your bike?"

He chuckled. "No. For not being there at times when you've needed me. I've been busy lately, but I want to be there for you as much as I can be. I want you to know...you do something to me."

"Makes me want to break into song," she said, then sang the first line of the Cole Porter song, You Do Something to Me, Irv used to sing in the shower.

A crease formed in Evan's brow. "I must sound ridiculous."

She enclosed one of his hands in hers. "I didn't mean to make fun of you."

The set of his jaw and his steady gaze conveyed his seriousness. "I mean it, Becca. I'm drawn to you in a way I haven't felt in a long time. I know you're only beginning to recover from your trauma, but I want to be around when you're ready to love again."

She didn't know what to say.

Fortunately, he did. "I've been alone a long time. I'm ready to settle down with the right woman and start a family."

That seized her interest. "You want children?"

"As many as my wife does. I want to be a father."

Her heart melted. Before her sat one of the

sexiest men alive, reporting to her he wanted the same thing she did. What was preventing her from throwing her arms around his neck, if not her unhealed heart? "I've wanted to have a child for a long time."

"What stopped you?"

"David wasn't ready. I had a feeling he'd never be ready, or that he didn't want children at all."

"Too bad. Personally, I'd have a kid already if I'd only met the right woman sooner."

"You know, you have never mentioned any of your prior relationships."

"There's not much to tell. I married once when I was too young. I tied the knot on the rebound to forget someone I loved. I made a big mistake and ended up divorced in my mid-twenties. I've had a couple semi-serious relationships since then, but nothing worked out. I carried a torch for my first love a long time. But it's all over now, and I'm prepared to make a commitment to you whenever you say the word."

"What makes you so sure I'm the right one?"

He raised her hand to his lips, turned it over, and gently kissed her palm. A sexy, but scary sensation sizzled up her arm.

"Because I love your intelligence and sense of humor. The way your eyes light up when you're excited. The playful, but also the more serious side of you. The more time I spend with you, the more I like you. That hasn't happened with anyone else in a long time. I'm more certain than I've ever been about anything in my entire life. Take your time, but when you're ready, I'll be there."

It took every ounce of her will power not to give in to him. How long could she hold out against such a sincere expression of desire? And how long would she want to? She didn't have to answer the question because it was rhetorical. In the meantime, she wanted to be sure her interest wasn't just a reaction to an ounce of his ardor coupled with a pound of her loneliness. She didn't want to make the same mistake twice in picking the wrong person for the wrong reason. Especially since she couldn't be certain whether she could trust him.

She glanced over at Evan, and his warm smile lit a fire in her. She wanted to take her time with him, but staring at him made her wonder if it would be possible.

Chapter Eight

My feet ached from standing for hours, but I felt gratified by the applause when I wrapped up the lecture for the day. Surprised by the number of seminar participants who rushed the podium to speak with me about Rachel's case, I was pleased I had made an impression on this sophisticated group. I answered all their questions as completely as possible without giving away the next day's lecture, and prepared to leave for the night. After folding my notes into my briefcase, I turned to see Adrian at my side.

"You're right, Sarah, I'm hooked. You can't leave me hanging this way."

"Want to see me?" I joked. "You'll have to be patient and wait for the conclusion tomorrow. It'll be worth it."

He groaned. "No fair. This case is amazing. I want more now."

The look in his eyes told me he wanted more from me, too. Self-conscious, I lowered my gaze and straightened my forest-green suit jacket. After a full day of lecturing, I knew I looked frumpy and tired, but when I glanced back up, he followed my hand with his eyes. To distract both of us, I picked up my cup and carried it to the table in the rear of the room. He followed.

"You're not going to reveal anything to me, even though we're compadres?"

I placed the cup on a tray. "No way, no how.

You wait like the rest."

He narrowed his eyes. "How about for a price?"

"What are you offering?"

"A drink at the bar to loosen your lips."

The way he said it made it hard to resist. "I wish I could, but I have to go back to my office and see a couple of clients."

"Too bad," he said, looking deflated. "Can we take a rain check for tomorrow after the conference ends? You can't schedule patients on a Friday night. It's against the law."

I laughed. "That might work. Check with me in the morning."

He looked at me with a smug expression. "A little commitment phobic, are we? You sound as scared as Becca. Don't you wonder if your own fears might stand in the way of your helping her?"

I took a step back. "Ouch. You talk about not being fair. How can you judge me based on one statement? Are you always this quick to jump to conclusions?"

He didn't say anything or change his expression.

"I have tentative plans with my sister tomorrow night. I'll check with her to see if we're still on, and let you know first thing." I glanced at my watch. "'I'd better go now."

"Let me walk you to your car. Are you in the garage?"

I nodded. "I'm glad you're going with me. I was mugged a couple of weeks ago outside my office, and I'm still a little nervous about going into deserted places alone. I'd appreciate the company."

We made our way to the elevator. While we waited for it to arrive, he turned to me. "What do you think about Becca falling for this Evan fellow soon after her husband's murder? Do you think it's premature, a symptom of an underlying emotional problem?"

The elevator doors opened and we entered. "I think it may be partly related to her grief and a mild depression, but I also see it as a combination of her inability to form a healthy attachment with her husband, coupled with an intense attraction to an apparently interested and interesting man."

"It's a little soon though, don't you think? Did you discourage her from getting involved?"

"I did my part, but she had her own doubts, too."

He leveled his baby blues on me and I felt myself melt. "Understandable under the circumstances."

Grateful when the elevator stopped and we were forced to step out, I said, "Perhaps. As you know, relationships can be scary. To paraphrase the Wizard of Oz, you put yourself on the line when you trust someone with an organ as easily broken as your heart."

"Is that what happened to you?"

We approached my car and I fumbled for my keys. "We're not talking about me."

"We're not?

It sounded like he was onto me. I strode more briskly now.

He caught up. "No one can give you any guarantees, but ultimately there's only one person who can truly betray you and let you down. Yourself."

He was right, although I didn't want to admit it. I would rather hold onto my role as victim, with my ex as victimizer. I know in my heart I'm the one who let myself down. I recognized the signs of a brewing storm long before it materialized, but I ignored all the warning signs. And after Ken left, I refused to do anything about my bitterness and distrust.

"I hope you're as helpful with your patients as you've been with me."

He stopped me with a hand on my arm and rotated me toward him. "I'm sorry. I didn't mean to upset you. I like you, Sarah, enough to want to be your friend. I'd never intentionally hurt you."

I patted the hand holding my arm. "You didn't hurt me. What you said stung a little, but I know you're right. I have to face the facts whether I like them or not." I strutted up to my silver sedan and opened the door, while he stood by. Before ducking into my seat, I glanced back. "I wish I could talk longer, but I do have appointments." Our eyes met and held for one long, hot moment. "I'll see you first thing tomorrow."

"Goodnight," he said and unexpectedly brushed my lips with his before sauntering off.

Breathless, I stood watching him, tingling from

head to toe.

This man has pushed all my alarm buttons, but I was too intrigued to flee. I had a queasy sensation in my gut, but I know it's only fear and couldn't be counted on as feedback. Deep down, I'm too curious not to see more of Adrian Farley. And it's time I stop giving into my fear about men and take a risk. While my head cautioned me about starting something new, I knew I was already caught in a trap I might not choose to escape.

Later that same evening, after closing the office door behind my last patient, I picked up the receiver and dialed my sister Lara's number.

She answered after a couple of rings. "Sis, why the pleasure of a call this evening? I can only speak a few minutes. I have to get Dicky off to bed."

"Sit down." I waited a moment and then said, "I think I'm having a nervous breakdown. I met the most amazing man today. A psychologist from Pittsburgh. I need psychiatric help, but you're the best I can do at this late hour."

"Dr. Lara at your service." I heard her yell at Dicky. "Sorry. I'm up to my ass in Legos. Let me take this into the next room." Again I heard a muffled voice and then she came back on the line. "Kids! Can't live with 'em, can't live without 'em. Now, what was it you were telling me about some hottie you met today? Go ahead and make my day."

"I'm going nuts. He's too good to be true. Too good looking. Too smart. Too polished. He's just too perfect. What the hell does he see in me?"

Lara made a "tsk" sound with her tongue. "What I do. You're a fabulously successful woman and a joy to be around. That's what he sees."

My heart swelled. How lucky I am to have such a loving sister! "I love you, too, even if you're a terrible liar. I guess it's been too long a time since I met anyone I'm even remotely attracted to. After what happened with Ken, I'm still unsure I can trust anyone new. Or myself to make a good decision."

Another yell for Dicky to stop tossing his toys. "Sorry again. He becomes cranky when he's tired."

"Am I keeping you away from putting him down? I can call you later."

"Are you kidding? This is the best news I've heard in a long time. I thought I'd never hear this from you again, considering how hard you took the thing with Ken. It's a relief to hear you say someone interests you."

"I wouldn't be bothering you at Dicky's bedtime if I wasn't having a major panic attack. I'm not sure what I should do. He wants to take me out after the conference tomorrow, but besides our plans, I'm wondering whether I should start anything new. This guy might just be too slick."

Lara sighed. "What the hell are you waiting for? The Pope to convert? It's been over nine months since Ken moved out. It's time for you to start dating again!

This one sounds too good to pass up."

"Maybe too good to be true."

Of course Lara had it right. As much as I'd like to, I couldn't keep using Ken's betrayal and my subsequent suspiciousness as excuses for not moving on. I'd never let one of my clients get away with that one. Why would I let myself? It might be easier to hold onto past hurts than to risk inviting new ones, but it isn't healthy, and wouldn't make me happy. It's time to pull my head out of the hole it's been in, and face reality.

"Does it mean you're breaking our date?" I asked.

"We can do it another time. I'm only biology to you. Go out with this man and see if he's chemistry. You need to expand your curriculum."

"All right, I'll go. But you better be there if it's a bust and I need a shoulder to sob on."

"You know I will."

With the receiver stuck under my chin, I began to place client notes in a file. "It's late, and I'd better be heading home. I have a few things to put away before I can leave for the night."

"Where are you calling from?" Was that a subtle surge of anxiety in Lara's voice?

"The office. I'm leaving right now."

An awkward silence descended between us before her voice came back on the line. "It's dark, are you going to be all right? Where are you parked?"

How sweet of Lara to be concerned after my recent attack! "Don't worry. I bought the pepper spray your Will suggested, and I carry it with me all the time. I wouldn't leave home without it. I'll be fine."

"Will you call me the moment you get home?"

"How silly of me. If I hadn't called you now, I wouldn't have worried you. Of course I'll phone you."

After I hung up, I smiled. If Lara wanted me safe, she'd never let me date again. But she is and I am. I locked the office door and headed toward the elevator. All Lara cares about is saving my butt, she doesn't give a damn about protecting my heart.

Chapter Nine

With a rap on the microphone, I cleared my throat. "We're about to begin this morning's lecture. Please take your seats."

I glanced around the conference room. Adrian entered from the rear and made his way to the coffee table. Others wandered back to their seats. I waited patiently for the chatter to subside.

When all were seated and the room fell silent, I continued.

"Good morning! I hope you had a refreshing night's sleep and are ready for a full day of Rebecca Rosen and company. As you may recall, I left Becca after a harrowing chase by an unrecognizable stranger." I saw numerous nods in the audience. "The next morning, Becca awoke with a horrible headache, and unrelenting doubts about whether she had been stalked, or had merely imagined it. Had it actually happened, or had she experienced a post-traumatic triggered hallucination? At the encouragement of her mother, during her daily call, Becca agreed to report what she had experienced to the police, and stopped by the station on her way home from work. She followed the officer on duty down a long hallway to Sally Mills' office..."

Whether it was the Wanted posters over the intake desk or the hollow echo of footsteps against concrete floor and bare walls, something about the police station always gave Becca the creeps. A sour scent of suspicion and a subtle sense of fear permeated the precinct on Market Street, left behind by the ghosts of prior arrests and interrogations. Becca followed the cop on duty to Mills' office and entered at Mills' prompting.

Mills had been working on a file, but closed it when Becca took a seat across the desk from her. "What can I do for you today?"

Becca plunged into an explanation of her recent stalking ordeal, doing her best to ignore Mills' overtly cordial but obviously officious demeanor. No matter what she said or how she said it, Mills never seemed terribly convinced of her veracity. It came as no surprise when, at the completion of her story, Mills looked at her with an incredulous stare.

"You never saw the man's face, and you're not even certain he was the one following you onto the subway car? Is that correct?"

What could she say to sway Mills? She was tempted to exaggerate the story to make it more convincing, but equally determined to remain honest. If caught in the tiniest of lies, she would only look more culpable. "No, I'm not certain, but it appeared as if I was being pursued."

Mills jotted a note. "Besides a sense of threat, do you have anything else we can go on?"

Becca shook her head, feeling foolish. "I guess I shouldn't have reported this incident."

"It's not that, it's just that you're not giving us

anything substantial, which seems to be pretty much the story with this case. If you expect us to follow up, we'll need more than a gut feeling and a black trench coat."

"I understand." Becca glanced down at her foot, in perpetual motion, and back up, in time to catch Mills watching her. "Do you have any new leads?"

The policewoman frowned. "There is one thing. I'm glad you showed up today because we were about to ask you to come by anyway." She opened a file and glanced down at it. "We found a hair attached to the bloody rag wrapped around your butcher knife and we've analyzed it. We need to take hair samples from everyone associated with your husband—including you. I'd like to take one right away."

The hair might finally vindicate her. "Doesn't the color tell you anything?"

"Not enough. We'll need the sample."

"I have nothing to hide. I'll give you whatever you want."

"Good," the cop said. "By the way, have you hired a lawyer yet?"

Any sense of relief had been short lived. "Why are you asking?"

"Just precautionary."

"Does that mean I'm your primary suspect?"

The detective's gaze didn't waver. "Until we have more to go on, you're the only suspect. Stay close to home." She rose. "Come with me and we'll take the sample."

Becca rose, but could no longer hear the din of the bustling police station over the roar of blood in her head. As she suspected, the police had short-listed their suspects and would not be looking further. She fought off a mental image of herself in a striped suit behind bars. For the first time it dawned on her she might be the only one who could vindicate herself. The only one with the motivation to find the real killer.

But could she identify him on her own?

A knock on the door surprised Becca. "Who is it?"

"Evan. Let me in."

Damn. "Wait a sec." She plucked a tissue from a box at her side and wiped away tears streaking down her face. With a couple of deep, calming breaths, she quieted her sobs. In the bathroom, she washed away the long black trails of mascara streaking down her cheeks, and drew a comb through her disheveled hair. She didn't want to look like the poster child for despair.

Evan knocked again. "Are you going to leave me out here all night?"

With one last glance in the mirror to make certain she had erased all evidence of her outburst, she opened the door and let him in.

Evan's gaze traveled around the room at the mess Becca had left in her normally ordered apartment, then fixed on her. "Are you okay? Have you been crying?"

"Come." She led him to the sofa and took the seat beside him. "I guess I'll never have much of a career as an illusionist. Talk about wearing your emotions on your sleeve! Mine are written across my forehead in neon."

"What's wrong?" he asked, sounding concerned. He took her hand and held onto it tightly.

"Nothing that Gloria Allred or a one-way ticket to Paraguay couldn't fix."

"No joking. I want to know what's happening with you."

"The police believe I murdered my husband. They told me as much today."

"Oh..." He caressed her hand. "How could they possibly think it was you?"

She wiped away a tear. "They don't have another suspect. I guess I'm it."

"I don't believe this," he stammered. "I never thought—"

"No one did, except the PPD."

"What motive could you possibly have?"

"They have a witness who's willing to testify I was having marital problems. Somehow they're building a case around it."

He made a face. "If every wife who's unhappy with her husband were to do him in, there wouldn't be too many men left."

"The cops don't see it that way. To make

matters worse, David and I were the only known persons in the apartment that night."

"I'm sure they'll find another more plausible suspect."

"They don't seem to be looking too hard."

"Too bad." He squeezed her hand. "I know this is a difficult time for you, but it's important to stay strong and have faith."

"Don't go philosophical on me."

"I know, I know," he said. "But you have it in you to cope whether you know it or not. You have to access your inner wisdom and courage at times like this."

This sounded a little pat, but she appreciated his desire to soothe her anxiety. She wasn't surprised the police would focus on her. Who else would they think did this? Isn't it usually the spouse?

"Right now my insides feel like mush. I'm going to need your support."

"You can take all you need; I give it to you freely. I'll be by your side through whatever happens." He brought her hand to his lips and kissed it. "Have you called an attorney?"

"I've interviewed a couple and I'm meeting with one tomorrow. If I'm comfortable with her, I'll retain her."

"Good. That's the first step."

"What's the next step?"

"You'll let me take care of you." He pulled her into his arms and held her close.

She tensed at his touch. Why did she always react this way? She wanted so much to trust him, but nothing seemed to overcome her reservations. It took her a good minute before she could relax in his arms.

Before she knew it, she clung to him; weeping against his chest, venting her anguish in unrelenting sobs that wracked her entire body. He held her near enough to feel the heat rising off his skin; smell the subtle but sexy scent of aftershave. She burrowed closer to him; never wanted to let him go.

He ran his hand over her hair; wrapped her in a comforting hug. When her breathing finally slowed, she glanced up into his eyes and, suddenly, she wanted him more than she had ever wanted anyone. For once, she didn't feel the need to pull back when he lowered his lips to hers. With his kiss, she sizzled with desire.

All at once, the desire transformed into fear. She pulled away. "I can't."

He looked confused. "I don't understand..."

"I'm sorry, I have too much going on in my life. I don't need any more complications."

"Ouch! I'm a complication then?"

She took his chin in her hand and turned his head toward her. "Of course not. I didn't mean to imply that. You mean the world to me. I need you more than you can imagine. I shouldn't have said what I did. Just give me a little more time."

His eyes held hers. "Of course. I don't want to be a burden to you."

"You could never be a burden to me. I'm crazy about you and when the time is right, I'll show you exactly how I feel."

"I'm going to hold you to that promise," he said.

"And I'm going to hold you, too."

According to one of my psychology professors at the University of Pennsylvania, no one can predict human behavior. This axiom has always proven to be true in my practice.

Becca's next psychotherapy session confirmed the tenet one more time. Even while telling me the story of her encounter with the police, and her progress locating the right attorney, she had an unusual glimmer in her eyes, an expression I could only describe as joy. Intrigued, I questioned the dissonance between what she said and how she said it.

"I don't know how to tell you this, Sarah, but I think I might be falling for Evan." She spoke so softly I had to lean forward in my seat to hear her.

Although taken aback by the suddenness of her revelation, I tried not to show her my surprise. "When did you come to that conclusion?"

"The other night. I'm as shocked about this as anyone. I didn't know I could feel this way about anyone so soon after David's death. It's changed the complexion of everything."

"I see," I said, even though I couldn't completely decipher what impact this news might have on Becca's treatment. "Can you tell me why the change of heart?"

"Evan's been there for me lately, in a way no one else has."

I took a sip of water and considered the consequences of Becca's pronouncement. It would be premature for Becca to jump into a new relationship without resolving her feelings about the last one, but that wasn't my primary concern. The best therapeutic work takes place when a client experiences an ego-dystonic state, or one of internal strife, rather than an ego-syntonic state, where they are no longer experiencing conflict or confusion. They're far less apt to do the difficult and painful work of delving deeply into their subconscious mind when they're no longer in distress. Something as simple as falling in love can become an impediment to therapeutic progress, and in this case, might be the ego's way of distracting Becca from the real work which needed to be done.

"How do you think it will look to the police when they discover you're in a new relationship?"

"I don't know. I hadn't thought about that. I guess it might look fishy, but you know as well as I do my relationship with Evan has nothing to do with David's death."

"Since you say you're under suspicion, you need to consider how you will explain yourself."

"I'll tell them the truth." She threw up her hands. "But they won't believe me. I can't say... I'll have to think about it."

"When you say Evan's been there for you, can you explain what you mean?"

Her face lit up again. "I think he's in love with me, too. He's attentive and supportive, and the more time I spend with him, the happier I feel. Even with everything that's been happening, having him around has been amazing."

"And you? What do you think you can offer him right now?"

She fidgeted with her fingers. "Good question. I've been such a mess lately, and I'm sure I take way more than I give."

"Let me ask you something. What do you know about love?"

Becca laughed. "What's there to know? It's a fabulous feeling. That's what I know."

I shook my head. "You're wrong. Love isn't a feeling at all."

She squinted at me with doubt. "What do you mean? Everyone knows love's a feeling."

"And you think 'everyone' knows best? They're aware of what's in their own best interest? What you're feeling might not be love at all—but rather, infatuation. A delightful experience, no doubt, but a time-limited one. Infatuation is a temporary state. Love lasts."

She looked unconvinced. "So how do you define

love?"

"To me, love is a commitment to nurture, respect, and support the integrity and growth of another person. Love doesn't affect you like a drug, like infatuation does. It's gentle and develops over time. Love can evolve out of infatuation, because our feelings of attraction cement us to another person long enough to experience them for who they truly are, but it's a far richer experience with greater longevity."

I took another sip of water while she pondered the implication of what I had said. "How many people do you know who have been together more than a couple of years, and are in what you would describe as a loving relationship?"

She had to think about this. "Not many."

"Yet all those couples entered into relationships thinking they were in love. Just like you. What they were feeling was infatuation. They were thrilled to have another person show interest in them and they felt, perhaps for the first time in their lives, their emotional and physical needs were being met. They tied themselves to this person, assuming this state of fulfillment would continue indefinitely.

"Unfortunately, the elation runs its course in a year or two and then dissipates. When that happens, they're left with the same fears and feelings they had before, coupled with a real sense of disappointment after being smitten. That's when the troubles begin.

"Without a good understanding of what love is and how to achieve it, they begin to believe their partner is the enemy. They think the other person is withholding what had been given freely before.

"This often leads them to attack one another. There are many ways to attack another person besides verbal abuse or physical violence. Silence and withholding attention are two others."

Becca nodded. "Like my dad."

"Exactly. I don't mean to dissuade you from a relationship with Evan, but it's important that you understand what you're getting yourself into. You need to ask yourself: is this a good time to begin a new relationship? Whether you've given yourself enough of a chance to process through what happened with David, and grieve his loss? If you are healed enough from your recent trauma to move on? I think these are questions you need to explore before you make a commitment to anyone new."

She looked down at her hands, busy knitting an invisible scarf, and refused to meet my eye. I prayed I hadn't lost her, but it was my job to help her take a good look at her motivation before making any major changes in her life.

Finally, she raised her head in a defiant gesture. "I've been asking myself those same questions, but it's too late. There doesn't seem to be any way to alter the path I'm on. Like it or not, I'm too far gone."

"I see," I said, and this time I did get the picture. "How will this affect your goals in therapy?"

"It shouldn't affect them at all. No matter what develops between Evan and me, I plan to continue working with you. I can't have a healthy relationship with him unless I have one with myself. Besides, nothing has changed for the better outside of my relationship with Evan."

I gave her a reassuring smile, hoping she meant what she said. "I'm glad to hear that."

In addition to my concern Becca might be taking on more than she could handle with Evan, it would have been disappointing to lose her as a patient prior to meeting her therapeutic goals. As long as she remained in therapy, our relationship might act as a safety net if the one with Evan went awry—a definite possibility, considering her state of mind. In other words, I wanted to be there for Becca when she was ready to be there for herself.

After her therapy session in Queen's Village, Becca met Evan at a lunch counter around the corner. She ordered corned beef on rye and he chose a vegetarian whole wheat wrap with eggplant and bell peppers.

While they waited to be served, he inquired about her session.

"It was thought-provoking as always," she said. "We spoke about a lot of different things."

"Like what?" he asked, reaching across her for sweetener to put in his herbal tea. He poured a packet in his cup and then looked back up at her.

"Like...well...like love, for instance. Here's a question for you. Do you know the meaning of love?"

Before he could answer, their dishes were unceremoniously dumped on the table with a mind-boggling clatter by a skinny waitress who obviously didn't indulge in the overstuffed sandwiches or rich desserts served at the deli.

After the waitress retreated, he said, "I believe I do. It's a mystical union between two people leading to a deepened awareness, connection, and understanding on both their parts."

"That's beautiful! I should have known you would come up with exactly the right answer."

"Why do you ask?"

Becca swallowed a bite of her sandwich. "Because I can't say I've ever thought too deeply about the subject. What passed between my parents couldn't be called love. Most of the time what had been referred to as love was either inauthentic and over the top, or downright nasty."

He smiled at her, tenderness blanketing his face. "I plan to teach you everything I know about love," he said, then reached across the table and took her hand.

A spark passed between them, but she quickly withdrew her hand from his and looked away.

When she glanced at him again, he stared down at the table, refusing to let her meet his eyes. "Is that all you spoke about? Are you going to counseling or a lonely hearts club?"

At his remark, she jerked her head up to stare at him.

He raised a hand. "I don't know why I said that. I didn't mean..."

She hammered her cup against the table with a decided thwack. "Believe me, we don't spend most of our sessions discussing my love life. We talk about all kinds of different things."

"What then?"

"You name it. Now do you mind if we change the subject?"

He cocked his head in a boyish gesture of appeasement. "I didn't mean to intrude, but I'd like to get to know you better, and this seems the fastest way in."

"You could ask me a direct question about myself."

"Alright, I can do that. Do you talk much about your rape and David's murder?"

She laughed. "I didn't mean about my therapy. I meant about me."

"Answer my question."

"Of course, silly. That's the reason I'm seeing a therapist: to work out my feelings about what happened. I want to pick up the pieces and go back to living a normal life."

He took a sip of herbal tea. "You don't see your life as normal now?"

"Hardly. I'm still traumatized, and don't you ever forget it. I expect to be treated with the utmost care." She smiled, which eased the tension that smoldered between them like a newly lit log.

"Have you tried to recreate what happened the night of the murder, to see if you can identify the intruder?"

"We've been more focused on what happened to me as a child."

Evan made a face. "Are you kidding me? You have enough to deal with in the present. I can't believe your therapist would insist on doing the Freudian frug on your psyche. Are you sure you're not wasting your time?"

Becca sat back and stared at Evan. She couldn't believe his attitude. What had gotten into him? He typically erred on the side of patience and understanding. Was he betraying a different part of himself? "Why are you opposed to my therapy? Is there some reason you would want to discourage me from looking back?"

"Now what purpose would that serve?"

"Maybe you don't want me to remember something?"

He shook his head. "I'm not sure what you're talking about. I don't particularly believe in traditional therapy. Too many practitioners spend their sessions dwelling on the past. And their patients remain stuck in time."

"Well, I'm not one of them because I'm actually beginning to feel better. I rarely have nightmares anymore, and I'm happier than I've been in months. Now let's forget about my therapy and talk about other things."

She immediately turned the topic to his course work, and the conversation slowly drifted away from her psychotherapy to his studies, but a nagging sense of irritation, like a bitter aftertaste, stayed with her long afterwards. She resented his meddling in her affairs without any first hand knowledge of them, and questioning the difficult, often wrenching work she was doing. She also questioned his motivation for undermining her effort. Maybe Sarah had been right; maybe she couldn't make a good decision about a man so soon after her trauma. She had to wonder about her feelings toward Evan. Was she ready for a serious relationship with him? Even while he droned on about meditation, her mind traveled somewhere else—miles away from him.

After work the next day, Becca surveyed the street outside her apartment building. After her recent encounter with the stalker, she couldn't go anywhere without looking over her shoulder.

Inside the apartment, the dim, late afternoon December light filtered through shuttered windows. She flicked the switch to the overhead and carried a bag of *Whole Food's* groceries to the kitchen counter. Cecil made his grand entrance and rubbed up against her leg. She petted him and fed him before putting the groceries away. Finished at last, she undressed and tugged on her blue fleece sweats and slippers for a quiet evening at home.

Back in the kitchen, she put water on for tea when the phone rang. She quickly placed the tea kettle on the stove and grabbed the receiver before the answer message began. A muted male voice, as though spoken through a distortion device, said, "You must have thought you heard the last of me, but you haven't. I keep an eye on you all the time."

Becca's heart skipped a beat. "Where are you?" she asked, while sidling over to the bay window that overlooked the street. She stood behind the curtains, pulling them back just enough to peruse the block. No one who fit the stalker's description in her head stood within view.

"You can't see me, but I watch your every move. I haven't forgotten you. Never forget me..."

"Stop bothering me!" she yelled into the phone. "Leave me alone!" She heard the line go dead.

Shaken, she immediately phoned the police and reported the call. With curtain closed, she leaned back against the wall, feeling helpless. Then she caught sight of the blinking light on the message machine. Hoping it indicated an earlier call from the stalker, as evidence for the police, she pressed the button. Instead, Uncle Paulie's voice filled the room.

"Hi sweetheart. I've inquired after you repeatedly, but your mother keeps telling me you're too busy for a visit. But I finally convinced her to give me your number so I could call you myself. She wants to do dinner on Sunday with the whole family, and is hoping you'll come. I hope so, too. I'd love to see you. Give her a holler. Bye until then." Click.

At the sound of Paulie's voice, Becca faltered. Damn, only hours before she had convinced herself she was doing much better, but the back-to-back calls had sent her into a tailspin. Had she only been fooling herself?

She would bet her newly minted paycheck Julie had convinced Paulie to call, and Becca reached for the phone to offer her regrets when something stopped her. As much as she resented Julie's manipulation, and found spending time with Paulie repugnant, she couldn't put the inevitable off indefinitely. To spend one evening with her family, as uncomfortable as it may be, might kick up enough dust to expose what lurked beneath her anxiety. The time had arrived to face her fears...and her family.

She straightened. This time when she lifted the receiver, she knew exactly what to say. She dialed Julie's number and waited for her mother's nasal voice to come over the line.

Chapter Ten

With the patient count down, Becca left the hospital an hour earlier than normal. She couldn't wait for the trip home from work to end, so she could curl up on her couch for a much-needed nap. She dragged herself off the El and trudged the three blocks to her building, up the front steps and into the foyer, anticipating the moment she could lie back and close her eyes.

Then she opened her front door to a startling sight.

The apartment had been torn apart. CDs and DVDs were strewn on the floor; books were piled into a mound. A ceramic sculpture lay on it's side, broken. Jagged pieces scattered about. From her angle, she could peer into the bedroom, where drawers had been jerked open and their contents hurled onto the carpet. Closets were emptied, and the furniture had been moved. Every item she owned had been dumped or damaged.

An awareness the perpetrator might be lurking about sliced through the fog that had descended upon her, and her apprehension intensified. She knew she should back out the door immediately, but she couldn't tear herself away from the destruction derby in front of her. She gaped at it and groaned, a heavy despair settling over her, mingling with the now-familiar sense of vulnerability and victimization.

Finally she pulled herself away, closed the door carefully behind her, and left to find Evan at home in his condo. When he opened his door and spotted her expression, he hurried her inside.

"What's the matter? What's going on?"

Still in shock, she could barely catch her breath long enough to explain after her sprint up the flight of stairs. "S...S...Someone broke into my apartment. I don't know if they're still in there. I'm afraid to go in alone."

"Good thinking. Have you called the police?"

"I came directly here."

He handed her the phone after dialing the number she gave him for Sally Mills. A man came on the line.

She sniffled back tears. "Is Detective Mills there?"

"She's off today. I'm Lieutenant Wantabe. Can I help you?"

"My apartment's been broken into. Whoever did it might be inside. I don't want to go back in there."

"I'll send a car over right away. What's the name and address?"

After giving her information and case number, she listened to a muffled voice bark out orders. Then he came back on the line. "Where are you now?"

"A neighbor's."

"Sit tight. A car will be there in a few minutes."

She waited with Evan until the sound of sirens shrieking down the street alerted them to the approaching police. The police officers they encountered in front of her building told them to remain outside when they entered the apartment, guns drawn. By the time she and Evan were allowed in, the police had swarmed the premises, looking into closets, behind curtains, under furniture, and in the bathroom. Most of her possessions seemed to be all accounted for, including her television, surround sound, medication and jewelry. The police came up empty-handed, except for the discovery of an open window in the living room that had been closed when she left in the morning.

"You might have surprised the intruder, and they bolted before taking too much," one of the cops said.

In the midst of the mayhem, Lieutenant Wantabe arrived. Although only around five-foot-five, he was a powerfully built Asian in a preppy-looking navy-blue pea coat and red scarf. He handed her a card and glanced around. "Whoever did this wasn't into interior design."

She followed his gaze and again felt deflated. "It's a mess, isn't it?"

He pushed back his hat and rubbed his high forehead. "Don't you have a burglar alarm here?"

She nodded. "I was late for work and forgot to set it."

"Have any idea what they were after?"

She shook her head. "Nope."

"Doesn't look like they missed much. I contacted Detective Mills after I spoke with you. She told me about the rape and murder. Do you think this break-in has anything to do with it?"

Becca spotted blood on her palm and realized she had been unconsciously digging her nails into her own flesh. She wrung her hands in despair. "Jesus. Why else would anyone do this?"

Wantabe took another look around. "Looks like we have our work cut out for us. Officer Jefferson here will take a full report. We want you to go through everything, and itemize anything missing. It's important you do a thorough job."

"I hope you guys don't think I did this myself."

Wantabe shrugged. "I've seen suspects do all kinds of crazy-ass things to throw us off their trail. Hopefully you're not one of them."

That he was cynical enough to believe she'd stoop to this level just to take suspicion off herself was beyond wildest imagination. What a perverted view of humanity! "You have to be kidding. I'd never do such a thing."

After he left, she gave her account to Jefferson and waited with Evan on the curb while the police cars pulled away. Back inside, she began to mechanically put her apartment back in order. Her first course of business, locate Cecil. She discovered him crouching under the bed in terror. It took several minutes to coax him out before she could go back to straightening her surroundings.

Her desk drawers hung open and had obviously been rifled through. As she put her paperwork back in order, she realized the box containing all her personal and business cards was missing. She checked a second time to satisfy herself of its disappearance. "Damn," she called to Evan. "They took my card file."

Evan, who had been busy picking her clothes off the floor, looked over at her with a shake of his head. "What will we discover next?"

It didn't take long to answer his question. While straightening the disheveled living room bookcase, she noticed the missing picture. "Shit!"

Evan appeared in the doorway with a coat over one arm and a hanger in his hand. "What?"

"There's a photo missing of me when I was ten."

He stood there, shaking his head. "I remember it. Why that?"

"I don't understand. This gets creepier by the minute..."

Evan put down what he held, took her by the arm, and led her to sit on the bed. "You've done enough for now. You've been frantically cleaning since the police left. You look exhausted. Rest."

She nodded her acquiescence, but as soon as she sat still, the tears tumbled. She had been through too much lately. Ashamed she couldn't contain herself in front of him, she wiped tears away with trembling fingertips as fast as she could. "This is awful."

Evan watched her through worried eyes, then took a seat beside her and draped an arm over her shoulder. "It sure is. Whoever did this must have been pretty desperate."

"Or fucked up." She spat out the words, stunned by the surge of outrage that rose up in her like a sudden storm.

"Yeah, could be, but maybe they had a purpose."

She stared at him, confounded. Why would he try to justify bad behavior? "You might be a spiritual kinda guy, but you aren't a saint yet. You don't need to attribute a higher order to this low-life. Whatever this asshole's motivation is, he's made me feel totally violated. In my opinion, he's just a criminal, and that's that."

Hands on her shoulders, Evan turned her toward him. "We might never know why he did this, but knowing might not make it easier on you anyway." He brushed away another tear. "This must hurt a lot."

He obviously knew the right thing to say because it made the tears fall faster. "Worse than hurt. I've been having trouble sleeping again. And when I do nod off, I wake up in the middle of the night in terror. My appetite's gone, and I hardly ever laugh anymore. All this is wearing me down."

"Understandable." He drew her closer. "You've been through hell and it isn't letting up. Perhaps there's something I can do to help."

"Stay with me tonight. I need to know you're here. Don't leave me."

"I wasn't planning on going anywhere." He trailed a finger across her cheek until it settled beneath her chin.

With a tilt of her head upwards, he lowered his lips to hers. Although tempted to pull away, the heat of his kiss, coupled with the intensity of her need for him, slowly thawed her frozen fear. She had many things to do before her apartment resumed any semblance of order, but she gave in to her desire for protection and passion, allowing him to kiss her over and over again. She ached for him now as she'd never ached for anyone before.

Slowly he nibbled his way down her neck, sending off waves of desire. His fingers gently crawled under her sweater and over her bra. She could feel her nipple harden at his touch, as the waves turned into tsunamis, the passion so powerful all she could do was surrender to it.

When he started to pull the sweater over her head, she helped him and arched her back into him so he could easily release her bra. He lowered his head to her nipple and took it into his mouth, suckling it until she was about to burst from pleasure mixed with pain. Slowly his fingers descended to the button on her jeans and he opened it with a flick of his wrist. He pulled down the zipper and slipped his fingers beneath her panties and between her legs. Waves of intense desire washed through her.

Unable to withstand the intensity of her passion for him, she lowered her hand under the waistband of his sweatpants. But the moment she took his penis into her hand, alarm bells blared in her mind and immediately shut off all other feelings but fear.

She froze, no longer able to respond to him.

Noticing this, he pulled back, searching her face for an explanation.

"What's wrong?" he asked in a husky voice.

She only wished she knew. She wanted him; why had she reacted this way?

She reached out and stroked his face. "I'm sorry. It's not that I don't want you. I've just gone as far as I can for now..."

He nodded, took her hand into his and gently, sensuously, kissed her fingertips, one by one. "No problem," he said. "I'll wait for you, no matter how long it takes."

His understanding swelled her heart and made her all the more frustrated with herself.

Evan agreed to spend the night with her. But after their earlier foreplay interruptus, she limited their intimacy to kissing, fondling, and sleeping together with their clothes on, unprepared for anything more. In the middle of the night, she awoke to find herself alone in bed. Curious, and a little thirsty, she rose to fetch a glass of water. She found him in the living room, whispering into his cell phone. She overheard him say, "I'm sorry I couldn't make it. I had an unexpected assignment. I'll call you in the morning."

The second he spied her, he flipped the phone shut, looking a little nervous. "What are you doing up?"

"I'm thirsty. What was that about?"

"I stood up an appointment with an instructor this evening."

She glanced at the clock and immediately doubted his story. "You mean to tell me you called your professor at two in the morning? Is this a nocturnal course? Metaphysics for the insomniac?"

"I only left a message..."

"And what made you lie? Why didn't you just tell the truth?"

He shrugged. "I wasn't sure if you'd want me to."

"I don't know what this has to do with me. Don't you think your professor might catch wind that this elusive assignment of yours is a myth? You could get into trouble with your program!"

"Nah. Don't you worry about it. I can take care of myself." He gave her a gentle shove in the direction of the kitchen. "I'll meet you back in bed."

Becca made her way to the sink, wondering whether Evan had lied to her, and why. Which made her question if he had intentionally deceived her every time he made excuses for not being available. As much as she wanted to believe in him, could she trust him?

Becca poured herself a glass of water and carried it back toward the bedroom. She wanted to shake off her suspicions before climbing back into bed, but they continued to nag at her like a persistent cough, long after she had settled in next to Evan for the night. Uncertain what to make of his actions, because he hadn't answered her questions or put her concerns to rest, she tossed and turned. Was she disturbed because she had caught him in a lie, or were her doubts merely anxiety because of their growing closeness? Whatever it was, her apprehension had been primed enough to keep a watchful distance from him. Perhaps he would prove himself to be trustworthy in the long run, but that would have to be seen. She couldn't afford another disappointment in her life.

Or any more danger.

Becca drove through sluggish rush hour traffic on her way to Julie and Irv's house for dinner. Although uneasy, she had put on her Sunday best: a sleek purple sheath with black pumps and a string of pearls, wanting to appear calm and in control. The Self-Assured Professional was the image she sought to convey. On the way out, she had stopped by Evan's, soaking up his admiration and quite a few kisses. At a stop light, she fixed her dusty-rose lipstick in the rearview mirror, not wanting to give herself away to her mom.

She pulled into the circular driveway of the stone Tudor and parked behind Julie's silver Acura, taking a moment to prepare herself for the family encounter. She reviewed her purpose for being there and chanted a number of affirmations to fortify herself—a skill she had picked up from Evan. Once everyone had arrived, she would ask a number of well-rehearsed questions about her early years. She could only hope her family would answer her honestly.

With one last glance in the mirror, she stepped

from the car and approached the massive double doors. Dwarfed in the glass, she looked as small and nervous as she felt.

A knock, and Julie flung the door open, exclaiming over Becca's outfit and her new hair cut. In the family room, she offered Becca a glass of Chablis, which she accepted gladly. A quick glance around the room made it clear Paulie had yet to arrive. This offered her an unexpected opportunity to prep herself for his appearance. At the bar, Becca joined her elderly maternal aunt in a drink. She attempted to make small talk, but was easily distracted by movement near the front door.

After thirty minutes of stealthy glances toward the foyer, Paulie had failed to materialize. Julie finally entered from the kitchen to announce he had called and would be late, but said they should start the meal without him. The hand supporting Becca on the bar faltered for a fraction of a second, but she quickly reestablished her hold.

The family took their time, wandering in groups of twos and threes into the dining room, then reconvened around the stately cherry-wood table. Becca followed after the others and seated herself beside the empty chair officially saved for Paulie. Although glad to have more time to prepare for Paulie's arrival, now that she had made the decision to face the family, she just wanted to get it over with. When she raised her wine glass, her palms were moist. She had to wipe them off with a napkin before taking a sip, or risk spilling bright burgundy liquid on Julie's lacy bleached-white tablecloth.

Julie's helper Maria brought plates of rib roast, roasted potatoes, and asparagus spears to the table. Once the guests had been served, the decibel level substantially subsided as everyone went to work, masticating in busied silence. The room became so quiet she could hear the click of forks against plates, the screech of a chair leg against the wood floor, the drip, drip, drip of coffee from a nearby percolator. Her family loved to eat and dedicated themselves to a meal as if eating it would affect the future of humanity.

Becca kept a nervous eye on the front door, watching for Paulie's belated entrance. As the minutes slipped away, so did her composure. She played with her food, unable to eat.

Julie noticed. "Aren't you hungry? The roast is marvelous. Try some."

To appease Julie and shift the spotlight away, she took a tiny bite. "Yummy. You outdid yourself, Mom."

"Eat up. Don't be shy." Julie speared another piece and dropped it onto her plate. Becca had to suppress a groan.

"I wonder where Paulie is? He's so late," she fretted, unable to keep her mind on anything else.

"You're right." Julie put down her fork. "I better give him a call, see what's keeping him." She left for the kitchen and returned a couple minutes later with a pout plastered to her lightly-lined, perpetually-tanned face—even in the midst of a Philadelphia winter. "He has car trouble. He's not sure he'll make it tonight. He hasn't even left his house."

That took all the air out of Becca's planned performance. She slumped in her seat, wondering whether Paulie felt as reluctant to break bread with her as she was with him. All his apparent interest in her must have been mustered by Julie's not-so-gentle nudge.

Once she realized the futility of confronting her family without Paulie, she found she could truly relax and enjoy herself. She cut a piece of roast beef and slathered it with horseradish sauce.

Julie took her seat. "We'll have to go on without him."

Becca heard the angry edge in her voice, which made her wonder who would feel the cut from that blade.

Julie turned to her. "Why are you slumping, young woman? Haven't I told you a million times to sit up straight? It's bad for your posture."

It hadn't taken long for Julie to find her displaced target. Why was it so often her?

Becca resisted the urge to tell Julie to go to hell. It had never worked in the past, why would it work now? Especially in front of all these guests. She let her mother's frustration wash over her, and turned to her cousin Bob. No use playing Julie's game by Julie's rules; she would only end up a loser. Besides, her mood had lightened too much to let Julie needle her. Of course, the time would come when she'd have to deal with her family and her fears. But if she could hold her own with Julie, she could stand up to the rest of them. At least she hoped so.

"To be a good psychotherapist, you have to walk a fine line between empathy and detachment," I explained to the audience. "Of course we all tread the same narrow path in our personal relationships, but the potential consequences of not doing it well are much greater when dealing with a bruised or broken client. While every one of us wants to be emotionally attuned to our clients' suffering, we don't want to lose our objectivity. And we especially don't want to be the ones to pilot their wayward course. They need to learn to navigate the rocky shoals of their own seas. It's not our job to steer the rudder—only to offer them a sexton and a map, so they can make their own way.

"Becca arrived at the next session a little late—a sign of developing resistance to the treatment, and of her growing transference with me. As Sigmund Freud first pointed out, the transference principle is pivotal to all therapeutic gains. Only after a client has drawn an emotional correlation between the therapist and someone who hurt them in the past, can they begin to work through their painful and difficult early relationships in real time. That's when the true therapy begins."

In my office, Becca refused to make eye contact with me and seemed in no hurry to sit. I offered her the space she seemed to require and gave her ample time to take her seat before I asked her what was going on.

She stared off into the distance, not answering right away. Finally, she said, "I don't believe I'm getting anywhere with this therapy, Sarah. I'm thinking of quitting."

Not at all surprised, it would have been easy for me to point out the obvious reason for her resistance, but I knew that wouldn't be the most helpful approach. I needed to listen to her concerns first; to empathize with her. As you know, empathic listening is the foundation of any therapeutic relationship, and therefore the basis for all progress.

"My life's more complicated since I've been coming to see you," she continued. "My nightmares are back again, and I'm a mess. I hate to say this, Sarah, but I don't think you're helping me at all."

"I'm sorry you're going through all this," I said, echoing her concerns. "It sounds like you're in a miserable place."

"You can say that again."

"I hope you realize anyone going through what you are would feel worse before they felt better."

She shot me a dubious look.

Before she could counter me, I continued. "It's painful to tear away the defenses which appear to protect you, but really keep you from learning your truth. As these impediments give way and your secrets are revealed, you're bound to feel more vulnerable and frightened. What you're going through is quite common, but it's also quite uncomfortable. It's normal to want to cut and run at this point in your treatment."

She sat forward, her body tense like a runner at the starting line. "But it's all futile. I don't think I'm making any progress."

I watched her, noting the slight twitch beneath her right eye. Then I glanced down and glimpsed her playing with her fingers. Her nervousness informed me, even if she didn't realize it, how close she was to a breakthrough. She did what most clients do under the circumstances: try to find a way to distance themselves from the therapy before they have to face something painful or shameful. I decided to force the issue, knowing I was taking a big chance with her. My intervention could inadvertently backfire and cause her to terminate treatment prematurely; but, then again, what did I have to lose under the circumstances? She might go anyway.

"It sounds to me like you're getting close to a deeper knowing, and it's the nature of the truth that is bothering you. Let's see what I can do to help you. Why don't you make yourself comfortable?"

She hesitated, looking as if she couldn't decide how to react. "I don't know..." she said, and stared out the window for several minutes. She seemed to be torn between the two sides of herself: the one resistant to doing the work and the other, willing to do anything to get past the misery and fear. "Okay," she finally said, not appearing okay at all. She lay back on the couch.

I released a silent sigh, grateful she had given into her cooperative nature. "Now, close your eyes," I prompted, "and take a couple of deep breaths. Then picture yourself as a little girl of eight or nine, and let me know when you have the image."

"I have it."

"Good," I said. "Now, I want you to place the child in a room with her parents, but somewhere she can't be seen. She could be behind a curtain or under a table, or anywhere hidden from view." I gave her a moment to follow my suggestion. "From her vantage point, have her watch what's going on in the room and report what you see to me."

After a short silence, Becca said, "My mom and dad are in the family room together, but they're not alone. Someone's with them."

"Who's that someone?"

Again silence. Just when I thought she wasn't going to answer, she said softly, "Uncle Paulie. He's come to tell them a secret."

"What do you hear him say?"

"He tells them I've been a bad girl. I don't listen to him. He's worried about me." She began to cry.

"My mother tells him she's heard enough. She doesn't want to hear anymore about it, but my dad says she should listen to Paulie. They start to argue and my mom starts to leave the room, but my uncle grabs her arm."

"And?"

A slight tremble passed through her. "He says my dad's right, she never listens to him. She's been ignoring him for years just because she doesn't agree with how he lives his life. He tells her this will come back to haunt her, but she pushes Paulie away. Her face is scarlet and she's angry. I'm scared, but before she can do anything, Paulie races out of the house and *slams the door behind him."*

"How does all this make little Becca feel?"

"Scared. Ashamed. Alone. Like no one will ever like her again."

"Is there anything more you can tell me?"

She shakes her head. "No...nothing."

"How would you like to help little Becca feel better?"

"How can I?"

"You can visualize the woman you are today enter the room where Becca is hidden. See yourself go over to the little girl you once were, and scoop her up into your arms. Carry her off to a safe place where you can hold her and comfort her, until you begin to feel a sense of peace and a sense of safety pervading every cell in your body. Then, and only then, take a deep breath and slowly come back into this room."

I waited for Becca to open her eyes and lever herself upright. "You okay?"

Becca nodded.

"Tell me what the scene meant to you?"

"That I feel like a bad kid inside who's done something terribly wrong and deserves to be punished and humiliated. No wonder I've put up with abuse and belittlement for as long as I have."

"Sounds like you're on to something significant there. And even though you have no idea what the something might be, I can assure you it's never as

terrible as it feels. That's the nature of our secrets. They're like forgotten food in the fridge. When they're left locked up inside for a long time, they spoil. The fact they appear putrid convinces us we've done something heinous we can never allow out into the light of day. But once we face our secrets, they're never as rotten as they seem. Instead of being humiliated and degraded by the revelation, we're relieved of the incredible burden of self-loathing we've been carrying around for years. You know what they say, you're only as sick as your secrets and, once they're no longer secrets, you're no longer sick."

She rocked back and forth in an effort to soothe herself. "I don't know. I might be worse off than your typical patient."

"I doubt that. But no matter what, it will not affect my feelings toward you one iota."

She allowed her eyes to meet mine for the first time since coming out of her trance. "I hope not."

I rose and made my way over to her, helping her to her feet. "I know not." Gratitude for her courage and perseverance welled up inside. I gave her a hug. We had overcome a therapeutic hurdle, and were on our way to the next stage of treatment. "I have an assignment for you this week. I want you to spend time every day with little Becca. I want you to comfort and reassure her you'll be there for her, no matter what she's done. Tell her she can trust you, because her trust is essential for you to do the work you need to do."

Becca made her way to the door a little dazed. "Okay, I can do that."

I knew I would do everything in my power to support and respect Becca's growth. There would be steeper hills ahead for her, but she had made it over the first pass and she could make it over the rest. She had proven her courage and capability to tackle the trail ahead of her. If only I have the wisdom and strength to continue to guide her on her path!

"Let's take a break and we'll reconvene in fifteen minutes."

The words barely escaped my lips before I spotted Adrian Farley rise and approach the podium.

"You look lovely this morning."

I smiled shyly, pleased he had noticed I dressed to impress in my cobalt suit and white blouse. My sister Lara always said those colors complemented my olive complexion and brought out the faint honey highlights in my ordinarily dull brown hair and eyes. "You look well yourself. Did you have a good night?"

While I made my way to the coffee urn, he fell into step beside me. "Not as good as I would have had, if you had joined me." A mischievous twinkle illuminated his bright blue eyes. This man sizzled with sensuality in a way I had rarely run into. Lucky me—I think.

He poured a cup of coffee and offered it to me. "Have you considered my invitation for dinner this evening?"

Considered? I'd hardly slept a wink thinking about it. And I didn't feel tired at all. That's what a hearty dose of hormones mixed with adrenaline can do for you. "If the offer still stands, I'd love to take you up on it," I said before I had a chance to spook myself into changing my mind.

He took a sip of coffee. "Great! I think we'll have fun." Again the sparkle in his eyes.

Again the tingle in my thighs. "Where are you taking me?"

"A special little hideaway near the art museum, with the best Beef Wellington in the world. I discovered it the last time I was in Philly. You do eat beef, don't you?"

"Along with everything else. I adore Beef Wellington." And that isn't the only meat I savor. I stopped myself, unable to believe I'm thinking this way. It's totally out of character. What's gotten into me? Or perhaps I should ask, what do I want to get into me? There I go again.

We returned to the podium, where we stood watching the clock and sipping our drinks.

"You described an interesting session with Becca this morning."

"More than interesting," I added. "I believe it was the turning point in her treatment."

"Why?"

"Because I made a major breakthrough with her. With all the different hurdles to overcome in a therapeutic relationship, trust can either be diminished or enhanced at any stage. And everything is based on trust." I couldn't read his reaction.

"That's a given."

"When I led Becca back to the scene in her family room, she could have just as easily reacted with fright as with curiosity. I took a calculated risk. I was lucky she didn't end the therapy right then and there."

"As you said."

"After the session, Becca was hooked. She had broken through her self-recrimination and guilt. Even though she still didn't know how daunting her memories were, at least she realized they had happened to a scared and wounded child. This brought out her maternal protectiveness, and helped her to see what she had been afraid of all those years had been done by an innocent part of herself. This made it much less threatening."

He listened with furrowed brow. "Then you're going to tell us she revealed whatever was bothering her in short order?"

"Not exactly." I sipped my coffee, allowed the warm, black liquid to revitalize me for the next part of my presentation. "Just because she was willing to strip away the first layer of defense didn't mean she was willing to take it all off. I could liken the process to creeping out on a sheet of ice. No one rushes onto it for fear of falling through. Anyone with half a brain takes their time."

He gave me a seductive smile, but all I felt for a

second was fear. Silly me, what's that all about? My cell phone rang, and all I could think was, 'spared by the bell.'

"Could you excuse me? I need to answer this."

He saluted me. "We'll continue our conversation over lunch."

I pressed the answer button on my phone while watching him amble off. Lara's voice greeted me. "What's the latest on the greatest?"

"Perfect timing. I was just speaking with the object of my insanity the moment you called."

"I'm sorry to interrupt," she said, sounding truly regretful.

"Not at all. Every time I talk to him, I feel like I'm losing control over myself. I might act like a professional, but I feel like a teenager with a crush."

"I know you too well." She chuckled. "I'm sure you're behaving much more dignified."

"I don't know. He triggers something in me I didn't even know existed. I feel like I'm going into the proverbial oven. He's hot all right, but he may burn me. I'm not sure if he isn't coming on a little too strong."

"You're such a worry wart!" she said. "Relax and take things as they come. You don't have to marry this guy. You're only going out on a first date."

"Easy for you to say from the vantage point of a committed relationship. I'm the one who should be committed, and I don't necessarily mean in a relationship, if you catch my gist."

"Remember, Will and I started with a first date, too. Along with raging hormones and commitment phobia. You're not alone. Everyone goes through the same thing."

I smiled to myself. "You're right. It's ordinary, everyday anxiety and nothing more. It's only that I can't remember ever feeling this way to this degree, and I'm not sure whether what I feel is anticipation or pure, unadulterated terror."

"It's both and there's no way around it, so you might as well go along for the roller coaster ride. It's actually the exciting part of the amusement park we call relationship. Why not let go and enjoy it?"

"I can't wait for the Big Dipper." I stopped myself. I'd been so caught up in my problems, I hadn't asked her why she called. "To what can I attribute the pleasure of your call?"

She cleared her throat. "I wanted to know if you were free tomorrow night, and if you could find it in your heart to babysit? Will and I want an early release from parental confinement. Your excitement over this dude has made me see I owe it to myself and my husband to find a way to stimulate our marriage. I thought a date might help us, too."

I thought about how often Lara had been there for me with a ready hand and an open heart. "No problem. If worse comes to worse I'll bring Adrian along, but I doubt that'll be necessary after tonight. We'll be fortunate if we make it through the evening without loathing one another."

I heard Lara sigh. "The eternal optimist. Stop

worrying. Be happy."

"Maybe you need me this evening, and I can gracefully bow out of this date."

"You're not going to use me as an excuse to avoid this man, or any other," Lara said, exasperated. "The earliest you'll hear from me is tomorrow."

"Thanks a million," I joked. "Just when I need you the most." People wandered back to their seats, indicating break time had come to an end. "I have to go."

"Before you do, I have one last thing to say. It's not me who you need most. I'm not the one who will let you down. If anyone will, it's going to be you."

Damn, she was right. I've proven it to myself often enough. Perhaps, if I can generate enough courage, I won't wimp out for once. It could be different this time. I place my cell phone back in my purse with a shaky hand. Nervous or not, here I come. The time had come to let go of past wounds and take a chance on someone new. I glanced over at Adrian, taking his seat. All at once he looked like the future to me.

Chapter Eleven

Becca lowered the head on Mrs. Wilson's bed as the old woman had requested. She tucked the sheet under her before withdrawing the thermometer. Harriet Wilson's fever had hit an all-time high of 102 degrees, and her breathing sounded labored. If she didn't respond to the antibiotics and her bronchitis worsened, she would have to be transferred to Thomas Jefferson Hospital later in the day.

"I'll be back to check in on you in a few minutes."

To prove how sick she was, Harriet didn't offer her typical argument.

Becca strode directly to the nurses' station where she penned Wilson's stats into her chart. "I'm worried about Wilson," she announced to Angela over her shoulder. "Her fever refuses to break and she sounds terrible."

Angela stared at her through reddened eyes. Her hair hadn't been combed, her uniform was creased. She looked uncommonly unkempt.

Worried, Becca asked, "What's the matter with you?"

Angela shook her head and tears sprang into her eyes. Apparent Angela didn't wish to discuss her troubles in a public place, Becca coaxed her into an empty conference room at the end of the hall. She took a seat catty-corner to Angela at a long mahogany table.

"I only have a few minutes, but I want to know what's going on," Becca said.

Angela tried to explain, but tears garbled her words. Becca offered her a box of tissues from a nearby shelf.

"Why don't you take a second. When you're ready you'll have to repeat everything you just said."

Angela sobbed into the tissue. Concerned, Becca hovered over her with an arm around her shoulders, consoling her with reassuring words.

"It's Elliot, the idiot," Angela sniveled. "It's difficult to describe what's going on, but there's been a change in him. He's rarely around anymore like he used to be, and when he is, he's preoccupied and ignores me. I don't know if he's met someone new or what's going on, but something's changed." She started to cry again. "I don't know what to do. I've lost my appetite, and I haven't been able to sleep the last couple nights. I even had one of the docs prescribe sleeping pills today."

"Have you asked Elliot what's going on?"

"If I've asked him once, I've asked him a dozen times, but I always get the same response. Nothing's changed. Nothing's going on. But I don't believe him. He's different, I tell you. Distant. It's not good." She dabbled at tears gathered in the corners of her eyes. "He's breaking my heart."

"He's a doctor, right?"

Angela nodded.

"Perhaps he's preoccupied with his work. You

know as well as I do the life of an M.D. They're always busy. Besides, a doctor sees nasty and tragic things. Sometimes they don't know what to do for a patient who's suffering. It's possible he's just distracted."

Angela drew in a big breath. "You might be right, at least I hope you are. I know he's told me about a couple of his patients whose stories would upset Ming the Merciless."

"Why don't you give him a chance and watch what happens without drawing any conclusions. This too might pass, but before it does, you might push him away with your worries and accusations. Give it a little time."

"I haven't mentioned the strangest thing of all. Remember I mentioned Elliot has asked me about you? Well, he hasn't let up, and he seems annoyed when I don't know the answer to his questions."

Becca made a face. "Why me?"

"I told you it was odd. I've tried not to make too much of his questions, but they keep coming. To tell you the truth, sometimes they seem a little too personal."

This tidbit gave Becca the shivers. "Like what?"

"Like the other night he wanted to know where we went together after work. When I told him we sometimes go shopping, he wanted to know where, and what kinds of things we shopped for—"

"It only shows his interest in you—"

"Yeah, but then he wanted to know the kinds of

things you like to buy, you know, perfume, make-up, lines of clothing. It was too much."

The shivers turned to tremors. "Why would he want to know so much about me?"

"Same question I asked him, but he became irritated and mumbled something about wanting to know every detail of my life. This whole thing seems a little off."

"What if you were to take what he said at face value and try not to analyze him? Perhaps he's telling the truth. Wouldn't it be a relief to you?"

"Of course, you're right. I have to let go of all my suspicions. I keep telling myself that, but every time I see him and he treats me with indifference or asks me questions about you, I become more confused and upset."

An idea dawned on Becca. She leaned over the table. "Remember we spoke about all of us getting together? I'd like to meet this guy. It would give me a chance to psyche him out."

Angela rubbed her brow. "Yeah, it might work. I'd like your opinion."

A screechy sound proceeded a voice over the intercom calling for Becca Rosen to go to room 222. Harriet Wilson's room.

Becca sprang from her seat, but then hesitated. "I have to go, but are you going to be all right?" She didn't move until she received the go-ahead from Angela, then tore out the door and down the hall.

On her way to Harriet's room, she considered briefly what she had heard. Another chill pulsed through her. She was as suspicious as Angela about Elliot's intentions. Why the sudden change of heart? And the interest in a total stranger? None of this made much sense. For once, she needed to face the situation head on and meet this man, instead of avoiding an awkward scene. That had been her modus operandi for as long as she could remember. This time she had to learn the truth firsthand.

Drew had asked Becca out for dinner on four or five occasions, but she had put him off because she didn't want to lead him on. They had any number of long-winded phone conversations during the weeks following their coffee date, and the more she learned about him, the more she admired his integrity and willingness to be of service to others. Liking and respecting him only made it harder to consider letting him down.

The Friday before the holidays he finally convinced her to meet him for a celebratory drink at his favorite watering hole across from his office on Spruce Street. She arrived at the intimate upscale tavern a few minutes early in her most conservative brown suit and matching pumps. She wanted the message to be clear from her packaging—friendship is as far as I'm willing to take this.

Becca took a seat at the oak and brass bar and ordered a white wine. While she waited for Drew, she checked out the black and white velvet brocaded walls and red padded booths. The place looked like a swanky nightclub in a 1940s film, and she almost expected Humphrey Bogart or Ingrid Bergman to waltz through the door. Instead, the customers standing by the bar were downtown professionals in conservative business suits. And when the door opened and let in a blast of frigid air, it became apparent she was far from Casablanca.

The door opened once more, allowing in more cold air and Drew. He combed his fingers through long hair ruffled by the wind. With his jeans and tooled boots, he instantly stood out in the bar. She liked the fact he wasn't self-conscious or particularly concerned about fitting in with other people. She waved and he came straight over to her.

"Am I late? Have you been here long?"

The bartender set her drink down. "Only a few minutes." She reached in her purse to pay for the drink, but Drew stopped her.

"I'll take care of it." He pulled a five out of his wallet and slapped it on the counter. "Keep the change, Jim."

Jim looked pleased.

Drew hoisted her drink and coaster. "Let's find ourselves a table in the back. It's quieter there."

He led her to a booth where he ordered a Guinness. "You sure are a sight for sore eyes. It's been a long time since I've seen you. How are you doing?"

"Better." And she meant it this time. "It takes

time."

"I bet." He paid the waitress who brought his beer. "Do you want anything to eat?"

She shook her head and the waitress left.

He sipped his drink "Tell me how your parents are doing."

"Same as always. No major change I can see. How are yours?"

"They're good. Not that I get to see much of them these days, even though I live close by, but I call them regularly. My practice has started to take off, and I rarely have time to fight traffic to Ardmore any more."

She sat back. "What type of cases?"

"Interesting ones. Yesterday I received a referral for a class action lawsuit against the Cambridge Company of Camden, New Jersey. They have a coal-based generator that is a major polluter in South Camden. The area has had a recent surge in respiratory problems, especially in an elementary school by the plant. It should be an important case."

"You sound excited about it."

He chuckled. "I guess you could put it that way. It's a real challenge. The company has money up the wazoobees and can hire the best and brightest lawyers around. I'm a little intimidated, but I'll have a chance to do good for a community that doesn't have much of a voice."

"How wonderful you're able to represent them."

"How lucky I am to be asked to help out."

Again he had impressed with his sincerity and humility. What a terrific man! She had never met anyone like him. "Would it sound gauche if I ask how you make any money at this?"

He laughed again and his eyes sparkled with good humor. "Absolutely debased. Actually, I ask myself the same question, only I put it in the future tense. Can I ever make any money at this? I think so, but I'm not in it for the big bucks. Satisfaction and the knowledge I've done good is more important to me than my profit margin. I suppose that's hard to understand."

Not at all! Becca thought. What a gem. Listening to him made her regret meeting Evan first, but it was too late. Evan had already stolen his way into her affections. "How do you make a living?"

"Investments. When I worked for the Feds, I put every penny I could into real estate and the stock market. I have a few pennies to live on until my private practice becomes a little less private and impoverished. That's what gave me enough to buy my townhouse last July."

She cocked her head in a question. "I thought you moved here in September?"

"I did, but I found this terrific place, the price was right, and I bought it before I moved back. You'll have to come by and see it sometime."

Not in the near future. She didn't want to start something she couldn't finish.

He raised his glass and toasted her. "Enough

about me. I want to hear more about you."

He continued by asking her details about her work, her friends, and her social life. Later, after their second round of drinks and an appetizer platter, he made her promise she'd join him again for dinner and drinks, but sooner next time. She agreed with greater enthusiasm than she expected, feeling more guilt toward Evan than she expected. Which only confirmed her confusion concerning everything.

While Evan had won a place in her heart, Drew had so much going for him. She found him hard to resist, with his chiseled chin and bushy brows, and she didn't know if she wanted to. This only demonstrated how unprepared she was for anything more complicated than a friendship. She had fooled herself once into thinking she was ready for a relationship, but now she knew better. At that moment she promised herself she wouldn't make a commitment to anyone until she was certain about what she wanted. And that might be a long time coming.

"Becca arrived on time to the following week's session," I explained, "and the first thing she did, after mentioning how much she'd gotten out of the homework assignment, was to declare her decision to recommit to our work. Upon hearing this, I knew I had a time-limited window of opportunity to move Becca deeper into her repressed memory, before her resistance returned.

"Not wishing to get side-tracked and allow the

opportunity to pass, I quickly inquired into her readiness to replay the earlier incident in her parents' bedroom, to see if she could attach a face to the man on the bed. I noted how she reacted by bracing herself with a hand on the sofa arm.

"I guess I'm as ready as I'll ever be, Sarah."

"Then lie back," I directed her, "and let's go there."

I gave her a minute to position herself on the sofa and engage in the relaxation techniques that were part of preparation for the trance work, then instructed her to take herself back to her parents' bedroom and mentally revisit what had happened. I watched her eyes travel beneath their lids as she visualized the encounter.

"What is it you're seeing?"

She sighed. "It's not good... He's making me touch him...I don't want to do it...but he won't let me go...I'm scared...please don't hurt me..." Her voice sounded meek and childlike.

"Take your hand back and... when you're ready, look up at the man and tell me who you see."

"I can't see his face," she wailed. "I want to, but I can't see him."

"Don't be afraid. I'm here to help you. I won't let him hurt you. Take a closer look."

"It's no use...his face is a blur...I can't see him through the tears..."

The little girl must have been crying as hard as the woman before me. "Why don't you ask little Becca who she thinks it might be."

After a long moment of silence, she said, "P...Paulie. She thinks it might be her Uncle Paulie. That's why she doesn't like to be near him."

"See if you can attach Paulie's face to the man in the bedroom. Let me know how that feels."

"I don't know. I guess it feels about right...but I'm not sure. I wish I knew..." She wrapped her arms tightly around herself. "He seems to have a head of curly blond hair and Paulie's grew straight and brown. Wait...I remember my mother had a wig with curly blond hair. I used to try it on when playing dress up...I wonder if he's wearing it. And he has on thick dark glasses. Maybe he's in disguise and that's why I can't tell who he is. Do you think that's possible?"

It was beginning to make sense. "More than possible from what you're saying. It's likely, if he didn't want to be recognized and caught."

"Wow," she said. "To think I've been trying to put a face on him and all along he was in disguise. That sure complicates my attempts to identify him."

"It does, but it doesn't mean it's impossible. Don't give up just yet."

"How can I? I opened the can. I can't put the lid back on now." Becca opened haunted eyes, a stricken look on her pale face. "Oh God..."

"Yes." I allowed her a couple minutes to recover. "How do you feel?"

"Frustrated. Frightened." She fiddled with her

fingers. "I wish I could be sure it was Paulie who abused me."

"Trust the process. You will know in due time. In the meantime, do you think it's possible Paulie might have had something to do with your rape?"

"I don't know, but it sure seems coincidental he returned to town around the same time."

"What do you plan to do with all of your suspicions?"

"I'm going to report them to the police. I only hope Detective Mills takes me seriously for once, and follows up on my lead." She folded her arms around herself in a gesture of consolation. "I forgot to mention Mills called me a couple of days ago to tell me my hair sample didn't match the one on the rag."

"I'm surprised you didn't mention that earlier, but it's definitely good news. Does it mean you're no longer a suspect?"

She threw up her hands. "I wish! It certainly puts a crimp in their case against me, but since they don't have another possible culprit, I'm still numero uno, as far as I can tell. Maybe this will take them in a new direction."

"Let's hope." I rose, as did Becca, and I embraced her in a comforting hug. "You're doing good work here. Whatever happens, I know you'll come out of this a much wiser woman. All your effort will pay off. You'll see."

I sent a silent thank you off to the Universe for giving me the strength and openness to allow Becca to take this as far as she could. If I hadn't worked on my own childhood issues, I would never had been able to allow her the license to explore the hidden recesses of her past as freely as she was doing.

One thing therapy teaches you: you can't take anyone anywhere they're not willing to go. As a matter of fact, you can't take them anywhere you haven't gone yourself. A therapist is limited by the constrains of their client's willingness to do the work, coupled with their own emotional barriers. It's essential for every therapist to be aware of their own underlying conflict and motivation, before attempting to treat someone with Repressed Memory Syndrome.

Becca stepped back. "Wisdom wasn't exactly my aim in life, but if it's all I get out of this, I guess I shouldn't complain. No matter what the police believe, I'm going to discover the truth if it's the last thing I do."

I cringed. "Please be careful." With a vicious psychopathic killer on the loose, I prayed her quest didn't turn out to be exactly that.

Becca had barely entered the foyer of the Goldstein home when chimes announced Paulie's arrival. Julie let him in and ushered him over to where Becca busily removed her coat and scarf. He gave her an enthusiastic greeting, and Becca reluctantly returned his hug with a stiff one of her own.

"I didn't know you'd be here," he whispered

into her hair, sending a shudder down her spine.

She pulled away, shaken. "Mom surprised me with an invitation to dinner. She said it might be the only chance I'd have to visit with you for a while because you might be going back to California to clear up a few of your affairs."

Paulie turned to Julie with a bemused look on his face. "You make it sound as though I'll be away for months, but it should only take a week or two. Why didn't you tell me Becca was coming tonight? I bought her a little something I thought she'd enjoy. I think it's still in the trunk of the car. I'll go and fetch it."

"You already gave her enough" Julie said. But Paulie took off before she could stop him, and returned a few minutes later carrying a small gift bag. He handed it to Becca. "Open it."

Julie wrenched the bag from her hands. "This could have waited until after we ate. Let's go and have a cocktail in the family room. You can open it in there."

Irritated at the intrusion, Becca gritted her teeth against an urge to say something nasty and followed them into the family room, joining Irv in front of the fireplace. Julie poured them glasses of Chardonnay Paulie had brought with him from California.

"A toast to our finally getting together as a family." Julie raised her glass. They all lifted theirs. After everyone took a sip, Julie said, "Let's see what Paulie bought you, Becca."

Becca opened the bag with trembling fingers and extracted a bottle of *Raffinée*. Her knees nearly buckled. "Wow, my favorite. How did you know what perfume I wear?"

Paulie laughed. "Besides a great sense of smell, your mother gave away your secret."

Julie looked up in the middle of another sip of her wine. "I don't remember telling you anything of the sort. Maybe Irv did."

"You wouldn't remember my middle name if I didn't remind you. I asked you what Becca wanted for her birthday months ago. Sorry I'm late with this."

"You might have," Julie said, sipping her wine. "I just can't remember."

Becca stared at the bottle in her shaky hand and immediately placed it back in the bag. Did Julie tell him, or did he hear it from someone else? And who else would know about her preference, except Angela? "I'm glad we're finally together. I have so many questions for you."

Maria entered with a tray of crackers and crab claws, which she placed on the bar. Paulie took one bar stool and Becca another. "I've been wondering about something that happened to me years ago, and thought you might be able to set me straight."

"Setting people straight isn't my specialty, but go ahead," Paulie joked.

"I sort of remember you babysitting me when I was little."

Julie poured her another glass. "Once in a great while. My baby brother was old enough to have an active social life by the time you came along. I know my memory's not great, but as I recall, he wasn't available too often to babysit—much to my chagrin." She sent Paulie a mock look of exasperation.

"But you did on occasion, right?"

"Rarely after you turned five."

That didn't jibe with Becca's recollection, but even a couple times would have given him a chance to molest her. "If Paulie didn't babysit me, who did?"

Julie thought. "There was a nice young man named Adam who lived around the corner from us. He babysat for me most of the time. Then there was a teenager a few houses down. I believe her name was Melissa. She helped out on occasion."

Dizzy, Becca decided to lighten up on the wine. "You're saying Paulie rarely watched me when you and dad went out?"

"Why do you ask?"

All eyes were on her. No use trying to fool them. Time to bring her suspicions out in the open. "I have reason to believe whoever babysat me, also..." she took a deep breath, "...also molested me..." The words rushed out in one sustained breath before she could fully consider the ramifications.

A plate shattered to the floor in a violent crash. Everyone looked startled, especially Paulie. Julie leapt to her feet and took off for the kitchen, returning with a broom. She swept up the shards as they all watched without a word.

Paulie stared at her through the saddest eyes she had ever seen. "I can't believe you'd think I could do that," he stammered. "I don't know what to say."

Neither did she. She had opened a door that would never close again. Becca looked down at the Berber carpet, refusing to meet his eyes.

Julie placed the broom aside, came around the bar, and wrapped an arm around her shoulders. "You've been under tremendous pressure since David's murder. You're understandably upset and not thinking clearly." She turned toward Paulie. "Please don't be angry. I'm sure this is nothing and we can clear up any misunderstanding. Why don't you boys grab a bite in the dining room while we girls go upstairs to talk for a few minutes."

"But—" Before Becca could say anything more, Julie placed a hand under her elbow and navigated her toward her old bedroom.

Once inside the room, Julie turned to her with a beet-red face and eyes that flashed with anger. "Where the hell did that accusation come from! Are you going out of your way to make things miserable for everyone else? I know you've been in pain lately, but that's no reason to take it out on the rest of us!"

No use holding back any longer. Time to tell all. "I'm sorry this has made you uncomfortable, Mom, but I've been in therapy the last couple of months, and it's surfaced I was molested as a child. I'm hoping to be able to find out who did it and to connect the dots between my recent rape and my earlier one."

"How can you be sure of that? At least sure

enough to make such an accusation. You're really out of order here."

She wasn't sure of anything anymore. "I'm having flashbacks and memories of the abuse."

"You know children have faulty memories," Julie said, staring off in the distance, uncharacteristically quiet for a minute. "Assuming what you say is true, what makes you think these two incidents are connected? They're years apart. Couldn't they have been committed by two separate people?"

"They could be, but my nightmares tell me otherwise. From what I can gather, the same person committed both acts. The police think I lied to them about the rape and I'm somehow involved in the murder. I can't possibly exonerate myself and protect myself against a madman who's still on the loose, unless I can figure out who did it. And why."

Julie watched her closely as you would an unpredictable child. "Even if it's true, why Paulie? He had nothing to do with it."

Rage flared up in her with unexpected urgency. "How do you know? And why would you want to protect him instead of me? You're the one who left me unsupervised, with a sociopath who raped me! What type of judgment does that show?"

Julie stared at her, eyes wide, mouth gaping open. For the first time ever she didn't have a quick retort. "But...I never meant..."

"Screw what you meant to do! What does it matter in the face of what happened to me? It was your job as a mother to shelter me! A fine job you did."

Tears filled Julie's eyes. "I only meant the best for you. I would never have done anything to intentionally harm you."

"Intentional or not, you left me in the hands of a rapist. And you're going to have to live with that for the rest of your life. The least you can do is help me out here." She plopped down on the bed. "I realize Paulie's your baby brother, and you don't want to believe he could do such a heinous thing, but how do you know what he's capable of? I'm your daughter, for crying out loud. Aren't I the one you should be protecting? Not him!"

"Of course, but I can't possibly think he'd do such a thing to his own niece."

"If Paulie didn't, then who did?" The taste of tears filled the back of her throat. Would she ever figure this out?

"I wish I could help you, but I don't believe it was Paulie. He wasn't even around much."

"Then I have to find out who. What can you tell me about the Adam kid? What was he like?"

A furrow formed on Julie's brow. "Let's see... I believe he was about sixteen or so when he babysat you. A lanky but cute kid with brown hair which used to fall over his black-rimmed glasses. I remember him being polite to me and your dad. I can't imagine he would have done anything untoward to you."

"Well, somebody did, and they might have come back for more."

"Are you sure you were molested? We were so close. Wouldn't you have said something to me?" Julie mused.

"Obviously not."

Julie looked demoralized. "I wish you had come to me. Maybe I could have intervened."

"That would have been nice, but you knew I was having major psychological problems. You even took me to a psychiatrist who hospitalized me. Didn't it ever dawn on you there might be something going on that disturbed me that much?"

"I didn't know...didn't make the connection." Julie took a seat next to her on the bed. "Explain one thing to me. How can you depend on your dreams to make a connection between the past and the present?"

"In my nightmares, whoever molested me keeps coming back for more. But it's something else: it's also the cologne. I smelled it the night of the rape and I think it's the same one the molester wore. It's called *Aramis*."

"But that's a common cologne! Many men wear it. Why, your dad even has a bottle, although I've never known him to wear it much."

"Oh." She hadn't thought about the cologne being in the house all along. Maybe whoever molested her used Irv's cologne. Or maybe it was Irv. She quickly banished the thought. "I never considered that."

"What?" Julie asked.

Becca chose not to answer. "Mom, I don't know

what to do. I feel like I'm falling apart. I have trouble sleeping, and when I do, I end up waking up in a cold sweat from a nightmare. This is becoming unbearable."

To her surprise, Julie bundled her up into sheltering arms. Because she rarely thought of her mother as a friend or an ally, this demonstration of love caught her unprepared.

"Whatever happens, Becca, I want you to know I'm here. I might have let you down in the past, but you can count on me now."

Her heart swelled with gratitude at her mother's support, which surprised her, and made her aware her feelings toward Julie were beginning to mutate from anger into a greater acceptance. She even experienced a degree of respect for Julie's know-how in handling the awkward situation downstairs. "Thanks, Mom, I appreciate it."

Julie held her for a long minute, then pushed away in her typically brusque manner. For once it failed to bother Becca. "Now, dry your eyes and let's go down to dinner," Julie said. "I'll go ahead and make excuses to Paulie while you ready yourself. But be down soon or I'll come up to get you."

Becca waited until Julie had left the room before gathering herself. She didn't want to pursue her suspicions around Paulie and lose the momentary sense of camaraderie she shared with her mother, but she still hadn't crossed him off her short-list of suspects. For now she would wait and watch. If she took her time and remained open to clues, more would be revealed.

Later that same evening, Becca paced Evan's dark-stained living room floor, listening as the sound of her heels click against wood, then echo off the tall white walls and cathedral ceiling. "I don't know what to believe. Paulie says he rarely babysat for me and wasn't even in Philly at the time of my attack. He said he could produce proof he was in California, but we'll see if it ever materializes." She scratched her head. "The plot sickens. If it wasn't him, who could it have been?"

Evan watched her from his perch on the arm of his boxy, brown futon. "Do you know how many crimes go unsolved? Most of them. Why do this to yourself and your family? It's been over six months since the incident. Relax and allow the police to do their work."

"I don't think I can," she said, pacing. "Besides the fact I'm their primary suspect, I don't think I'll be able to let down my guard, knowing there's someone lurking about who has me in his sights." She stopped in front of Evan. "All I ever wanted was a normal life! Now look at what I have."

"Maybe normal isn't all it's cracked up to be. Look at me. I ended up studying all last night, and never left the condo. If that's how you define a normal life, it leaves a lot to be desired."

"But you said you were going to the library last night. I distinctly remember you telling me that was the reason you couldn't join me for dinner."

"Oh, I went there earlier. Right after clinic. No, I had to study for my exam last night."

"Oh, I guess I heard you wrong." Or did she? "Anyway, it has to be a heck of a lot better than this insanity. All I'm asking for are answers, yet all I get are more questions. I don't think I'll ever be able to get on with my life until I figure out what happened." She took a seat on the futon. "It's strange hearing myself say I've put my life on hold, but it rings true."

He sauntered over to the ceiling-high bookshelves lining one wall of his condo, removed a book, and handed it to her.

She read the title, *Man's Search for Meaning* by Victor Frankel. "What's this about?" she asked, thumbing through the book.

He took a seat beside her. "Frankel was a Nazi concentration camp survivor who experienced the most horrendous treatment any human being can imagine, and yet, because of his attitude and outlook, he came through the war in one piece physically and emotionally. According to him, with the right perspective, you can walk through hell and come out a better person. He points out you can't always control what happens to you, but you can control how you react to it. Read it, you'll see."

"What are you trying to tell me?"

"Only that you don't have to put your life on hold while you wait to find out who raped you." He draped an arm around her shoulder. "You can make a decision to go on with your life and take things as they come." He drew her closer. "And remember, you're not alone. I'm here with you. As a matter of fact, I want to be with you when you go on this manhunt. From now on, I'd like you to take me along."

He smiled down at her with a look of tenderness. Then it mutated into desire. He began to lower his lips to hers, but she pushed him away. Not ready for a repeat of their last encounter, she could no longer be sure she really trusted him. She doubted everyone now, and he was no exception. "Not now."

Flushed, he ran his hand through his layered hair, looking so appealing she was tempted to ignore her reservations.

"What's the matter?"

She crossed her fingers behind her. "I have to leave for the hospital in an hour to cover the evening shift for Angela." The moment she said this, guilt at telling a half-truth nibbled at her.

"Is there anyone to cover for you?"

Gazing into his beseeching eyes made her wish there was. Or did she? Too confused to choose, she stood. "I have to go ready myself. I'll give you a holler tomorrow."

His expression turned serious. "Do I get another chance soon?"

How could she answer him? Although attracted to him, she didn't know her own feelings. Now with Drew in the equation, she couldn't even try to make sense of it all.

She gave him a gentle nudge. "We'll see about that," she said, and fled his condo before he could probe any further. She had too many questions herself to give

him any answers. And even if she knew, she wasn't
sure she'd be ready to say.

Chapter Twelve

An ache in my belly signaled lunchtime, and I noticed a handful of my audience fidgeting in their seats. "Before we take our lunch break, I'd like to share with you my definition of a psychopath. On the surface psychopaths are charming, intelligent, likable, and often successful, but underneath they're shallow, unfeeling, superficial, and lack empathy. What you see is not what you get. One thing of note is that psychopaths often have a 'secret life,' and are elusive and unavailable. If you observe these traits in someone, those could be the first indicators of psychopathology. Let's end here for the morning and meet back after lunch, at precisely two."

People rose from their seats. I glanced down at my notes to double-check where I stopped, and heard them start toward the door. A couple of hard-core types ignored their hunger pangs and wandered up to the podium for clarification or questions. Once through with them, I glanced about, but failed to spy Adrian. Against my will, my heart sank.

Much to my relief, the door to the men's room opened and he reentered the conference room, heading straight over to where I stood.

"Going to lunch, Sarah? I'm treating."

I laughed; our lunches are included in the cost of the conference. "Same time, same table?"

"You're on."

As we made our way to the lunch room, we chatted about the conference attendees. He observed that one of the men had a toupee which looked more like a Stainmaster carpet sample than real hair, and I pointed out the sexy young woman in the too-tight, low-cut spandex top—as if he hadn't noticed. Today, lunch was being served cafeteria style, and we carried trays full of food to the table. I had more on my plate than I normally eat, but I was famished after a day and a half on my feet.

After we both had a chance to take a few bites, he asked, "What do women see in psychopaths?"

I shook my head at his question. "I would like to remind you, not all women are attracted to psychopaths. Most women who are prey to these guys have been abused themselves, and aren't able to read the more obvious signals. The psychopath's existence depends upon an ability to dazzle and manipulate. They're predators. Lying and pouring on the charm are survival tactics for them. One way they lure their victims is by figuring out what the woman wants most in the world, and offering it to her. It's only after the fish is hooked that their true nature surfaces. While psychopaths are particularly adept at overcoming someone's resistance, women with good instincts can avoid them, or at least recognize one, before he's done too much damage to her."

"What is their 'true nature?'" he asked between bites of meatball sandwich.

"Rage. They're full of anger and violence. But why am I telling you this? You've heard it all before."

He smiled. "I still love hearing it from you."

Oh my God, I thought. *I can't believe how*

obvious Adrian is and how well it works with me.
"What a flirt you are."

"I'm a lot more than that."

"I don't know if I can take much more."

He captured my gaze and said in a husky voice, "I think you can."

I took a sip of my iced tea to cool down.

"Sarah, what's your interest in this type of case?"

I put down my glass and considered how much to reveal, deciding it would be prudent to keep my real reasons to myself. "It's a fascinating case. You said so yourself."

"No doubt, I sense it holds a personal attraction for you."

Bull's eye! "You're quite good at this, aren't you?" I meant what I said. His knowing look confirmed he was clever enough to recognize the truth.

"There's more to this than you're saying."

"You're right. I do have a personal motivation, but how did you figure it out?"

"Just a hunch. Are you going to share it with me?"

Ordinarily I wouldn't, but something about Adrian propelled me to be bolder than usual, and maybe a little more reckless. "There's a similarity between my childhood and Becca's, but not as much as you might think. We're both children of abuse, but mine wasn't sexual."

His expression turned serious. "I see."

What did he see? I wondered. A woman still struggling with the residue of a difficult childhood, who can't always trust her own judgment where men are concerned? Who has had trouble standing up for her own truth with others? Because that's the woman I see.

Suddenly self-conscious, I said, "I don't advertise this, and I hope you'll keep it to yourself."

"Of course," he reassured me. "I had no intention of telling anyone else."

I took the ketchup and gave it a couple of strong shakes before it flooded out onto my fries. "I believe, as psychotherapists, we find clients with similar conflicts to be the most compelling. Don't you?"

"Yes," he agreed. "I do."

"And there's nothing wrong with that, as long as we've done our homework. To the degree we're still struggling with old ghosts and buried wreckage, we'll be handicapped in helping them."

He took the ketchup I offered him and put a dollop on his plate. I was amazed at his portion control after my fiasco. "What about you? Do you feel you're healed enough to help Becca?"

"If I didn't, I wouldn't have taken her case," I said, but I suddenly had the sense of being found out. This made me wonder if I still bore obvious wounds. But what if I did? Did it affect Becca's therapy? Or my judgment? In answer to my own questions, I decided to revisit my hypnotherapist, and see if there was more work to do. I made a mental note to call for an appointment the following week.

I glanced over at Adrian, and he grinned at me as if he knew something about me I didn't know. With that smirk plastered on his face I could only hope whatever it was, he was dead wrong.

"Please take your seats," I said. "We're ready to begin the afternoon session." A cacophony of sounds followed my announcement: the stomp of feet, lilt of voices, and creak of chairs. Then silence.

A woman's arm shot up over the sea of heads. "Sarah, could you clarify Becca's ambivalence toward Evan? Was she still grieving David's death, or was there another reason for her reaction?"

"Of course Becca still grieved her husband's untimely demise," I answered, "but what made her conflict more profound was her inability to trust herself and her judgment. As I'm sure you've gathered, she had been mildly depressed before the rape and murder, which was only exacerbated by the trauma. With her history of childhood abuse, compounded by her rape, her sexuality had been affected. Under the circumstances, how could she make healthy choices or have a fulfilling sexual relationship with anyone? Her tremendous attraction to Evan caused her to feel more alive around him, but deep down, she recognized her incapacity to have a functional romantic entanglement with anyone until she removed her major emotional roadblocks."

One of the dowdy social workers rose and asked, "Isn't it possible she saw something more in Evan than simply a crutch, Sarah? You make her sound cold and manipulative."

"Good point. I didn't mean to paint such a stark picture of her, and I certainly don't intend to imply she didn't have feelings toward him. I'm only saying she wasn't ready for an intimate relationship, and part of her knew this."

A serious-looking young man stood and I acknowledged him. He had a shaved head and an impressive viper tattoo on his forearm that snaked beneath the sleeve of his black tee-shirt "Why was Becca so passive to begin with?"

"Her passivity was a direct result of family dysfunction, combined with her sexual abuse. When a child's nature is repressed, like Becca's, by an overprotective parent, they tend to react in one of two ways. They either become passive and dependent, like Rebecca, or angry and rebellious, like many of your adolescent patients. The abuse Becca endured cemented those dysfunctional behavior traits, and they became what we call characterological. Even though passivity might appear harmless on the surface, underneath it lies a well of resentment. This explains Becca's reaction to her mother. As a colleague of mine would often say: 'There's nothing passive about passivity.'"

I glanced around. "If there are no other questions, I'd like to pick up where I left off this morning." No one responded, and I continued.

"The night after her family dinner, Becca arrived home late from St. John's after covering Angela's shift. Exhausted, she went straight to sleep, bypassing her usual cup of chamomile tea and before bed-time reading ritual."

The phone ringing in the middle of the night startled her awake. The time read 4:45 on her bedside clock. "Yes?" she answered, her heart hammering at the thought something might be wrong with Julie or Irv.

A woman's voice asked, "Is this Rebecca Rosen?"

Becca acknowledged groggily and the woman continued.

"I'm calling from the emergency room at Thomas Jefferson Hospital."

Now fully awake, Becca levered herself with one arm to a sitting position, squeezing the receiver closer to her ear. "What's wrong?"

"Your friend Angela Petrocelli was admitted a few minutes ago with severe abdominal distress. Since she doesn't have any family in town, she asked us to contact you."

"Is she all right?" Becca asked concerned, but also relieved it wasn't one of her parents with a heart-attack or a stroke.

"To be frank, she's not well at all."

"Tell her I'll be there as soon as I can."

Becca hung up the phone. Only apprehension about Angela's condition galvanized her to rise from beneath the warmth of her down comforter into the frigid night air. Shivering, she made a mad dash for the dresser, squirmed into her gray sweats, and gathered her burgundy fiber-filled jacket from the coat closet as she headed out the door. Outside, the street was deserted and eerily quiet. She could barely go five feet before fear of her stalker sent her racing back to the safety of the building. She had to decide what to do! Perhaps she could convince Evan to join her.

At Evan's building, she scurried to his condo and knocked lightly on his door, not wanting to disturb the neighbors. When he failed to appear, she pounded harder and called his name. Still no answer. Worried, she tried again, wondering where he might be at this time of night. She knew where he kept a spare key and considered letting herself in, but didn't feel right invading his privacy.

Instead, she took off at a sprint for her car. No matter what, she had to be at the hospital for Angela. She thrust open the car door and dove into the driver's seat, hammering down the door lock with an open palm. With no time to lose, she careened out of her hard-found parking space and screeched around a deserted city street corner to her destination, parking as close as she could to Jefferson Hospital's emergency room entrance.

At the late hour only a handful of nocturnal sufferers sat scattered throughout the waiting room. She sprinted past them to the front desk. "I'm here to see Angela Petrocelli!"

The nurse wore a grave expression. "Please come this way. Dr. Peters wants to speak with you."

The nurse showed her into the treatment area. "Wait here. Dr. Peters will be right with you."

Becca stood awkwardly by the nurses' station in the puke-green painted room divided by curtained cubicles. She shifted from one foot to the other, eager to hear about Angela. Minutes slipped by. Why hadn't she been taken to see Angela? What was the hold-up?

Finally, an overweight young woman approached Becca and held out a hand. She was thirty-something with curly red hair, warm brown eyes, and a pale complexion with freckles on her nose and cheeks. "Dr. Peters. I'm glad you could come."

"How's Angela, Doctor? Is she all right?"

Peters frowned. "She lapsed into a coma a couple minutes ago. We've decided to put her on life-support. She's being moved to the Intensive Care Unit right now."

The ICU! She knew this spelled serious. "Is she going to survive?"

"We don't know. We're doing the best we can, but she came in here gravely ill. We're not sure what the problem is, but we're running tests as we speak." Peters pursed her lips. "Because she's a nurse and has access to medication, do you know if she took any opiates? Her pin-point pupils lead us to believe she may have overdosed on morphine."

Becca couldn't believe her ears. "Angela wouldn't even take an aspirin if she had a headache. I certainly don't think she would have taken morphine." Then she remembered the sleeping medication Angela had mentioned. "She was prescribed *Ambien* by a doctor we know, because she was having problems with her boyfriend and couldn't sleep. She might have taken too many."

"We'll look into it. Is her boyfriend named Elliot? Right before she lapsed into the coma she mentioned to one of the nurses she was with him this evening. We thought he might know what she ingested that made her ill."

"His first name is about the extent of what I know about him. He's a surgeon she's been dating for the past few months. Wait...I remember she mentioned he has a private practice in Center City, and he's associated with Hahnemann Hospital. That's all I can tell you."

"Okay, we'll call Hahnemann and see if we can locate him. If you remember anything else, please let me know. In the meantime, we've spoken to her mother in Erie and they've given us permission to perform lavage, and pump her stomach. We'll come and get you in the waiting room when we're done."

Becca drifted back into the waiting area and it soon became clear where it had gotten its name. The suspense made every minute seem like an hour. Unable to stay seated any longer than the time it took to leaf through a *Newsweek* magazine, she paced the floor, observing the people around her for the first time. Most of those waiting to be treated in the middle of the night appeared to be poor people who used the Emergency Room as they would a primary care physician. *Tattered and torn and tormented people,* Becca thought, *down on their luck in every way imaginable.*

Finally, the nurse called her to the emergency room desk. "Your friend is in the ICU on the third floor. Take the elevator down the hall to your right."

She took the stairs instead of the elevator to the Intensive Care Unit. After the night nurse cleared her with the doctor, she was led to Angela. The sight shocked her. Angela lay dwarfed by machines which hovered over her like mutant aliens monitoring her every respiration and heartbeat, feeding her through intravenous tubes. Beeps and bells provided background sounds in rhythm with flashing lights and digital displays. Her typically rich complexion had turned sallow, and her hair hung limp on her pillow. Every once in a while she would twitch, but otherwise she lay deathly still.

Frightened, Becca took a seat by the side of the bed and grasped onto Angela's sweaty hand. "Angela, it's Becca. I'm here."

For a good half-hour, Becca held onto Angela's hand like a life-line, murmuring to her in muted tones, hoping her voice might bring her friend back.

A nurse finally came by. "You better go. We have to take her levels. We'll let you back in at visiting time between ten and twelve."

What could she do in the meantime? Silly to remain at the hospital unless she could be of help. She should make herself useful. "I'll bet the ambulance driver didn't lock Angela's apartment. I should go by and button things up. Can I pick up anything for her while I'm there?"

The nurse considered. "She obviously doesn't need anything right away, but when she comes to she'll need a toothbrush and a robe."

"I'll be back at ten with her toiletries." She withdrew a pad and pen from her purse, wrote down her cell number, tore the page from the book, and handed it to the nurse, who glanced at it briefly before shoving it into her pocket. "That's where you can reach me if you need me in the meantime."

On her way out of the ICU she ran into Dr. Peters. "Any news on Angela?"

Peters shook her red ringlets. "Nothing yet, but we're doing our best. We have one of the best group of doctors in the city. Don't worry. If anyone can solve this mystery , they will."

She worried all right, but that didn't mean she could do anything. If they were the city's finest medical team and they couldn't discern what was wrong with Angela, who could? But would they find out in time to save her life?

Becca pushed open the door and let herself into Angela's empty apartment, along with stale air from the narrow hallway. One glance around informed her Angela had left in a hurry. Her always immaculate living room was a small disaster. The headpiece from her phone hung to the floor, a chair overturned, and a lampshade slanted cockeyed. A buzzing sound filled the air. Not wanting to leave fingerprints in case of foul play, she carefully replaced the receiver with her hand tucked into a jacket sleeve.

Righting the chair, she made her way into Angela's bathroom. The stench of vomit hit her at the same moment she spotted the path of dried mucus, flecked with red and black specks, dribbled across the bathroom floor. A similar trail flowed down the sides of the toilet. Her stomach cramped, imagining what Angela had gone through, alone, during her last hour in the apartment. Or had she been alone?

Becca opened the medicine cabinet to locate Angela's toothpaste, and spotted a container of *Ambien* on the bottom shelf. Then her gaze alighted on the shelf above, and the bottle of *Aramis* Angela had purchased for Elliot. She immediately noticed the tip of the label had been torn off when Angela removed the price tag. Otherwise, the bottle had been barely used. Dr. Peters had mentioned Angela's date with Elliot. Did he have anything to do with her sudden deteriorating condition?

On a hunch, she strode over to the bed stand, looking for Angela's address book. Inside the top drawer she found a barely used toothbrush and a comb with a couple of dark brown hairs, slightly fairer than Angela's. On impulse, she withdrew the hairs from the comb and placed them in an envelope from Angela's desk, sealing it. She didn't want to take a chance on leaving anything pertinent around, in case Elliot returned for his possessions. She considered taking the toothbrush and comb, but decided not to alarm him.

Becca knew she might be overly suspicious since there was no indication from the hospital of foul play, but after all she'd been through, she wouldn't put anything past anyone. She hoped Angela had only taken ill with a gastrointestinal virus and would fully recover; but just in case, Becca wanted to cover all contingencies. Her throat tightened at the thought of someone's harming her best friend. She loved Angela, and would do anything to protect her.

Then she spied Angela's cell phone on the floor by her fallen purse. She carefully scooped up the cell with a towel wrapped around her hand and opened the address book. Scrolling through Angela's contacts, she found Elliot's name—Elliot Schneider—and number. She immediately pressed it. With racing heart, she held the phone close to her ear and listened to it ring. After a couple rings a voice came online with a message, saying the phone number had been canceled or was no longer in service. It was most unusual for a doctor to cancel his number and not answer his calls, no matter the hour. Doctors always had an answering service and an emergency number. What if a patient was in trouble? She jotted down the number on her notepad, hoping it might lead somewhere.

She heard a noise in the hallway and froze. She had left the door ajar in case she needed to call for help, but now wished she hadn't. By stepping stealthily up to it, she sneaked a peak down the hall. Empty. She decided to lock the door behind her.

Back in the bedroom, she hurriedly put together a suitcase of Angela's personal belongings and exited the apartment, locking the door behind her. In the hallway, she imagined for a moment a whiff of cologne, which made her skin crawl. Out of the corner of her eye she spied a dark shadow steal into the stairwell. She froze with fear. Recovering quickly, she took the rickety lift downstairs and wondered, while it rattled and shimmied to a halt, if she was any safer in it than in an occupied stairwell. All she knew; she had to get out of the building!

Once back inside her car with locked doors, Becca took an audible breath of icy air. On instinct, she glanced back up at Angela's bedroom window and thought the curtains had parted a couple inches, but chalked the perception up to her fright-fueled imagination.

Fear, like a bad case of the flu, followed her all the way back to the hospital, where she spent the remainder of the night curled up in a chair outside of the ICU.

At first light, Becca unfolded herself from her cramped quarters in anticipation of the time she would be allowed to see Angela. Exhausted after a night of little sleep, she dragged herself straight to the bathroom and splashed cold water on her face; then to the dining hall for a quick cup of diluted coffee and a bowl of soggy oatmeal. Back outside the ICU, the wait agonized her. She flipped through a copy of *Cosmo*, barely able to concentrate on the articles: "Ten Ways to Satisfy Your Man"; "Twelve Ways to Lose Twelve Pounds." A small commotion caused her to raise her eyes in time to spot Sally Mills and her partner leaving the ICU. They marched right over to where she sat.

"What are you doing here?" Mills asked without so much as a good morning or a handshake.

"Visiting a friend," Becca answered. "I could ask you the same question!"

Mills studied her. "Mind if I ask your friend's name?"

"Angela Petrocelli. Why?"

"Funny how our paths continue to cross. We're here to see about Ms. Petrocelli, too."

Her throat constricted. "Are you saying there's a criminal investigation here?"

Mills nodded. "The toxicology report won't be back for at least ten days, but they suspect she's been poisoned. Know anything about that?"

Not at all surprised, Becca shook her head. "Are you sure?"

"Unless she's in the habit of taking poison or was exposed to it accidentally, it looks like a safe bet. What's your relationship with her?"

"We're friends. Is she going to be all right?"

Mills shrugged. "They don't know yet. There's been quite a bit of damage. Do you know anything that might help us to understand what happened?"

Not exactly bedside manner, but what did she expect from the police? "She had a date the last evening with a doctor she's been seeing. His name is Elliot Schneider and she's crazy about him."

Mills flipped open a notepad and scribbled

notes. "At least we now have a last name. Do you know anything else about him? Where he works? Where he lives? Anything?"

"Angela told me he's associated with Hahnemann Hospital, but you already know that from the doctor." She retrieved the notepad from her purse, tore off the piece with Elliot's number, and handed it to Mills. "Here's the number she had programmed into her cell. I tried it, but it's no longer working."

Mills took the slip from her.

"I wish I could help you more," Becca said. "I'd like to talk to him myself. I've been by Angela's apartment to pick up her toiletries, and there's a newer toothbrush in her night table." Becca pulled out the envelope with the hair from her jacket pocket and handed it to Mills. "I removed these hairs from a comb in the same drawer as the toothbrush."

Mills stared at her open-mouthed. "Do you realize you've tampered with evidence and contaminated it? No matter what these hairs uncover, we won't be able to use them or anything else in her apartment after you got through with it."

Yes, she knew, and she wasn't proud. "I was afraid Elliot might return to gather his belongings before anyone else had a chance to get in there. I have a feeling the hair might match the one on the rag, and I didn't want to leave it behind."

Obviously disgruntled, Mills smashed the book shut. "How can we prove the hair came from the apartment and you didn't plant it? I'll send it to the lab to see what it shows, but it's useless to us now." Mills frowned at her. "You know, Rosen, you seem to always be in the wrong place at the wrong time."

Becca stared down at the linoleum floor. No matter what she did, it seemed to further incriminate her. "One other thing. There's a bottle of *Aramis* Angela bought for Elliot in the medicine cabinet. You might want to check it out for fingerprints."

Mills' tough-looking partner stepped up. "Are you working this case for us or just working us?"

Mills elbowed him aside. "We'll check it out. We'll need you at the precinct later today to answer a couple more questions."

With a sinking feeling, and enough awareness to know she was in this deeper than she ever thought possible, she watched the detectives stride away.

"Come back, Angela...I miss you...I need you...don't leave me," Becca whispered into Angela's ear. She meant every word she uttered. Their friendship dated back to an isolated table in the rear of their high school cafeteria, where they both had gone to escape the pressure of not being in the cool crowd, and had extended to their days as roommates at Penn State. She had taken the job at St. John's to work alongside Angela and had stayed on, instead of seeking a more prestigious arrangement. They had been inseparable for many years.

But no matter what she said, Angela failed to respond. Her respirations were shallow and rattling, her complexion jaundiced and deteriorating. She lingered for days in a coma. At one point, a nurse mentioned they had started her on atropine, the antidote for organophosphorus poisoning. It seemed futile. With every phlegmy breath she drew, Angela appeared to be losing her battle.

By the fourth day, Becca refused to let go of Angela's hand, even after a nurse came by to tell her visiting hours were over. When a second nurse arrived with a firm warning, she tore herself away for home and a short nap, returning to the ICU at the earliest possible opportunity. Evan had stopped by in the late afternoon between classes, and waited with her outside the ICU until they let her in, but he had to leave to attend a seminar.

By the evening visit, Angela's skin had taken on an ashen pallor and her breathing had become more ragged. The nurses were as reassuring as they could be, but Becca could sense her friend slipping away. She again begged Angela to hang tough, but her words seemed pointless. She was powerless.

When visiting hours ended, she choose to stay nearby. She curled up in the same chair she had made her bed in the first morning, not far from the ICU. Even though she wouldn't be allowed back in until morning, she knew she had to remain close.

An hour later, she heard the Code Blue announcement. Two doctors and a bevy of nurses rushed past her into the ICU. With hammering heart, she trailed the last one in, where she watched from a distance while they tried to resuscitate Angela. Even from her vantage point, she could observe resignation on the doctors' faces. The doctor working on Angela finally stepped aside, and a nurse draped a sheet over her head.

A cry escaped Becca's lips, calling attention to her. A nearby nurse rushed over to comfort her, and led her to a seat by the nurses' station. With a box of tissues placed at her side, Becca leaned into the kind woman's side, and wept until there were few tears left.

The nurse removed the arm that encircled her and asked if Becca wanted to say goodbye to Angela before the orderly came to remove her from the unit. Between sobs, Becca confirmed she'd like that, and allowed the nurse to support her as she hobbled over to Angela's side.

She cautiously folded down the sheet to look upon Angela's pale face and a new round of tears began. The face before her bore little resemblance to the Angela she knew - the Angela with wise eyes and a radiant smile. It lacked everything that made Angela who she was.

Becca reached out and touched Angela's cheek. "I love you..." she managed to croak out before more tears choked her words.

When the nurse at last came over to tell her the orderlies had arrived, Becca needed help out of the ICU. Angela's death, on top of David's loss a mere six months earlier, was too much to bear. She had said her final farewell to Angela, and would never see her again! Emptiness and despair engulfed her.

She made her way with help to her car, consumed with thoughts about Angela and all they had been through together. She knew deep down inside, she could never, ever replace her dearest friend, or her joy when Angela was around, or her sense of innocence and open-hearted faith in others.

Angela's murder cemented the suspicions she had been harboring for months. Someone was out to damage and destroy. No one could be trusted. She would have to be on the alert from now on ,until she could figure out how to protect herself and those she loved from harm.

Chapter Thirteen

Every once in a while, something in our life proves to be a major tipping point. It could be a connection. A correction. A revelation. An idea or an event. For Mecca, that event was Angela's death, followed by a call days later from Sally Mills reporting the results of Angela's toxicology report. The cause of death was confirmed: Pesticide poisoning. Although Becca had undergone her own trauma months earlier, it had only solidified her coping mechanisms. Angela's murder, on the other hand, shocked her out of any remaining apathy.

Becca arrived at her next therapy session depressed, but strangely energized. I sat across from a different woman. A woman of determination. A woman with a mission. Her face set in a hard mask of misery and steely resolve, her muscles tensed like a runner at the starting line. She leveled her gaze upon me.

"I'm certain whoever killed Angela is the same person who murdered David."

I looked up from my notes. "What makes you so sure of that?"

She stared beyond me to a corner of the room. "The Aramis, in part...but it's more than that..."

She stood, walked over to the picture window overlooking the Philadelphia Parkway with an unobstructed view of the Rodin Museum, the sculpture of The Thinker in front. I had often gazed out at the statue myself and wondered what he was thinking. Now

I asked myself the same question of Becca.

Her back to me, she said, "It's more than a gut feeling. It's something in the marrow of my bones. A deep down knowing. Even the police think there's an association between the two murders, but they believe it's me. Maybe it is..." she mumbled.

Surprised ,I asked, "In what way?"

She swivelled around to face me. "I seem to be the one constant in this equation."

I walked over to stand with her by the window. "Is it possible whoever did this is trying to frame you, or at least get to you?"

"Perhaps..."

"How does that make you feel?"

The look in her eyes was sheer panic. "Like the walls are closing in on me and I can't escape. As if I'm stuck in one of my unrelenting nightmares."

"What do you plan to do about it?"

When I've asked her this question in the past, she often dipped her head in defeat. This day, she raised her chin in a defiant gesture. "I can't take the pain and uncertainty any longer. If the police won't do their job and protect me, I might have to do it myself."

I had to give her credit for her spirit, but I needed to temper my admiration with a hearty dose of reality. "Being proactive instead of waiting for others to do the job is admirable, but dangerous. Please, please, please be careful. A killer's out there who might not be far away— might even be in your life. It's important for you to take care of yourself. You still have the key to the safe house, don't you?"

She nodded. "I'll take care all right. But I'll also take care of business. I'm sick and tired of living in dread all the time. I don't want to spend the rest of my life looking over my shoulder— or under my bed. I've weathered enough intimidation."

I glanced over at Becca and all I could see was a slightly-built youthful-looking twenty-nine year old woman at risk. My stomach cramped at the notion someone in the world had Becca on his list of lives to destroy. I feared for her safety, but there was nothing anyone could do to insulate her. I did the only thing I could do - I quietly sent off a wish to the Universe for her well-being.

To take her mind off her troubles, Becca propped her feet up on the coffee table and channel-surfed the Sunday evening television shows. After flipping from NCIS to Desperate Housewives, she checked the time on the channel identification screen. 8:25. The dryer cycle would be winding down on her whites and she would have to go downstairs to the laundry room to remove and replace them with a load of colored clothes.

In her only clean sweats and a pair of flip-flops, she descended the backstairs of the building to the laundry room. The fresh odor of newly laundered clothes accosted her senses the moment she entered. A smell she adored, it made her feel clean, and something she rarely felt nowadays, in control. She removed her load from the dryer, placing pale yellow towels and floral print underwear on a work table, then busied herself folding towels and linens and stacking them on the table top.

Next, she turned to her underwear, but had barely begun to separate out panties before a sense something was missing arrested her. She counted the underpants, but couldn't believe her eyes. She had placed a week's worth of underwear in the hamper, but only five pairs remained. What had happened to the other two? She scrutinized the laundry basket, then searched the washer and dryer, but came up empty handed. Perhaps she had dropped them on her way down the first trip, but it was hard to believe she wouldn't have spotted them on the second.

She resisted the idea someone might have gotten into her laundry and taken her most intimate possessions. But how? And whom? Suddenly scared, she inspected the hall and stairwell for an intruder. With no one in sight, she hoisted the laundry basket and carried it upstairs.

Once inside the apartment, she marched into the bathroom to investigate whether she had left anything behind in the hamper, but found nothing. No clothes remained on the bed, not one item had fallen to the floor. Damn. It became more and more certain someone had been in her laundry.

Beside herself with yet another violation of her privacy, she returned to the living room where she double-checked windows and door to make sure they were locked before reclaiming her seat on the sofa. This intimidation had to stop. The thought of a stranger having her underwear— and God knows what he was doing with them— made her sick to her stomach. A taste of bile filled her throat and she swallowed down her indigestion.

She'd had it with the constant harassment. She wouldn't allow whoever was doing these things to get away with them any longer. The police hadn't been any help whatsoever. They seemed intent on believing she was making these incidents up to throw them off her trail. She couldn't tell her parents, because if they knew what was going on, they'd insist she move back in with them. And she was no longer sure she could trust anyone else—even Evan.

The only person she could rely on was herself. Even if she wasn't absolutely certain she was up to the challenge, what choice did she have? She folded her hands over her stomach, but the pressure did little to ease the churning in her gut. She had to figure out who was harassing her—if it was the last thing she did. And that thought scared her half to death.

Detective Sally Mills sat across the desk from Becca, a smile plastered on her lovely face. "I have good news and I have bad news. I'll begin with the good news."

Becca leaned forward silently praying for a reprieve, but knowing her prayers might prove as futile as any attempt she could make to bring Angela back to life.

"The hairs you handed me the other day

matched the hairs on the bloody rag."

Not surprised, she sat back. "What does that mean?"

Mills combed her hair back from her forehead and out of her eye. "Only that you have hair from the same person who's a suspect in your husband's murder. How did you say you put your hands on that hair?"

Becca didn't like her tone. "I told you already. I took them from a comb in Angela's bedside table."

"What comb? There was no comb, no toothbrush and no cologne. We found the sleeping pills you mentioned, but nothing else."

Bingo. The shadow had been real. It had stripped any evidence from the apartment. Interesting. She was on to something. "I'm not surprised."

"Why's that?"

"I told you the murderer would be back to get his things. That's why I took the hair to begin with."

Mills looked skeptical, equally as skeptical as Becca was scared. Everything added up to trouble for her. "Perhaps, but it doesn't let you off the hook. You could have planted the hair yourself, or had an accomplice for all we know."

Becca's saliva soured. No matter what happened, the trail always led back to her. Convinced she was involved, the police interpreted every piece of evidence as further proof of her culpability.

"By the way, we looked into that doctor you mentioned, but we can't locate anyone by that name.

There's no Dr. Elliot Schneider at Hahnemann, none in private practice and the only Elliot Schneider we found in all of Philadelphia died a few months ago of old age. Even the phone number was a dud. Seems it was one of those prepaid numbers and the contract was signed using a fake ID. We've tried tracing it down, but we keep coming up empty handed. So far we've run into a dead-end."

Damn, then her suspicions about Elliot were probably true.

She glanced up in time to see Mills studying her through narrowed eyes. "Do you have any idea why your friend would have emptied out both her savings and checking accounts the day before she was poisoned? Did she mention anything about it to you?"

Becca was stunned. Maybe in this case only the shadow knew. "No...nothing..."

"And do you have any idea what she did with the money? There's no trace of it at the apartment or on her."

"How could I? I didn't know anything about it."

Mills cocked a brow. "You were the last person in the apartment as far as we know."

"Look, I didn't take anything from there except the hair sample and some toiletries. What do I have to do to prove my innocence to you?"

"Find the real killer for starters."

"I thought that was your job, not mine. But you're not doing it. How about if I were to take a lie detector test and pass?"

Mills eyed her. "That might help, but I wouldn't recommend you do it without the advice of your attorney, who, by the way, called me the other day. Why isn't she here now?"

"She didn't want to waste my meager funds because I'm not officially a suspect. Isn't that true?"

Mills didn't answer. Instead she slapped a couple of her cards on the desk in front of Becca. "Have her call me again and we'll talk. In the meantime, sit tight. We'll be in touch."

Becca rolled her eyes. "I didn't expect anything else. You're becoming my closest and most consistent acquaintance."

Mills shrugged. "The way things are going, we might become a whole lot closer."

Becca's stomach cramped. The last thing she needed was the police on her back any more than they already were, but she couldn't shake them without better evidence. And she wasn't sure where to find it.

Drew raised his glass. "Since it's taken me weeks to entice you into going out, I'd like to toast our first dinner together."

Becca tapped his glass with hers. It had taken weeks because she had needed time to recover from the shock of Angela's death. Angela's family had returned from Erie to Philadelphia to bury Angela, and Becca had been busy helping them out and meeting with the police. The family had left only a week earlier, and things had finally settled down enough for Becca to make other plans.

"You've picked a great place to celebrate."

She glanced around the restaurant. *Salt*. Great name. Upscale decor. She admired the hanging art-glass lamp above their table, the modern metal wall sculpture over Drew's head. Decorations, lighting, and table settings had all been chosen with care and an eye for art and elegance. She only hoped the dinner lived up to the decor.

"Do you come here often?"

"Only on special occasions." He smiled, but his gaze remained steady and fully focused on her.

"It's lovely," she said, fingering the bone china plate and using it as an excuse to shift her gaze. "Truly lovely..."

"Like you."

At his words she looked up and met the full force of interest in his eyes.

"You've been so busy lately. What's going on with you?"

After taking a moment to consider how much to tell him, she gave him a sketchy outline of her legal troubles. He listened intently and asked her the appropriate questions, looking both intrigued and concerned. This was all the encouragement she needed to pour more of her problems out to him.

She began to babble on about the two murders in detail, until sensing the inappropriateness of what she was saying, she stopped herself. Even though his parents were best friends with hers, how much did she really know about him? How did she know she could trust him? At the moment, she didn't know who to trust.

"This conversation isn't exactly uplifting. Mind if I change the subject?"

"Whatever you wish." He watched her over the rim of his wine glass. "I have something I've wanted to ask you. There's a terrific Seurat exhibit at the Museum of Art. Have you been to see it?"

She appreciated his smooth segue into a less threatening topic. "I've been too busy these last few weeks. What did you think of it?"

"It's amazing. The curator did a smashing job of showing Seurat's development as an artist. You should go."

"Is Seurat a favorite of yours?"

Drew made a face. "I'm more of a fan of modern art. Mondrian, Marcel DuChamp, Jean Miro. How about you?"

Suddenly self-conscious, she played with her glass. "To be honest, I don't know much about art beyond Andy Warhol and Pablo Picasso."

His face lit up. "Then let me take you to the exhibit. It's a great place to begin your studies."

She could use the diversion. "Okay...you're on."

"How about music?" he asked. "What's your

favorite kind?"

Before she could answer, the waitress appeared with their plates. Hers was a work of art to match anything at the museum. Her lamb chops were surrounded by a medley of vegetables and topped with a tall sprig of parsley and a thin checkered wafer. The subtle scent of marinated meat and vegetables wafted to her. "This looks fabulous."

"Looks do not deceive. Dig in." Drew took a bite of his wafer. "Wait until you taste."

She did, and the lamb melted on her tongue; the vegetables cooked to perfection. She busied herself exploring the myriad tastes and sensations and failed at first to notice Drew staring at her. When she finally glanced up and caught his eye, he looked away.

"You like?"

"Wonderful," she said between bites of potato au gratin and carrot. "This is a treat."

"I think so, too." He smiled at her. "But you never told me what type of music you enjoy."

She had to think about it. "Rock, I guess. That seems to be what I listen to most often. U2 and Cold Play. I just discovered Muse. The usual suspects."

"Not bad choices." He put down his fork. "Do you ever listen to classical, or aren't you interested?"

"I can't say I do. I've heard all the popular pieces, but nothing too esoteric."

"Good," he said with a satisfied smile. "Then I can also be the one to expose you to some of my favorite composers, like Pachelbel and Chopin. I think you'll be impressed with what you hear."

She took a sip of white wine and let the liquid gold running down her throat warm her. Flatware tinkled nearby and voices rose. Laughter followed. The festive ambiance of the room along with the wine were beginning to weave their magic over her. Happiness filled her. When was the last time she felt this good? Certainly before Angela's death. The more time she spent with Drew, the more she enjoyed being with him.

"I'd like that," she said, wiping her mouth on her cloth napkin, folding it and setting it down on the table. It pleased her to meet a man eager to share what he loved with her, who didn't pressure her to share herself with him.

Lately, whenever she was with Evan, he wanted more from her than she was willing to give. She had told both Drew and Evan the same thing—she wasn't prepared for anything serious, but so far Drew had respected her boundaries more than Evan. Drew's attitude impressed her. She grew fonder of him every time she was with him.

She sat back in her seat. An undefinable something shifted inside of her as though a veil had been lifted and her vision cleared. She could see things for the first time as they really were. What she experienced of Drew and Evan in a bright, unfiltered light, didn't surprise her. In that instant, Evan looked less like someone she could rely on while Drew was becoming a trustworthy friend.

Drew sat forward. "Next Friday the Philadelphia

Orchestra will be playing at Symphony Hall. Want to go?"

If she took him up on his offer, it might mean she intended to keep on seeing him. Even deepen their relationship. Was she sure she wanted this? Emboldened by her developing feelings toward him as well as her wine-fueled euphoria, she raised her glass and toasted his. "I'd love to," she said, knowing she had just seized the gauntlet and accepted the challenge.

Chapter Fourteen

"Irv, our long lost daughter has been good enough to pay us old folks a visit. Go out and buy some lox and bagels in her honor," Julie called across the foyer to the family room.

Irv appeared in the doorway between the two rooms at the same time Becca handed her coat and hat to Julie. "I'll stop by Samson's. They have the freshest bagels." He gave Becca a quick kiss on the cheek, then shrugged into a green wool jacket with matching cap and black leather gloves.

His departure left Julie free to escort Becca to the kitchen for coffee.

Becca hoisted herself onto a bar stool by the counter and took the cup Julie held out to her.

"You never said to what we owe our typically unavailable offspring's unexpected early morning appearance," Julie offered with the cup.

Of late, Becca smiled so rarely her lips felt stiff when she lifted them. "That's a mouthful, Mom. I wanted to see how you and Dad were doing..."

Julie's sneer betrayed her skepticism.

"And ask you to fill in a few details about the babysitter you mentioned."

Julie plopped down on the stool beside her and uttered a disapproving grunt. "I should have known there was an ulterior motive for you to swing by...more than concern for your aging parents. Why don't we have a quiet breakfast and let this babysitter thing rest? I don't see what good it does to always drag up the past."

Becca took a sip of the strong brew and considered what to say next. "This has less to do with the past and more to do with the present."

"Like what?"

Becca could see disbelief in Julie's tired brown eyes. "He might know where I can find an old friend from the neighborhood. It would mean a lot to me if I could get in touch with him. Do you know where he might be?"

Julie shook her head. "Last time I spoke with his mother, Dorothy said he hadn't been in contact for a long time. He left town to join the navy and was stationed in Virginia. I'm not sure where he went from there."

"How long ago was that?"

"I'd say nine years. I don't know the last time Dorothy heard from him, but it's been years. He's even less attentive to his parents than you are..." she held up a hand, "but don't use his behavior as an excuse for yours."

Why did Julie always bring the conversation back to the same old place? "Are you still in contact with Dorothy?"

"On occasion. Your dad and I bump into her or Dan once in a while at the post office or quick store. Why?"

"Do they still live around here?"

"Over thirty years in the same house. Longer than us. More coffee?"

"Thanks." Becca held out her cup while Julie poured. Steam rose off the black liquid in quasi-human form, reminding her of the ghost she chased. "Do you know how I might get ahold of them?"

Julie put the pot down. "I might have their number in my address book. I could check for you."

"I'd appreciate that. I'd sure like to ask them about Adam and..."

Julie stopped her with a hand on her arm. "You won't say anything to them about what's going on with you? It would only upset them. They're lovely older people. I'd hate to see them hurt."

Impressed with Julie's concern for them, Becca patted the hand on her arm. "Of course not, Mom. There's no need for them to know about the abuse. As far as they're concerned, I'm only trying to find an old friend."

Julie sighed. "Good."

The front door slammed shut. Within seconds, Irv appeared in the kitchen carrying two grocery bags. Julie hopped off her stool with the grace and ease of a much younger woman to wrestle one from him. She placed the contents on the counter, lifted a knife from a block and began to slice an onion, a big red Jersey tomato and cucumbers on a wooden board. Without being told, Becca placed plates and napkins on the countertop and arranged the lox and vegetables on a serving platter. Soon the odor of toasted bagels and fresh fish filled the room and reminded her of their many Sunday brunches together over the years.

Irv handed Becca a toasted bagel which she slathered with cream cheese and topped with lox and tomato. She took a bite. Scrumptious. "Ummm, yummy," she said, smiling with satisfaction at one parent, then the other.

Julie stood by the sink nibbling on a half bagel and Irv had seated himself on the stool next to hers. To her amazement, Becca found herself enjoying the repeat performance of a now-rare family ritual. It had been such a long time since they had eaten breakfast together as a family, Becca had forgotten how comforting it could be. For the first time in a long time, she relished their closeness.

Which might be a sign of her newfound maturity. It reminded her of what she had learned in nursing school about premature infants forced by adversity to mature rapidly. She had been through so much over the past few months, it had taught her to see her parents in a whole new light: To look past their failings and foibles and appreciate all they'd done for her. She needed family and community now more than ever. She had lost more than she could ever replace.

Julie buzzed around making sure all coffee cups were filled and offering Becca a second bagel, which she prudently declined, but the gesture touched off a wave of warm feelings for the effort being made on her behalf. She enjoyed her parents more than any time since they took her to New York City to see her first Broadway play at the age of fifteen. In celebration, she clinked her coffee cup against Irv's raised one.

"Good health," he said, returning her smile.

It all seemed so simple now. If only she could build on what she already knew and the consistency of those who loved her, everything would be all right. She could recreate a sense of normalcy and belonging out of the ashes of her former life. She merely had to stay away from dangerous people and places. Stick with what she sensed to be safe. She could do it, she decided.

As long as no one stood in her way.

The phone at Dorothy and Dan Cantor's house rang a second time and Becca pressed the receiver closer to her ear. She prayed someone would answer and she could get this call over with. No matter how many times she practiced her approach to the Cantors, her spiel sounded unbelievable to her own ears. What would it sound like to them? She hardly remembered Adam, let alone buddied up with him. He must be at least five or six years her senior. How could she convince them she knew him well enough to have a friend in common?

After the fourth ring, she heard a click, followed by a woman's voice. "You have reached the Cantor residence. We're sorry we're unable to answer your call right now. Please leave a message and we'll get back to you when we return."

Becca croaked out her name and number before hurriedly hanging up, then slumped into a dining room chair. Damn. Disappointment at the delay in her plans was quickly followed by relief that, at least for today, she didn't have to face discouragement from Adam's folks. And even if they were willing to help her, would it really lead her anywhere useful?

A whistling sound came from the tea kettle. Becca managed to pry herself away from the comfort of the dining room table to fix herself a cup of green tea. Even though she had left her information on the Cantor's machine, she really didn't expect them to return her call. It had taken most of the morning to generate enough chutzpah to make the call, in a week she'd have to screw up the courage all over again.

The sound of her cell ringing snapped her out of her reverie. She flicked it open to hear Drew's smooth baritone.

"Hello, good looking. What's cooking?"

His silliness momentarily lightened her serious mood. "Nothing much. Just whittling away the day."

He whistled. "It's a big, bad, beautiful world outside and you're wasting the day. Why don't we meet at the art museum for that grand tour I promised you?"

She hesitated, not certain she was up to an outing in her present mood. "I don't know..."

"Why not?"

"I have a lot on my mind right now. I'm not sure I would be much company."

He made an exasperated sound. "You're not getting out of this one that easily. I don't expect anything from you. I only thought it would be fun to go out for awhile, and I'd like your company. It might lift your spirits. What do you say? Come on. Let's do it."

Becca didn't have to consider his offer for long. The thought of spending the day with Drew seemed a better alternative to her obsessive ruminating. "Okay, when?"

Two hours later she met Drew by the fountains in front of the Philadelphia Museum of Art. He had purchased a couple of cheese steaks on his way over, and offered her one. Even though frigid out, she had worn her down jacket and was quite comfortable joining him for a picnic on the stairs leading up to the museum. Drew excused himself long enough to bounce down gleaming marble steps to a coffee cart on the street below. When he returned, he handed her a latte. The drink warmed her, as did the arm he slung over her shoulders after they finished eating.

They spent a few minutes catching up with one another, before Drew helped Becca to her feet and led her into the museum, where he insisted on paying both their entry fees. Once inside the gallery, he seemed as excited as an adolescent with a new car. Taking her hand in his, he led her from one painting to another, sharing what he knew about Seurat and the French Impressionists. First stop: Seurat's most famous painting, *Un Demarche Apres-midi a l'Ile de la Grande Jatte*.

In front of the large bucolic canvas of people lounging around a park on a Sunday afternoon, Drew explained that Seurat had been the ultimate example of artist as scientist. He had spent most of his life studying color and linear structures, which he used in an art form known as Pointillism. With a hand over one of her eyes, Drew was able to demonstrate the many tiny dots that made up the painting and she grasped how painstaking the creative process must have been for Seurat. The palette and pixilated images were particularly pleasing to her eye, especially with her newfound knowledge of Seurat's creative process.

Next, Drew gestured enthusiastically toward another canvas. His passion had begun to rub off on her, and she laughed with delight at his exuberance. She was enjoying herself more than she could have imagined a mere two hours earlier; her pleasure and fondness for him, like appreciation for fine art, was renewed and enriched with each subsequent visit. If his parents weren't such good friends with hers, and if Evan wasn't in the picture, she might actually have considered a relationship with him. As it was, he was becoming a good friend.

After the museum, Becca invited Drew back to her apartment for a glass of wine along with a plate of brie and crackers. She had eaten too late in the day to consider a full meal, but both agreed they could handle a light bite.

Side-by-side on the couch, munching on goodies and sharing stories about their families, the chime of the doorbell surprised them. Becca raised her hands, palms up, and shook her head in a gesture of confusion.

"Expecting anyone?" he asked.

"No one at all. I'll check this out and be right back."

Becca opened the door to Evan's smiling face, stepped into the hallway and swiftly closed it to a crack behind her. "What are you doing here?"

Evan's face instantly transformed from joyful to perplexed. "I haven't seen you in a couple of days. I thought I should stop by and see if you were all right."

"Bad timing," she said. "I'd love to talk, but I have a friend over."

His eyes darkened. "What kind of friend?"

She shuffled from one foot to another, then croaked out, "A...a friend of the family. Nothing to be worried about. We visited the Seurat exhibit at the Museum of Art today and came back here for a nibble."

He made an effort to peer past her through the crack. "I thought you might want to go for a beer. Maybe your friend can join us."

"I don't think that will work. He has to leave soon."

He shook his head. "*He* has to go? What does that mean? Are you seeing someone else?"

"I don't know what you mean by seeing..."

"You know perfectly well what I mean." He quickly sequestered the gift bag he held behind his back.

She didn't know what to say. "Look, I don't want to argue with you. Please try to understand I have other friends and leave it at that. I'm sure you have friends, too."

"I hope you know what you're doing. I'll stop by tomorrow. We need to talk." He spun around and stalked away.

Early the next morning, Evan appeared at Becca's door.

Still half asleep, she had tossed on her red terry robe with black furry slippers before letting him into the apartment. "I wasn't expecting you this early." She rubbed the sleep out of her eyes.

He stared past her, but seemed satisfied no one else was there. "I have to go by the library, but I wanted to stop here first and give this to you." He held out a single scarlet rose. "It matches your robe."

And my eyes. "How kind of you." She inhaled its fragrant scent. "Come on in. I'll find a vase."

He took a seat on her sofa while Becca filled a stem vase and placed it on the coffee table. "Want a cup of tea? I'll put water on."

"I can pass. I just had coffee."

She took a seat catty-corner to him. "You feeling any better today?"

He stared at the ground, his expression guarded. "I'd feel a whole lot better if I knew what you were up to, bringing another guy around."

"I was telling the truth last night when I said that Drew's a family friend. You know where I stand on commitment right now. The only type of commitment I need is to a psychiatric ward."

A shadow passed over his eyes. "I thought we had something going on. Was I wrong?"

She reached for his hand, but he pulled his out of reach. "You know how much your friendship means to me, but I've been totally candid about my relationship readiness. I'm still too raw from the rape and murder. I couldn't make a good decision for myself if it jumped out and grabbed me. I need more time."

"I've waited for months now, but that was before you started seeing another man. It complicates everything. I trusted you and you've let me down."

She thrust a palm in his face. "Whoa. I never made any promises to you. I explained exactly where I was coming from before we even had a chance to get to know one another. If you have any expectations of me, it isn't because of anything I said."

"What if you decide you like this dude more than me? I don't know what I'd do. I don't want to lose you. Give me a chance. I can live up to anything you ask."

His sincerity did nothing to change her mind. She rose, went over to the window with a view of the street. Fresh snow had fallen overnight and covered everything in a pristine white coat. Bare branches dangled icicles. A solitary car drove past, the snow muffling its sound. Icy silence prevailed. Across the street a man in a wool coat, hat and gloves walked a Golden Retriever. It looked breathtaking, but stark - and lonely. She wrapped her arms around herself in response to a sudden chill.

"Please don't pressure me," she said to the partially frosted pane, her breath fogging the glass. "I'll let you know where I stand when I know myself."

"How long will that be?"

"I can't say..." The air stirred behind her, and she turned to see Evan at her side. He held out a gold gift bag with green ribbon. The same one as before. Surprised, she asked, "What's this?"

"I bought it for you yesterday, but I didn't have a chance to give it to you. I want you to have it now."

She tried to smile, but her effort was lame. "I can't accept another gift. The rose was enough."

He forced the bag into her hand. "Take it. I bought it for you. No one else would appreciate it."

Again she tried to give it back. Again he pressed her to take it. Realizing her refusal was futile, she reluctantly acquiesced. "Even if I accept this, it won't change anything."

"Yes, it will," he said. "It will make me feel a whole lot better."

She ached for him. For his obvious attempt to connect with her. For his desire. For his disappointment. But she also was wary of making commitments that she couldn't fulfill. "Okay." She tore open the bag, extracted a bottle of *Raffinée,* and gasped. As a friend had said the other day, *deja vu* all over again. "My favorite perfume. How did you know?"

"You mentioned it to me."

She couldn't remember doing anything of the sort, unless she told him about the broken bottle the first night he was over. The apartment did reek of it. "I don't recall..."

"It's one of my favorites, too. I wanted you to have it. That's all."

"Well, thanks..." She offered him a half-hearted hug. It was an odd coincidence that he and Paulie had both figured out her favorite scent. Either she was surrounded by amazingly perceptive people, or someone had gotten the inside scoop. A swift shiver coursed through her.

Evan must have noticed her reaction because he drew her closer. "I'll keep you safe if you'll only let me," he whispered into her hair. "Let me be there for you."

In what way? Normally being this near to him would have excited her. For once she was more shaken than stirred.

After a moment she relaxed into his embrace. Even though she was full of misgivings, his arms felt right around her. Was she being overly suspicious? The gift might only be a lovely gesture, nothing devious or dangerous at all.

Bewildered by her conflicted feelings, made more so by Drew, she broke away to the kitchen as soon as it seemed appropriate to refill her cup of tea. Once alone, she took a moment to reconsider. She had better watch her reaction to Evan. The minute she succumbed to his embrace, she relinquished her vigilance. She didn't want her emotions to short circuit her common sense. No matter what her heart told her, she had to follow her head. And she would - at any cost.

Last break of the conference and I was more than ready for it to end. Two full days on my feet were enough for me. I knew a couple of my colleagues could do week long seminars, but I wasn't one of them. Since I craved quiet time, I quickly answered a couple of questions, then went outdoors for a breath of spring air.

The Holiday Inn on City Line Avenue in Bala Cynwyd has a lovely courtyard. I found a lounge chair in the sun. Flower beds of fiery red gladiolas and bright yellow irises surrounded me. I tilted my head back and luxuriated in sunlight. What a beautiful May day.

The scent of sexy cologne reached me before a voice as warm as this spring day said, "I've been looking all over for you, Sarah," and caused me to open my eyes.

Adrian. He looked even more attractive than usual with the sun lighting a halo in his wavy, dark chocolate-brown hair. I shaded my eyes so I could feast them on him and patted my foot rest. "Join me."

"Are you avoiding me?" On closer inspection he looked strained.

"No. Should I be?" I waited, but he didn't answer. It's possible I was. Perhaps I had unconsciously avoided him, not wanting to wear our budding relationship thin before we even had a chance to get together, or because I was scared. Nothing new for me with men. Or perhaps I was having second thoughts because I wasn't totally comfortable with him. I doubted his true intention.

I stopped, not wishing to second guess myself any more than I already had. "I only wanted to take advantage of a few minutes in the sun. Isn't it glorious?"

He hesitated a moment longer, then took the seat I offer him. "I was worried you were giving me the slip. I looked all over for you to make sure we were still on for later, but couldn't locate you anywhere. You aren't planning to back out on me now, are you?"

I didn't know whether he was being overly anxious or just plain interested. The broad smile which crossed his chiseled face reassured me it was the latter. I certainly hoped so. I wanted this guy to turn out better than the last one.

"Don't worry. I'm not going anywhere but out with you. I've been fantasizing about the meal you promised me all day long." *And the dessert, too.*

His shoulders drooped. "Good. You had me worried there. I've been looking forward to this evening. I'd be disappointed if you backed out now."

His heart-felt true confession put an end to my earlier ruminations. I liked a man who could articulate his feelings, and it didn't hurt that he was also sophisticated, educated, and professional. This one had it all. The more I got to know him, the more I liked him—maybe enough to be in trouble. "What did you think about the earlier session?" I asked. "You haven't regaled me with your typical commentary."

He shrugged. "It certainly whetted my appetite for the denouement and final curtain. I'm curious if one of Becca's many admirers will turn out to be the perpetrator, or if it will be someone else."

I pinched my lips shut between thumb and forefinger. "I'm not telling. Any guesses?"

He narrowed his eyes conspiratorially. "Let's see. Drew's a great guy from what you've described, but he might be too good to be true. And Evan, well he's acting suspicious. Of course, what I remember from reading mysteries, it's never the obvious suspects. I'm baffled." He rubbed his brow. "You didn't entirely rule out Paulie. Even after what he told Becca, he could be lying to throw her off his track. And then there's Irv. I just don't know."

"Good. I'm glad I've left you guessing. That will keep everyone here for the remainder of the afternoon and awake until five. I hate to address a restless crowd."

"As for me, I'll be awake way past five." His eyes held a fire that warmed me more than the sun. He rose. "I better use the facilities before we reconvene. See you after five, Sarah." He saluted and strolled off.

I watched Adrian walk away with excitement. His broad shoulders and strong stride thrilled me. I couldn't wait to be with him. Still, I wasn't totally convinced he was for real and I didn't want to be let down by another man again. It would be too much to take this soon after Ken. I thought of an excuse for bowing out of our dinner this late in the day, but then reconsidered. It was way beyond that, and so was I. I

made a commitment. I had to take the risk, no matter
the results.

Chapter Fifteen

Unable to contact Adam's family, Becca decided instead to arrange a meeting with Paulie at a diner on Race Street the first Friday in February. She arrived early and located a booth in the rear of the fifties-style diner. Its décor was black and white checkered, plastic table tops, red vinyl booths, and a large, chrome-trimmed motorcycle in the middle of the room. The clientele ranged from harried business-types in wrinkled shirts and pleated slacks to teens in gangster wear, oversized tee-shirts and baggy pants. An old fashioned jukebox took up one corner and drew her attention. A couple of kids plied it with coins to coax it to play popular hip hop songs.

Paulie entered to the pulsating beat of 50 Cent. He wore a gray jacket over black jeans and looked like an aging backpacker with his cap pulled low over his balding head. When he spotted her, he came right over, rubbing his hands together.

"Not exactly California weather. How do you stand all this sunshine and balmy breezes?"

Becca tried to smile, without much success. "You bear it as long as you can and then you move to the sun belt."

"I seem to have gotten things backward." He took a seat on the bench across from her and ordered a hot chocolate, offering to buy her one.

With her stomach performing somersaults, she declined.

After he was served, he turned to her. "Why the big pow wow today?"

Becca froze. She didn't know where to start, or what scared her most. Was it running smack up against his denial, or learning the truth and not liking what she heard? He might even react with rage at her inquiry. She took a deep breath and pushed herself past her panic-induced inertia.

"I wanted to apologize for putting you on the spot in front of my folks the other night. I know it was awkward for you. It's just that I've been in therapy ever since David's death, and it was brought to my attention that I was molested around the age of six or seven. I need to figure out who did it to me." The words rushed out without another breath.

Paulie reached in his jacket pocket and pulled out a small pile of receipts that he slapped on the table. "I don't know if this helps, but here's proof I wasn't lying when I said I wasn't here in August. I didn't move back to Philly until September."

She fingered the receipts, turning over several. Dates verified his claim he was in California at the time, but he could have flown out for a couple of days. Anything was possible.

"Why me?" He took the pile and placed it back in his pocket. "Why do you think I had anything to do with this?"

"It all started the night of my parents' homecoming party for you last October. The *Aramis* you wore that night triggered a weird reaction in me."

"You do realize the *Aramis* I wore that night was a homecoming gift from one of the guests."

That stopped her. "A gift? From a guest? Do you know which one?"

"To be honest, I don't remember. I think it might have been one of your parents' friends. I received a number of gifts that night."

"I see. Then you don't typically wear *Aramis*?"

"No. Why?"

"Because it was the scent of *Aramis* that triggered the flashbacks and memories of being molested. To be honest with you, I've a distinct recollection of being with you at the time of the molestation. It's one of the few things I do remember."

He took a sip of hot chocolate, steam rising to cloud his wire rim glasses. Behind them, his eyes looked sad. Serious. Maybe even ashamed.

He cleared his throat and said softly, "I was there."

As if hit by a stray bullet, she jerked back. How proud Julie would be to see her posture now. "Then something did happen?"

He stared down at the table. "I wish I had said something sooner, but you begged me not to tell. You said the boy you were with had threatened to burn down the house and kill your cat if you told anyone. You were so distraught, I decided to bury the thing. I guess you did, too."

She sat back, tears blurring her vision. It had

happened. She wasn't insane. All her nightmares and terrors were real. She swallowed the lump that had formed in her throat. "What exactly do you know?"

"All I remember—you know this was over twenty years ago—is that I left work early one Saturday afternoon and swung by your house to talk your folks into going out for a bite. I knocked on the front door, but no one answered. Since the door had been left unlocked, as was typical of Irv when he left for a short errand, I let myself in. I heard loud music coming from upstairs and thought he might actually be home listening to the radio as he often did when he was alone."

He paused, looking uncomfortable. With elbows on table top, he fiddled with a napkin, constantly twisting it between his fingers until it began to fray. "The door was open to your parents' room and I glanced in to see you and a curly haired boy on the bed, partially undressed and ...well...fooling around." He flushed when he said the words and looked away from her. "I didn't know what to make of it. We didn't know much about child abuse in those days. I thought maybe you were experimenting with sex like a lot of kids do."

"What did you do next?"

"I yelled for you to stop doing what you were doing and to meet me downstairs. By the time you sauntered sheepishly into the living room with your head down, your friend had taken off out the back door. I never saw him again." He studied the pattern on the table top a long time before looking back up. "I'm sorry I didn't say anything to Julie when it happened. You might not have suffered like this if it hadn't been for my silence."

The tears she had restrained broke free. She tried to brush them away, but they fell fast and furiously. He had tears in his eyes also. They had both suffered in silence a long time because of what happened in that bedroom. "You don't have to feel guilty...things are always clearer in hind-sight."

"Thanks for your understanding. I only wish I knew then what I know now. I never would have remained quiet."

Even with his obvious sadness, she couldn't deny a slight doubt about his total veracity. He had good reason to cover up his role in her abuse. "Thank you for confirming my suspicions, but you could be of greater help if you'd tell me the boy's name."

He shook his head and the hat fell slant-wise. With long, slim fingers, he straightened it. "I'm afraid I never saw his face."

It made her less certain of his story. "Oh, that's too bad. Is there anything else you can tell me?"

He shook his head. "Sorry."

Nowhere near as much as I was. "I hope I'm not being too intrusive, but I have a couple more questions for you."

"Shoot."

"What happened between Julie and Irv.? As far back as I can remember, they've had this standoff. I've never understood the cause."

He stared past her. "I'm not sure how much I

should tell you..."

She reached across the table. "Please. I need to know. You held back one truth and you've regretted it. Don't keep this from me."

"I hear you." He toyed with the salt shaker. "You know your dad was drafted during Vietnam, right before your parents were supposed to get married. He served for two years and came back a different man. He'd always been reserved, but he returned sullen and withdrawn."

"But that still..."

He nodded. "I know there's something more. A couple years after he came home, Julie caught him sending money to a woman in Saigon. Seems he fathered a child when he was there. You know Julie. She never forgave him for cheating on her—even under the circumstances. Things were never the same between them."

"Wow." She sat back stunned. "Who would have thought?"

"And your other question?"

"It's about you. Why you've never married."

He didn't answer right away, as though he was considering what to say. "I'm in a relationship now, but he's in California wrapping up his affairs before moving out here."

Astonished this was the first she heard of it, she let out an involuntary gasp. "No one ever mentioned you were gay."

"I think Julie is still hoping I'll change my mind, as if I had a choice. But you know your mother."

She chuckled. "I sure do."

"I hope this only validates my contention that I wasn't the one who molested you. I'd never, ever, ever take advantage of a child like that, but especially a female one. I love women, but I'm not sexually attracted to them."

She believed him. In appreciation for his openness, she skirted the table to give him a big hug, which he returned with warmth and generosity. A sense of gratitude and understanding toward her family, and utter acceptance of each of their special qualities and quirks, welled up inside her.

But that left her back where she began. If Paulie was telling the truth, who was the boy in bed with her? And did he have anything to do with the two murders and her rape? This may have closed off one possible avenue, but it didn't open another. She'd just have to keep digging around until she discovered a crack in the case.

On a lazy Saturday in late February, Drew stopped by to take her to a nearby deli for brunch. How sweet of him. She relished her favorite morning meal of lox and bagel almost as much as she enjoyed his company.

Since snow had fallen overnight, along with the temperature, she bundled up in coat, hat, scarf, and gloves. He stood by and watched her layer clothing with a broad grin and a loving look. His good nature made him irresistible. She could just eat him up along with the bagel and cream cheese.

When she was appropriately attired for the weather, they left the apartment to a blast of what felt like arctic air that frosted her nose and cheeks with a light icy coating. She shivered and Drew wrapped an arm around her, drawing her close. She reacted by twining her arm around his waist.

Together they proceeded down Lombard to Samson Street. The lacy white flakes drifted onto porches, steps, car hoods, and a few alighted on the tip of Drew's nose. She reached out to brush them away, but he caught her hand in his. Their eyes met in a moment of mirth and magic, then she laughed and rushed on ahead to the deli door.

By the time they finished their sandwiches and paid the bill, the snow had subsided, but a winter chill still hung in the air. They made a mad dash back to her apartment to find shelter from the cold, but on turning onto her block, she ran smack into Evan.

"Oops. Sorry."

He stopped her with a hand on her shoulder. "Whoa there. Where are you going in such a hurry?"

Drew strode up beside her. "We were in a hurry to get home. Didn't mean any harm."

Evan's eyes widened. "We...?"

Becca looked from one man to the other. "Evan, this is my friend Drew."

Evan looked paler than the snow. "This is the *friend* you were telling me about?"

With a wary expression, Drew squared his shoulders and took on a belligerent stance. Watching him, Evan tensed.

Worried, she placed herself between the two men. "Drew and I were at Zeke's for a sandwich." She wanted desperately to defuse the situation.

Evan stared down his competition while addressing her. "So this is why I've seen so little of you the last few weeks? No wonder you're too busy to get together with me. You do look occupied."

His agitation was unmistakable. She automatically flashed her palm in front of his face. "You're wrong. I've seen Drew a couple of times since Angela's death, but not anymore than I've seen you. Most of the time I've opted to be alone."

Evan shook his head in disbelief. "You weren't alone when I visited you the other night, and you don't look too alone now. Not with Drew here tagging along."

Drew took her by the arm and moved her out of the way. "Listen to me. Becca's a big girl. She has the right to choose who she wants to be with, and right now that happens to be me. Isn't that clear?"

Evan's eyes flashed pure fury, and she could barely breathe wondering what he would do next. For a moment he looked as if he might draw back and punch Drew on his exposed nose. Instead, he shook his head, pivoted on his heels and strode up the street in a huff.

They watched Evan storm away, then Drew grasped her trembling hand and led her indoors. "I'm worried about you living near that guy. He's scary. I want you to do whatever you can to protect yourself from him."

Becca chuckled. She knew Evan well enough to be confident he wouldn't harm her, even in a jealous rage. Or...did...she? "He's harmless. I'm not afraid of him."

"That's not the point. Women are hurt all the time by the men they trust. I think you need to take measures to safeguard yourself."

He was right, even if she didn't want to admit it to herself. "What do you suggest I do?"

"Report what just happened to the police."

She threw up her hands. "That's a waste of time. They're more likely to be on my tail, not his. Besides, I don't believe Evan would do me harm, no matter how upset he is."

Drew kept a level gaze. "I'll vouch for you. This guy might be trouble. They have to check him out. I know what to say that will motivate them. I didn't go to law school for nothing."

That intrigued her. "Like what?"

"Let me handle it."

They continued to discuss this over cups of steaming hot chocolate, but whatever she said to defend Evan, Drew had an answer. Still, she refused to let him wear her down with his insistence.

"Be fair to Evan. He hasn't done anything heinous that I know about. Let's not make any more of this than there is."

Later, after Drew asked her to reconsider for the tenth time, then left to do paperwork at his office, she carried another cup of hot chocolate into the living room. As angry as Evan had been, she ached for him. His reaction to spotting her with Drew demonstrated how much she meant to him. Even his restraint in not hitting Drew was out of respect for her.

She couldn't deny someone out there had destroyed the lives of two people who were close to her and had done damage to hers, but she didn't want to believe it was Evan. Even so, she would have to avoid being alone with him until she could be certain he meant her no harm. She had come to rely more on Drew in recent days and she meant to keep it that way for now.

All at once she realized she'd been collecting evidence in favor of Drew and against Evan the past few weeks. Perhaps he was the perpetrator, but it could just as easily be someone else. So why him? Was it intuition, or was it because they had grown too close—she cared too much---she was running scared?

After another long shift at St. John's, Becca couldn't wait to be home. She entered her building and was about to turn the lock in her door when the faint odor of *Aramis* filled her nostrils and chilled her to the bone.

Without hesitation, she withdrew her key and made her way to the curb. Not knowing who to contact after her recent encounter with Evan, she frantically dialed Drew. On the third ring, he picked up the call.

"Drew, I think someone's been in my building again. I'm afraid to go in alone, in case he's there. Could you swing by and give me a hand?"

"How do you know he's been there?"

"There's the scent of cologne in the air. I'd recognize the odor anywhere."

"Are you okay? Where are you now?"

"I'm fine. I'm outside the building."

"Good... Wait a sec."

She heard a muffled commotion in the background. Drew yelled something unintelligible, then he was back on the line.

"Stay put. I'll be over as fast as my car will carry me."

Fifteen minutes later, Drew pulled up to the curb where she met him. They entered the building together. The odor had subsided, but her heartbeat hadn't. No wonder she could no longer smell the cologne, she could barely inhale out of fright.

After surveying the hallway and stairwell, they crept into the apartment. Drew insisted on circumnavigating the two main rooms to search under, behind and inside every possible hiding place. He came up empty handed, except for locating Cecil huddled in a corner of the bedroom with his back up. "It looks like we're alone. I can't see that anything has been touched."

Becca collapsed into a chair, hand over heart. "I hope I wasn't overreacting, but this constant sense of threat is so unnerving, it's wearing me down. I don't know what to do. I've reported the fact I'm being stalked to the police, but they don't seem to be taking anything I say too seriously."

He took a seat on the armrest of the sofa, gathered her hand into his. "Let's get out of here. I'll finish up a few things at work and we can go out for something to eat. You shouldn't be alone right now."

She nodded. "Okay, but first I have one phone call I have to make before I go anywhere."

"Who to?"

"Just some neighbors of my parents. I've been trying to reach them for awhile, but I heard from Julie they were on vacation and just got back yesterday. I want to arrange a meeting with them."

"Would it be too nosy of me to ask what for?"

She shrugged. "I want to find out about their son. He's an old friend of mine."

He eyed her suspiciously. "Another old friend. That sounds familiar."

"You're not going to do an Evan on me, are you?"

He playfully grimaced. "Never. Don't let me

stand in your way. Give them a call." He picked a magazine off the side-table and flipped through it.

For privacy Becca made her way into the bedroom. This time when the phone rang, Dorothy answered on the first ring.

"Mrs. Cantor. This is Rebecca Rosen, Julie and Irv Goldstein's daughter. Do you remember me?"

"Of course I do, dear. How are you?"

The gentleness of the old woman's voice put Becca immediately at ease. "Actually I have been better..."

"We've heard about your loss. We're terribly sorry."

"Thank you. I appreciate that." She hesitated, not sure how to continue. "I'm wondering if you could help me with something."

"What is it, dear?"

"I'd like to stop by and talk with you about Adam. You know we were friends and he babysat for me on occasion. After all I've been through, I'm eager to connect with my old friends and find out what happened to them."

The line seemed to go dead. "Hello, hello, are you still there..." she asked, then Dorothy's shaky voice came back on the line.

"To be honest, dear, I don't hear much from Adam anymore since he moved away from home. I don't know if I can be of much help to you."

Becca gripped the phone. "I think you can be.

It's important. I'm planning a neighborhood reunion. Please let me come by. I'll explain it all then."

Another hesitation. "I don't know, dear. My husband doesn't like to talk about Adam. I don't think it will work out."

"But... "

"I'm sorry, but Dan's coming into the room. I can't talk about this now. I wish I could help you, but I can't. I have to go..."

The line went dead.

"Hello...hello..." Becca clutched the receiver to her ear, not wanting to believe Dorothy had hung up on her.

In suspense for weeks wondering what she would learn about Adam, Dorothy's reaction had only amplified the intrigue. It seemed like she might be on to something, but, unless she found another way in, she would always be out of luck.

She heard Drew say something to Cecil, then rumble around the room. No use keeping him waiting. With a resolute thump, she placed the receiver back in its cradle and made a pact with herself. She would pursue this lead, no matter the cost. Somehow, somewhere, she would figure out a way to get to Dorothy Cantor.

As today demonstrated, she was in too much danger not to try whatever proved possible.

Chapter Sixteen

Across the street from the Cantor house, Becca shifted from one foot to another and rubbed her arms for warmth. She had learned from Julie that Dan Cantor played cards at Sam's on Wednesday nights. She watched him leave the house and waited in the cold until his car drove off.

The second he turned the corner, she crossed the street and knocked on the Cantor's door. A minute later, she heard Dorothy yell, "Who's there?"

Not wanting to frighten the poor woman, Becca immediately identified herself. Much to her relief, the door opened a crack and a woman, who appeared at least ten years older than Julie, with gray hair, numerous wrinkles and lines that etched gullies around her mouth, peered out. "What is it?"

Becca stepped closer. "As I said on the phone, I'm looking for Adam. I'm hoping you can help me out."

"I'm sorry, dear, but I told you I don't know where he's at. I really can't help you."

Dorothy started to close the door, but Becca slapped her hand against it. "I only want to ask you a couple of questions. What can it hurt?"

The woman looked shocked by her reaction. "Why is this so important to you?"

She had to think fast. "I gave him something of mine I value and I want to see if I can get it back.

Please give me a moment of your time."

Dorothy considered with a frown. "Okay, but only a few questions. I have things to do."

Becca agreed to her terms and entered the clean but cluttered living room of the Cantor home. Two overstuffed, mauve sofas vied for space with numerous oversized display cabinets. Kitsch covered everything. A scan of the room revealed artificial plants of all shapes and sizes, shelves full of pottery and pictures, numerous vases, and other sundries. Dorothy had to move magazines from an armchair so Becca could sit.

"Would you like a cup of tea, dear?" Dorothy inquired.

Not particularly thirsty, but eager to prolong her visit, Becca agreed to the drink.

Dorothy retreated to what Becca would guess was an equally claustrophobic kitchen and, after a few minutes of clatter, returned with a steaming cup. She shoved aside a couple of pictures and a book, then placed the tea on an ornately carved walnut coffee table in front of Becca.

Dorothy took a seat on one of the sofas which offered Becca an opportunity to observe how thin the woman was. The hands she placed in her lap trembled.

"You look well, dear. How are your parents?"

To put Dorothy at ease, she updated her exclusively on the positive details of Julie and Irv's life. Dorothy listened closely and smiled broadly when Becca told her the part about Irv's crusade against an invading monster mouse. and how he managed to vanquish the formidable foe.

"I'm sorry to show up this late, but I just left my parents' house and stopped by on impulse."

Dorothy sighed. "It's for the best, since Dan's not here. It's hard for me to find any time alone since he retired. How can I help you, dear?"

Becca sat forward, every muscle tensed. "I know you haven't heard from Adam in a while, but do you have any idea where he could be?"

Dorothy squinted in concentration. "I don't know if I should tell you this, but since it's so important to you, I will. Last time we heard from Adam, he'd been picked up on a drug possession charge and wanted us to bail him out of jail."

Dorothy appeared to be the least likely parent to have an addict for a son, and know how to handle him. "What did you do?"

"Dan and I had an equity line on the house which we tapped to help him out. He promised to pay us back." She looked stricken. "After he left jail, we never heard from him again." Misery deepened the lines on Dorothy's face.

A lump filled Becca's throat. "I'm so sorry to hear he did that to you. Do you have any idea if he's in the Philadelphia area?"

"Last I heard, but who knows if he stayed around or left town once he was out of jail."

"Wouldn't he have been on probation? Doesn't that make it hard for him to leave the city?"

Dorothy stared off into the distance. "Adam's behavior has been unpredictable ever since he started using drugs. I can't tell you what he did or what he'd do."

"It's been so long since I've seen him. Do you happen to have any recent photos of him?"

Dorothy revived a little at the request. "He left home shortly after high school, but I still have his yearbook. Would you like to see it?"

Would she ever. "I'd love to."

Dorothy left the room and returned with the yearbook in hand. Becca joined her on the loveseat where she flipped through pages until she landed on one covered with row upon row of smiling faces. She pointed to a picture in the middle of the page of a young man with brown hair and glasses. A geeky looking kid. No one would ever think of him as a future drug addict of America.

"That's him." Dorothy touched the picture tenderly.

Becca took the book from Dorothy and scrutinized the face. The boy in the photo didn't resemble anyone she knew, but if she imagined him twenty years older with contact lenses, it might be a stretch, but he looked a little like Evan Frankin. Yes, once she stared at the picture long enough, she could definitely see the resemblance. If only she had one of those computer age-enhanced photos like the ones of missing children on milk cartons. That would help a lot. But without that type of assistance, she would have to rely on a mental image, which suggested a similarity around the eyes and nose. "Do you have a copy of this picture I can borrow?"

"No, dear. This is the only one I have and, even if Adam has let me down, I want a reminder of the darling boy he once was."

Becca nodded her understanding and studied the photo. She wanted to memorize it before handing the book back to Dorothy.

Dorothy took the book from her, stared at the picture and sighed again. She closed the book. "Can I do anything else for you, dear?"

She had reached a dead-end. "No, but thank you for sharing that with me. I'm keeping my fingers crossed Adam will make a recovery and become part of your family again. If he does, here's my number." She handed Dorothy a slip of paper with her cell number scribbled on it.

Dorothy placed the paper on the coffee table alongside the pile of magazines. Becca was tempted to put it in a less cluttered place, but couldn't see any.

Dorothy saw her to the door. "Are you sure there isn't anything else I can do for you, dear?"

"No, you did plenty. Thank you." Becca gave Dorothy a quick hug and left.

Back in her car she started the engine and watched exhaust snake upwards in her rearview mirror. The car rattled from the cold and the engine coughed a couple times as if it was missing. She waited while it warmed, watching an SUV meander down the street, and thought about the distraught parents with their addicted son. Her heart went out to them.

Funny how at the least likely times your eyes are opened. She had gone to Dorothy's to learn about Adam's whereabouts and failed, but she had come away a whole lot wiser.

For as far back as she could remember, she had wanted more than anything else in the world to have a child, but she hadn't thought through the possible consequences of that decision until now. After meeting with Dorothy tonight, she realized the reality might be a far cry from her fantasy. Any romantic idea she harbored that a child would bring her ultimate gratification, could turn out to be quite the opposite. A child wouldn't necessarily bring her the joy and self-fulfillment she craved. Like Dorothy, she might have to be willing to hold that child in her heart—even if she had to keep it at arm's length. Was she ready for that responsibility?

She pulled away from the curb with the picture of Adam still imprinted on her mind. Her next stop: Evan's place. Her pulse stuttered at the thought of what she might find there. But, no matter what, she had to connect the dots and find out if Evan was actually Adam.

I glanced down at my notes. "Hypnotherapy has been a major component of traditional psychotherapy ever since Sigmund Freud borrowed the technique from Franz Anton Mesmer, the father of mesmerism, including it in his repertoire of tools for treating hysteria. 'Hysteria' in the late 19th and early 20th centuries is what we now refer to as stress on one end of the spectrum and post traumatic stress disorder at the opposite extreme. Freud found that hypnosis could be used with hysterical patients to bypass the defenses erected by the unconscious mind to protect itself. It's a trick of sorts. A way to convince the mind to work with the therapist instead of against her.

"Later, in the mid-twentieth century, Milton Erickson revived the use of hypnosis in his practice and became the most influential of all modern hypnotherapists. His techniques are used today by a new generation of psychotherapists, including myself.

"During our next therapy session, I again employed the form of hypnotherapy I refer to as trance work to lead Becca back to the day she had previously described in her parents' bedroom. Again, as before, I asked her to revisit the scene unfolding before her, but this time I suggested she go deeper and describe in detail every nuance of her mental image.

Becca quickly became restless. She rolled her head from side to side and squirmed, indicating to me that she had psychologically arrived at the right junction of time, space and event, for me to make my move. "What are you experiencing?" I asked.

"He's sitting next to me and wants me to play a game with him."

"*Who's* sitting next to you?"

"I can't see his face, Sarah...Oh God, he's taking off his glasses and putting them down on the floor."

It was time to give her a gentle nudge. "What's preventing you from seeing him?"

"He won't let me..."

"How is he stopping you?"

Again her voice took on a childlike quality. "He said he'd kill me, my cat Max and my mom...I can't do it."

"You're no longer a child. He can't harm you now."

She gasped. "Yes, he can and he will."

"Does that mean he's the man who's been stalking you?"

She began to rock herself. "I think he's the one..."

"Go on. What else can you tell me?"

"He's bigger than me and stronger. He's trying to push me down, but I struggle to get away. He tells me to relax and not be so formal."

"That's a strange thing to say."

"He starts to unbutton his shirt. Oh, look at his hand. He's wearing a school ring with a large blue stone." She sniffed the air. "And he smells of cologne, like he just put some on."

"Good detail. Is it the same cologne your Uncle wore?"

"I don't know...I think so... Oh no, he's trying to remove my top."

She began to make sounds like a frightened animal. Concerned about her reaction, and on the alert for any developments, I didn't want to interrupt the flow and miss an opportunity to take her beyond where she'd gone before. As gently as possible I asked her to describe what happened next.

Her reaction was immediate and firm. "No!" she roared and sat bolt upright, eyes open. "I can't do this anymore."

I gave her a minute to calm down. "What just happened?"

"I don't want to do this...he hurt me," she wailed pitifully, like a child in pain.

Worried about her, I took the seat beside her on the sofa. "It's okay," I assured her. "Don't worry. We're making terrific progress."

Becca looked at me with desperation in her eyes. "I'm such a mess, Sarah..."

"No you're not..."

She quivered all over as though she'd just come in from the cold. "I'll never figure this thing out. I'm doomed to live with it haunting me forever. I know what he did and it's not pretty, but I might never know who did it..."

"That's not so," I assured her. "You've moved further along today. Each time we meet, we get closer to the truth."

She looked up at me with such hope and trust in her eyes, it nearly broke my heart. "You think so?" she asked in a thin voice.

"I definitely do. Don't give up on yourself. You're heading in the right direction, but we can't hurry the process. Rest assured it's progressing at the right pace."

She blew her nose on the tissue I handed her. "I hope you're right. I want to know who did this to me before he has a chance to do it again." She gazed at me with wide-eyed hope, tempered with doubt.

I hugged her to me. "You will. You'll see." And I meant it. From experience, I knew these types of revelations were like a new bloom and blossomed on their own schedule, but she was making headway. Now if she would only hang on, she would figure it all out. Soon, I thought, but hopefully soon enough.

Through splayed fingers, Becca levered open the mini blinds covering her apartment window and watched Evan pull away from the curb in his aging compact. She waited until he turned the corner before making her way next door to his building. He had mentioned an acupuncture class in the morning, which provided her with an opportunity to investigate his condo.

Investigate. What a funny word. She had begun to sound like the detectives on the case. Shows what eight months of being a "person of interest" could do for your vocabulary. She laughed to herself, just in time to catch the curious stare of a man she passed on the second floor landing.

At Evan's door, she scanned the hallway, then reached up to retrieve the key hidden above the jamb. To her relief, her fingers collided with cold, hard metal and she was able to coax the key into her hand. The click of the lock was a sweet sound. She replaced the key and slipped into the condo unseen, quietly closing the door behind her. Smooth. With a sigh, she leaned back against the closed door, waiting for the hammering of her heart to subside.

With no time to lose, she strode directly to the bathroom medicine cabinet. Inside, she discovered his toothbrush and mouthwash below row upon row of vitamins and minerals in containers of all shapes and sizes. She picked up one and read the label, L-Tryptophan. Whew. What the heck was that? Another read Beta Carotene. One was vitamin E, another fish oil. The list of supplements was dizzying.

She pushed a number of the bottles aside, feeling guilty for going through Evan's home uninvited, but spied no sign of anything suspect. No cologne. No contacts. Nothing.

In his bathroom closet, she searched under and behind fluffy white terry cloth towels, but came up empty-handed.

The top of Evan's dresser supported a few bottles of cologne and massage oil, but still no *Aramis*. So far she had struck out. No evidence. No culprit. No go.

Then she spotted the picture of Evan as a boy

half-hidden behind the cologne bottle. He couldn't have been more than nine or ten, but the picture remotely resembled the one Dorothy had shown her. A few years had passed between this picture and the one of Adam in the yearbook, but this could be the same kid. When she picked up the photo to study it, a school ring with a large blue stone was next to it. Exactly like the one she remembered. Her hopes dimmed.

She had lingered in the condo too long to be on the safe side. She double-checked the premises, making sure to put every single item back where she had found it. Evan's hairbrush lay next to a box of coins and paraphernalia in his top dresser drawer. She removed a handful of hairs from between the bristles and placed them in an envelope she had brought along for the occasion with Evan's name scribbled on the back. With the envelope sealed, she put it into her jeans pocket.

She wandered back into the living room, but instead of finding what she sought, all she discovered were shelves of self-help and spiritual books, stacks of new age and ethnic music discs and, on the bottom shelf, a box of audio-visual equipment that looked like something out of a spaceship cockpit. The directions on the back of the box said it could be used to create a state of mind referred to as "alpha, where you will experience deeper peace and more focused awareness." Exactly what she needed at the moment.

For good measure, she took one last glance in his coat closet before leaving and was about to shut the door when she caught sight of a black sleeve behind a brown wool coat. She pushed the wool coat aside to reveal a black trench coat. Her gut wrenched at the sight.

The turn of the doorknob startled her into a state of intense alertness without the use of expensive mind-altering equipment. The front door began to open and Becca bolted for the bedroom, stole behind the door and prayed she hadn't been witnessed. The sound of someone moving about the condo was drowned out by the pounding of the pulse in her head.

Who could be here and what did they want? If it was Evan, what could she tell him in explanation? Instead of trying to figure out what to say when she didn't know to whom she'd say it, she peered around the door and saw a woman with black hair in a ponytail placing a mop against the far wall. The cleaning lady. While able to breathe freely again, Becca realized she still had a dilemma. How to explain her presence in Evan's typically empty, but now overcrowded, apartment?

Since the truth would never do, she had to come up with a big fat lie. Fortifying herself with a deep breath, she waltzed into the living room. "Good morning," she announced breezily. "Evan told me you'd be here. I told him I would leave after you arrived." She marched out the door before the woman could ask her any questions.

Back in her apartment, Becca slumped into a dining room chair and lowered her head into her hands. The class ring and trench coat had certainly cemented her suspicions about Evan. She would drop off his hair sample with Mills on the way into work, but she already suspected what the analysis would show.

Mentally she placed a checkmark beside Evan's name on her list of potential suspects, believing she had found her man. Too bad. She was so fond of him, it was hard to admit she had been wrong. A deep sense of regret nagged at her.

She glanced up at the clock. She'd have to leave for work soon. Everything in her rebelled against the idea of leaving her nest just yet. She was in too much emotional distress to take care of anyone but herself.

On impulse, she called Drew, knowing it would be useful to talk things over with a friend. Communication had always been her way of problem-solving her disappointments, her rejections, her lapses of judgment. She could add this one to her growing list.

Later that day at an intimate Queen's Village tavern, Drew sipped on a martini and listened with apparent interest to Becca's tale. Occasionally he would interject a thought or opinion, but for the most part, he merely served as an attentive ear - the way she liked it. Only by listening to herself could Becca discern what was going on inside her own head. Otherwise, all the multiplicity of errant pixels would never come together and form a coherent picture in her mind.

When she finished updating Drew on what happened in Evan's apartment, he shook an index finger at her. "Now that you've found your man, why don't you turn it over to the police and give this thing a rest? I mean, you go over it all the time, clogging your mind with unanswerable questions to insoluble problems. A few days off to let everything percolate wouldn't hurt one bit, and it might help you to see things in a different light." He took another sip of his drink and put the glass down. "Want another wine?" He signaled for the barmaid.

Hadn't she made herself clear on the seriousness of her situation and the necessity of doing something sooner rather than later? Was he listening as attentively as he led her to believe? "I don't think this can wait."

"Nonsense. It's time for you to take a break." The waitress came by and he ordered another drink.

She declined, surprised to hear him request a second martini. She had never seen him drink more than a beer before.

He turned back to her. "Let's have some fun and take your mind off of your worries. They'll still be there when you get back to them."

She shook her head with vigor. "I can't do that. The fact there's a killer on the loose won't change because I need a break. I have to do everything in my power to tie this up as quickly as I can."

He sat back and leaned the chair onto its hind legs, a small smile creasing his lips. "Come on. There's nothing more you can do. Besides, what's going to happen if you lighten up a little except you might be happier. Maybe Becca will have a good time for a change. Relax a little. Scary thought, huh? Might be a trifle too much for her to handle."

She hated when people referred to her in third person, but she had to concede his point in spite of her resistance. Solving these crimes had become her raison d'être; her motivation for climbing out of bed in the morning and for everything else she did throughout the day. The thought of a time-out scared the living daylights out of her. And it was more than simply fear of the killer's next move—it was also fear of hers.

"Say I do that— I mean take time off for a couple days—"

"A couple days is hardly enough."

"Wait a minute. It's my life and I'm going to set the agenda." Where did that come from? She marveled at her gutsiness. "But say I go along with your scheme and something awful happens. Where would I be then?"

His drink served, he paid for it and took a gulp. "Exactly where you are now. Trying to figure out 'who done it' and how it was done."

He might have that right. "Okay, so from this moment on for the next two days, I'm going to put this crime to bed and trust that the police will do their job. Then what?"

He sat upright and reached across the table. "Come with me. Let me show you the best time you've had in months—maybe years. Let's dance, play, howl at the moon. Whatever we can do to take your mind off your troubles."

"What about work?"

"You are a party pooper, Becca Rosen. Okay, we'll follow my prescription only after we're finished working. Does that make you feel any better?"

She rolled her eyes. "All right... I'll do it, but where do we start?"

"Let's start with a real date, movies, dinner, the works. What do you say?"

She didn't know what to say. Part of her wanted to sit around and fret over the loss of her blossoming relationship with Evan, but she knew she'd be better off without him, even if it hurt. "When do you want to do this...date?"

"How about right now?"

She hadn't had a moment after leaving St. John's to even powder her nose or reapply her lipstick. "I'd say okay, but I need to wash up and refresh. Don't you live nearby? Why don't we go by your place."

Drew looked perplexed. "I don't know... I haven't cleaned all week. I'd hate you to see my townhouse in its present condition."

"Don't worry, I can look past the clutter. You only moved in a few months ago, I don't expect the Taj Mahal. I'm excited to see it."

"It'd be a lot more thrilling if I had the time to pick up my underwear first. Are you sure you want to see my skivvies? Perhaps we can postpone your visit until another time when I'm more prepared."

She laughed at his modesty. "Nope. We're going now. Don't be self-conscious. I won't judge you on the brand name of your briefs." She stood. "Let's go."

He grasped her arm. "All right...it's your funeral."

She took his arm and pulled him upright. "Come on. There's no backing out now."

For either of them.

Chapter Seventeen

Becca stood at the bottom of the landing leading up to Drew's townhome and admired the lovely two-story structure. A boxy building made of brick with a small front porch, it had multi-paned windows with mint green trim surrounded by forest green shutters and a dark green porch with mint green railing. She squeezed his arm. "You've been holding out on me, Drew. This house is darling."

He ruffled her hair. "Almost as cute as you."

For the first time that day, she could sense the tension lose its grip on her muscles; could breathe deeply. "I can't wait to see what's inside."

He gave her head a gentle rap with his knuckles. "Me, too."

He led the way inside, flicked on a light and illuminated a large living room with a stately brown leather sofa and an oak rocker. It looked a little like she would imagine a lawyer's office might.

"Nice." She strode over to the fireplace with a large mantel covered with pictures of Drew and his parents, Lisa and Sam. Her eyes alighted on a family portrait, which must have been taken when Drew was an adolescent. He had on glasses and a self-conscious grin. "Is that you?"

He came up beside her and turned the picture toward the wall where she could no longer view it. "Lousy picture. I'm embarrassed to have anyone see it."

"Why? You were cute."

"More like a nerd. Come with me. I'll show you around."

He led her into a small but adequate kitchen, with a large old-fashioned gas stove that took up most of one wall, and into a conventional dining room with French doors. Beyond the doors was a courtyard.

"Oh, you have a garden," she said. "I love gardens. May I see yours?"

"Sure." He opened the door and a cold blast of winter rushed in. "Are you certain you want to go out in this?"

"I haven't removed my coat yet. Let's go." She stepped into another world outside the French doors. A world of flowerless roses strangled by spindly vines; large lifeless azaleas beside straggly evergreen bushes. A gray, dreary world of death and dying. The decrepit little garden gave her the creeps. She hugged herself. "Burr, it's cold out here. How about if we go back in?"

"What did I tell you?" he asked, not putting up any resistance. "As much as I love gardening in the spring, it's not one of my winter sports.

He loved gardening? Where did she hear that one before? Wasn't it from Angela about Elliot? She would be worried, if she hadn't already pinpointed the perpetrator.

On her way into the house, she passed a couple sacks of potting soil leaning against the wall. Half-hidden behind them, sat a large container of *Diazinon*. Again she was reminded of Angela.

Back inside, Drew helped her out of her red wool coat and tossed it over a couple of other items of his clothing on a ladder-back dining room chair. She had to admit he had been truthful. The place was in shambles. Not out of the ordinary for a single working man.

"How about a glass of red zinfandel?" he asked her.

"Okay, I guess. It might warm me up?"

He left to fetch the drinks and she took a seat on the sofa, attempting to read an article on biofuels in a *New Yorker Magazine* that had been tossed to the ground. He returned with two glasses and a bottle, poured her a glass of deep burgundy wine and set the bottle in front of her on the coffee table.

"If you'll excuse me, I have to use the bathroom. I'll be right back," he said.

Right back was more than ten minutes, according to her watch, which she consulted innumerable times. He took the seat beside her on the couch.

"Sorry I took so long, but I needed to straighten up. Now the skivvies are where they belong."

"No problem. I've been reading an interesting article on global warming. Guess it's something we need to pay more attention to."

"I'd say. It's certainly hotter in here since you arrived."

A heated look filled his deep blue eyes, giving

her the shivers. Why? Something felt wrong, but she wasn't sure whether it was real or her typical response to an available and attractive man.

He slid a little nearer to her, but she backed off. "I've wanted to get to know you better for a long time. You have no idea what this means to me."

He moved closer still and she could go no farther with the sofa arm scraping her thigh. "You know I'm not ready..."

"Don't be silly— we've seen enough of each other. What are we waiting for?" With that, he lowered his lips to hers.

Instead of passion all she could feel was panic. His taste, his smell, his touch...Everything about him disturbed her. She pushed him away. "No. Not now."

He watched her through half-shut, hungry eyes. "When then? You can't keep putting me off. You know how crazy I am about you. It's not fair for you to play hard-to-get any longer. Come here."

He grasped her arm and drew her toward him, but she broke away.

"Don't be ridiculous, Becca. You know we were meant to be together. Loosen up and relax. Don't be so formal."

At those words a siren went off in her head. Sick to her stomach, she gulped down the bile that rose into her throat. "I'm not feeling well..."

He eyed her suspiciously. "What's the matter?"

"An upset stomach. You have to understand, I

had a stressful day. I'm under a tremendous amount of strain." Nausea stopped her words. "I have to use your bathroom." Again he gripped her arm and this time she couldn't break away. She had to make her point. "If I don't go soon...I'm going to be sick all over your carpet."

With an angry frown, he grudgingly let go of her arm. "It's through the bedroom, but don't take too long."

She heard a menacing tone in his voice. "I won't. I promise."

Before he could stop her, she hoisted her purse and took off for the bathroom on quivering legs. Everything at the moment spelled disaster to her. Perhaps it was intuition. Perhaps it was something more. Her instincts told her she was in deep danger.

She swiftly closed and locked the bathroom door behind her, sprinted over to the medicine cabinet. With no time to lose, she shoved aside shaving cream and a container of contact lens solution and came upon a bottle of _Aramis_ tucked away in the back of the cabinet. It had a tiny corner of the label torn off. Identical to the one missing from Angela's apartment.

She rummaged through a stack of blue and green towels in the linen closet and then, on a hunch, dug into a hamper full of dirty clothes. At the bottom of the pile, her fingers felt silky material. She pulled out a pair of her missing panties. The ones stolen from her laundry. She was in serious trouble. Her hands trembled when she replaced them in the heap.

Jesus. What was he doing in here for so long?

Covering his tracks?

She had found enough evidence to satisfy her, but with hair taken from the brush resting on top of the toilet tank, perhaps she could make a solid case with the police. She coaxed the hairs from the bristles, placed them in her pants pocket and readied herself to face Drew.

A knock at the door made her heart lurch. "What's going on in there? Are you okay? You're taking an awfully long time."

She watched the knob turn with terror—then it stopped. "I'm fine," she said, but her voice quacked with fear. "I'll only be a couple more minutes."

She waited breathlessly, watching while his shoes blocked light beneath the door. Like in her nightmares. Finally the shoes moved away. She heard the sound of his footsteps retreating, willed herself to stop shaking. She couldn't face him in her present condition and would have to wait out her reaction.

A plan. She needed a plan or she would never get away from him. Without fully thinking it through, she whipped the cell phone from her purse and dialed Julie's number. Luckily Julie answered on the second ring. "Mom," she whispered. "I need your help."

'What?' Julie asked. "What's going on?"

"I can't explain right now, but I need you to call me in five minutes. Do you understand? Five minutes. No more. No less."

"What are you up to now, Becca?"

"Just do as I ask. My life depends on it." She hung up before her mother could ask any more questions.

Drawing a number of deep breaths, as she did in therapy, helped her to compose herself enough to face Drew. She abandoned the sanctity of the bathroom, trudged past Drew's dresser, where she noted a couple pieces of jewelry carelessly strewn on top. Upon closer inspection, one of them turned out to be a school ring with a large blue stone. She couldn't go any further. Everything added up to danger. Drew looked more and more like the man behind the mystery. She was in grave jeopardy.

In the living room, Drew was pouring himself another glass of wine—or was it his third or fourth? Her palms moistened at the thought he might be tipsy on top of terrorizing. A lethal combination.

He looked up with a scowl. "You sure took your good ol' time." Rage rimmed his words.

She wanted to defuse his anger or she'd never make it out of there in one piece. "Sorry. I'm not doing well. I didn't mean for my problems to come between us."

"Well, they have," he said in a petulant voice.

She took a seat on the nearby chair, purposely not sitting too close to him. "I'm ready to go out now."

He poured wine into her glass to top it off. "There's no rush. Finish your drink."

He raised his glass and she reluctantly raised hers. "To Becca. The love of my life." He spat out the words sounding inebriated as well as pissed off.

She half-smiled. "What a thing to say."

"If you don't believe me, look at what I bought you. I was goin' to give it to you later, but it seems like I should do it now." He lifted a gift bag from under the coffee table and handed it to her.

Inside was a bottle of *Raffinée*. Stunned, she stared at the bottle a long time. Since he hadn't been to see Julie since the party, how could he know of her preference for the perfume, except from Angela? Her stomach turned sour again. "My favorite. How did you know?"

"I didn't, but it's my favorite, too. Why don't you put some on for me?"

The phone rang. Grateful to Julie for following directions, Becca answered it with a trembling hand. "Yes... Oh no... How bad is it? How soon do you want me there? Okay."

On the other end of the line, Julie kept asking her what the hell she was doing, but Becca ignored her mother's questions. "All right. You don't have to call back. I'll be right over."

She flipped the cell shut and glanced over at Drew. "That's the hospital. One of my patients has made a turn for the worse, and he's asked to see me. If I don't get there within the hour, he'll be gone."

Drew sneered. "I've never heard of a nurse on duty. You're not on-call. Let the doctors take care of him."

"You don't understand. He's been in and out of the hospital for years, and he's dying now. I need to be by his side at this time. If I don't do this, I'll feel guilty for the rest of my life. I know you wouldn't wish that on me."

"How do you know what I want?"

She didn't respond, but instead shrugged into her coat in an attempt to scoot out the door before he could stop her. But the moment she started for the door, he put himself between her and it.

"You're not going anywhere without me."

With legs wobbling beneath her and blood pulsing through her veins, she couldn't conjure up an immediate rebuttal. She racked her brain, but before she could piece together an argument, he said, "I have an idea. How 'bout I come with you."

What could she do with him in an unreasonable state of mind, physically blocking her escape? "All right, but they won't let you onto the ward. You'll have to wait for me in the waiting room."

"I can do that." He grabbed his coat and followed her out the door. "I'll drive."

She had to think fast. "But you've had more wine than I did and you don't know the way. Why don't I drive?"

He looked at her through hooded eyes, suddenly appearing sober. "Don't you worry. I know how to go."

She shuddered, but not out of surprise. Of course he knew the way. He had been there before, incognito. And he never intended it to be a friendly visit.

At the entrance to St. John's, Becca raced ahead of Drew to put a barrier between him and the new receptionist. The white-haired, heavy-set woman looked up with a start at Becca's brusque approach.

"What are you doing here? Isn't it your day off?"

She had to take control of the conversation. "I'm here to see Miller in 206. My friend Drew came along for the ride. Would you please find him a good magazine and a nice cup of coffee while he waits for me?"

"Since you're visiting, you can take your friend back with you."

Damn. This wasn't going well at all. Becca silently mouthed the word 'no', but she could see the lack of comprehension on Jane's pudgy face. "Mr. Miller's ill. It wouldn't be appropriate to bring anyone into his room. Please help me out here."

Drew stepped up. "No problem for me. I'm not 'fraid of getting sick. I won't be in your way."

Becca's stomach turned. This wasn't going the way she had planned in the car. "You don't understand. Miller's close to ninety years old. In his condition any outsider carrying a bug would kill him."

Drew cut his eyes to her. "I thought you said he

was dying."

"Mr. Miller's dying? I hadn't heard anything," the kindly, but clueless woman said.

"He's close to death, but you never know when a patient will take a turn for the better and pull through. I can't take the risk of bringing an outsider into his room under the circumstances. You agreed to wait for me out here, or I never would have permitted you to join me."

Drew looked at her through wary eyes, and with raised voice asked, "Are you sure you're telling me the truth? This sounds kinda fishy."

"What purpose would lying to you serve? I don't have time to debate this with you now. Go with Jane to the waiting room and I'll be back when I can break away."

Drew shook his head vehemently. "Nah. I don't think so. I'm stickin' with you." And he began to move in the direction of the ward.

She grabbed his arm, terrified. If she didn't restrain him, her only hope for escape would evaporate. "You can't do this. You promised to wait for me. This isn't going to work..."

His eyes narrowed. "Why's it important to leave me out here? I don't see why I can't join-"

With all the commotion, the security guard entered from the hall. He was a big man, much bulkier than Drew, and he carried a gun on his hip. "Any trouble here?"

"No... No problem at all. My friend here is going to wait for me in the lobby while I visit a patient. He's fully cooperative. Aren't you, Drew?"

Drew didn't say anything, but he gave her the meanest look she could ever imagine. "I'm not doin' anything of the sort..."

The security guard stepped closer to Drew. "The lady here's the boss. I hope you're not gonna make me escort you outside."

"Who says?"

The guard laid a hand on his weapon. "I do."

Drew looked from the security guard to her with a sneer. "Ya got your way this time, but don't plan on gettin' it again."

She turned to Jane. "Please show Drew to a chair."

When Jane came out from behind her desk and indicated the waiting area, he reluctantly followed. The moment she saw them trot off, Becca bolted for the ward, sprinting through the heavy doors that separated the lobby from the hospital. The doors closed behind her and she groaned with relief.

But she had no time to dally. She'd arrived in Drew's car and would be at a disadvantage leaving on foot. As quickly as her shaky legs would carry her, she made her way to the rear exit of the building and sprinted the five blocks to Market Street, where she hailed a cab. At her building, she hurried inside to gather her necessities.

Cecil waited on the area rug for her. He stretched, yawned and sauntered after her to the bedroom where he rubbed up against her leg. With no time to waste, she ignored him in favor of tossing a handful of clothing and toiletries into a suitcase.

Cecil must have picked up on her mood because he followed her every move, meowing incessantly. *This cat's uncanny,* Becca thought. *How does he know when I'm in trouble?* She stooped down and scooped him up into her arms. "I love you," she said into his fragrant and abundant fur. "I'm sorry I can't take you with me, but Julie's allergic to cats. I promise I'll be back to rescue you from loneliness and boredom just as soon as I can."

She held onto him much longer than she deemed safe, reluctant to let him loose. His purring reminded her of all she had lost; her husband, her best friend, her dignity, her sense of security. Now her home and her cat. Bundling him closer, she allowed herself a minute of aching sadness before she placed him down on her favorite chair. Back in the kitchen, she filled his bowl with a large helping of Kibble and left two bowls full of water.

"I'll be back in a couple days," she promised him with a ruffle to his fur, before racing for the door.

Outside, Becca scanned the street for Drew, then made a mad dash to her car. She tossed the suitcase onto the backseat and gunned the engine. Right before she pulled away from the curb, she glanced back to see Drew's gray BMW turn the corner. She slammed her foot onto the accelerator and roared out of her parking spot in a squeal of wheels.

In panic, she sped through a red light and made the next right, careening up the street by weaving in and out of thick traffic. After a second sudden turn, she glanced in her rearview mirror, but failed to spot Drew's car. Even though relieved, she knew she'd never be safe with him in the world; that no matter where she went or what she did, he'd find her. That was the one thing she could depend on.

She picked up speed and veered onto the expressway ramp.

Irv hoisted Becca's suitcases up the stairs to her old bedroom and Julie took her by the arm, ushered her into the kitchen. "Not that I'm not thrilled at having you here, but after that bizarre call and your sudden appearance, explain to me what this is all about."

Adrenaline raced through Becca's veins after her narrow escape and wild ride, with a detour to the police station to report what had happened and drop off the hair sample from Drew's brush.

"I'll explain in a minute, but first, I could use a cup of tea." She heaved herself onto a bar stool. "Something herbal. Do you have chamomile?"

"Just green. Will that do?"

"Sure," Becca said, rubbing her temples.

While it wouldn't be a far stretch for Drew to figure out she was at Julie and Irv's, he would never make an appearance with them around. For the moment, she was safe, but this was a temporary arrangement. She had to find other digs soon.

She watched Julie heat a mug of tea in the microwave. What would Evan think about nuking the tea? It seemed like a sacrilege. The thought of Evan saddened her. She had treated him so poorly. Funny, he was the one she should have believed in, not Drew. She owed Evan an apology.

Julie plopped the mug onto the counter and took an adjacent stool. "What's going on?"

After a deep sip of warm comfort, Becca lunged into a long-winded—but how could it be otherwise— explanation of what she'd been through that day. Julie sat stone-faced, listening. "I don't know if I'm even safe here, but I didn't know where else to turn..."

Julie raised a hand to stop her. "You did exactly the right thing coming to your dad and me. We might not be much, but we're your parents and we'd do anything in the world to keep you safe."

Touched by the kindness after her ordeal, Becca's eyes filled with tears. "Thanks, Mom. I have a key to my therapist friend's apartment that I plan to use because no one will know I'm there, but I wanted to see you first."

"You know you can stay here with us."

"I know I'm welcome here, but so does Drew. I'll be better off there."

"Okay...but we'll be here when you need us." Julie picked up a napkin and handed it to her.

Becca blew her nose unceremoniously and dabbed at her eyes. "I need an answer to a question that's been bothering me. Do you know if I was ever alone in the house with Drew? Please do your best to remember. It's important I know."

Julie stared down at her folded hands for an extraordinarily long time, but Becca knew better than to interrupt her. Finally, she raised her head. Tears filled her eyes and spilled down her cheeks. "I feel so guilty. I can't even tell you how horrible I feel."

Becca hadn't expected this reaction. She patted Julie's shoulder.

"Five years ago, Paulie told me about the incident in the bedroom. He had kept it a secret all those years, but couldn't keep it from me any longer. He wrote me a letter explaining what he'd seen. I didn't want to believe him. I told him he must have remembered it wrong. He was young and had a distorted perception of what happened. I refused to accept what he reported." She hesitated, wiped tears with the back of her hand.

Becca held out her napkin. "Want to share?"

Julie took it from her. "I couldn't admit I had let you down like I did. That I hadn't protected you. I couldn't face it, even though I suspected something terrible had gone wrong after your nervous breakdown. I was in denial..." She lowered her head into her hands and wept.

Becca slung an arm around her mother's shoulders. "Don't worry, Mom. There's no need to beat yourself up any more than you already have. I forgive you."

Julie thrust her arms around Becca's neck and buried her head into Becca's hair. And sobbed.

Becca held onto her mother while she cried, and a warm sensation settled over her. For the first time in years, Becca experienced what she could only describe as pure unadulterated love for her mother. Now it all made sense. With all the self-recrimination Julie had carried around, no wonder she was often defensive and overprotective. Becca drew her mother closer, no longer afraid of the unbreakable bond between them. She could take care of herself. She didn't have to keep her mother at arm's length.

"I love you, Mom."

"I'm so sorry." Julie sobbed into her hair. "I shouldn't have left you alone with that boy. I should have been a better mother. If I could do it all over again, I'd never have left your side. I'd have pinned my heart to yours."

Becca couldn't help but picture the image Julie painted with her words. And, all at once, her sadness and love and gratitude coalesced in an unexpected spasm of laughter. Julie straightened and stared open-mouthed at Becca, who nearly doubled over in a mixture of misery and mirth. Convulsive laughter kept coming in waves and she was helpless to restrain it. Before she knew it, Julie had joined in and they both laughed so long and so hard that the sound summoned Irv into the kitchen.

He looked from his wife to his daughter with a bemused smile. "What's gotten into you two?"

"Nothing," Julie said between bursts of laughter.

"Mom and I are conjoined twins." Becca joked. "We're joined at the heart."

That triggered another round of laughter.

Irv watched them for a minute, then shook his head. "You girls," he said, and left the kitchen.

Julie glanced over at Becca with a conspiratorial grin. "He'll never understand us, but we know what page we're on."

"The funny page," Becca said, and they guffawed again.

Becca finally stopped laughing long enough to draw a breath and wipe away the tears that streaked down her cheeks. "I need to know one more thing, Mom. Will you be there if I need you?"

"What a question. There's no limit on my love."

And for the first time in years, Becca's love for her mother knew no limits either.

Chapter Eighteen

A call from Detective Mills the following day confirmed Becca's suspicions. Under a Comparison Microscope the hairs from Drew's townhouse matched the hairs on the rag and those from the comb in Angela's apartment. While the lab would run mitochondrial DNA tests on the sample, the police were 99.9% certain they had a match.

Becca immediately offered to come down to the station and meet with Mills, but Mills cautioned against it. While she explained this sample, like the last one, couldn't be used as evidence, she had sent two officers over to Drew's to pick him up for questioning. She told Becca to sit tight and wait for a call.

Becca could hardly contain herself. Her detective work had paid off and she was eager to participate in the investigation. She restlessly paced the studio apartment where she was sequestered.

A second call from Mills came thirty minutes later.

"Are you sure of the address?" the detective asked. "We're here at the one you gave us, but the place has been abandoned. No one lives here."

They compared notes and sure enough, Mills had the right house.

"Strange. Drew said he owned the house. Why would he leave it like that?" Becca scratched her head. "Will you be there for a time? I'd like to see for myself."

"I won't, but a couple of other detectives will stay behind to snoop around for any evidence. I have calls to make. I'm going to find out who owns this building and what they know about your so-called friend. I'll let the other officers know you'll be by and they'll let you in."

For once she heard acceptance in Mills' voice, but she was too grounded in her certainty to have been disturbed even if Mills didn't believe her. "Please don't call him my friend. He's no friend of mine, I can promise you that." She hung up the phone, changed into jeans, boots, and a charcoal wool sweater before she headed over to Drew's. She arrived to find the house empty of furnishing as described. Two officers were busy dusting the premises for fingerprints.

"Any luck?" she asked the tall good-looking officer who let her in.

"Not much. Looks like the suspect wiped the place clean. We found a couple sets of prints in the bathroom, but they don't match."

At the word suspect, she perked up. Good news. She was no longer the only one in their sights. "One set of fingerprints might be mine. I hope this doesn't complicate your job."

The cop smiled. "My job is complicated. You're welcome to look around, but don't touch anything."

She traveled from room to room, revisiting her evening with Drew. Where had he gone? Drew wasn't the type to vanish completely, sight unseen. He was more likely to make a statement. Wreak revenge.

By the time she reached the bedroom, her sense that something might be wrong had transformed into full-blown fear. She snagged the officer's attention. "Do you think you could take me by my apartment? I have a weird feeling Drew might have been there and I don't want to go in alone."

"Give us a couple more minutes to finish up here and we'll be glad to run you by."

"Thanks." Not wanting to be underfoot, she left to take a seat on the outside steps, but it was the worst thing she could have done.

Alone, her fear turned into panic and she could barely sit still. To cope, she rose to pace the sidewalk in front of the house, vaguely aware of stares from behind the curtains of neighboring townhouses and from passersby drawn by curiosity to the taped-off house.

Finally, the two detectives joined her on the street and helped her into the back of their police cruiser. At her apartment building, the good-looking African-American cop insisted on going in first to make sure no one was lurking around the premises. Becca watched while his pock-marked partner checked out the street and alley, then entered the building. A couple minutes later he returned.

"No one's inside, but I have bad news—"

She knew what he was going to say before the words left his lips. With a loud moan, she dashed past him into the apartment and rushed to the bedroom, where she spotted Cecil on the bed—and stopped dead. The cat lay perfectly still, spread out as though asleep on her plum satin quilt. Too still with all the commotion. She approached him on tiptoes, tears stinging her throat and eyes, and gingerly picked him up into her arms. His head fell backwards at an unnatural angle, his neck broken.

She crushed Cecil to her chest and buried her head in his fur—the silky-soft fur she loved to touch. Tears now flowed fast and furiously. How could she ever live with herself for bringing such a violent fate upon her best friend, her husband, and now her long-time buddy and loyal companion? She had let them all down. Even with the policemen circulating about, she allowed herself a good long cry.

What might have happened to her if she had been in the apartment at the time?And what might still happen with Drew on the loose? Intense terror doubled her over. The tall cop came up beside her.

"I'm sorry about your cat," he said with kindness. "Are you all right?"

She tried to dry her eyes, but the tears kept coming. "As okay as I can be right now."

He reached over with gloved fingers, lifted a piece of paper off the spot where Cecil had been lying and read, "Never forget me. I'll never forget you."

Her stomach churned.

The cop studied the letter. "Our first piece of material evidence. We don't usually collect evidence after a feline homicide, but this is different. We'll be checking around to see what else we can find."

Mute with grief, Becca took a seat on the far side of the bed and buried her head in Cecil's fur. She must have remained that way for at least ten minutes before she heard Evan's voice beside her. She looked up and into his worried eyes.

"I was on my way home and spied the police car. I thought you might need me. It wasn't easy to talk my way in here. What's going on, Becca?" He glanced down at Cecil in her arms. "Is he dead?"

She nodded. He lowered himself onto the bed beside her, encircling her in his arms. With her head against his shoulder, she started to sob again. She could no longer support her own weight, so she let his strong arms hold her upright.

Finally drained, she laid Cecil gently down on the bedspread. At Evan's coaxing, she finished what she had to do with the police, then allowed him to lead her to his condo. He helped her into bed, made her a cup of hot jasmine tea and watched over her while she slept the rest of the day away.

By nightfall, she revived a little, but had no appetite for the split pea soup he placed on the side table. He took a seat at the foot of the bed.

"Feeling any better?" he asked.

"A little, thanks to you."

"I wish I could do more. I feel as if I'm partly to blame for not being there when you needed me, but I wasn't sure you wanted me around."

She nodded thoughtfully. "Maybe I'm the one who needs to make amends to you. I had the mistaken idea I couldn't trust you. I was so deluded. I'm sorry I treated you the way I did."

He took her hand. "It's understandable under the circumstances. You were confused."

"I didn't know if I could believe you."

"I guess my behavior didn't help. It's just that...well...I love you, Becca, and I was riddled with jealousy and fear."

She smiled to herself, remembering her therapy session. "How do you know it's love you feel? Are you sure it's not infatuation?"

He gave her a quizzical look.

"I mean, how do you tell them apart?"

"Now who's the metaphysical scholar?" He took her into his arms. "I don't care what you call it. I don't care if you call it eros, agape, or puppy love. Call it inspiration for my money. All I know is, I feel more attached to you than I've ever felt to anyone else. Enough that I want to spend the rest of my life with you."

"Are you serious?"

He looked her in the eye. "I've never been more serious in my whole life." To prove it, he kissed her with such tenderness. For an instance, it quieted the storm raging inside.

"I'm not thinking too clearly at the moment. I'll have to consider your proposal when I'm feeling a little more able."

"I'd expect nothing less," he said, and gave her an affectionate squeeze. "Whatever you decide, I only hope we can put this damn thing behind us."

But she knew better. Drew hadn't given up on her after all these years, why would he let her go now? She burrowed her head against Evan's shoulder, but even his closeness felt like temporary comfort. With Drew in the world, there was nowhere to hide.

At a sniveling sound I glanced up to see one of the two hefty social workers drying her eyes. Beside her, another woman squirmed in her seat. Most eyes were fixed on me, although I caught one of the men in the back of the room with closed lids.

A woman with silver-gray hair in a canary-yellow tailored suit raised her hand. "It's unusual for any of our patients to undergo as profound a transformation as Becca did over such a short period of time."

"You're right," I agreed. "As you well know, when someone's been violated as a child, they're often dysfunctional as an adult. They learn to shut out more than just memories of the abuse. They become so skilled at denial as a survival mechanism that they detach from their own feelings and experience little real compassion or connection to others. But a series of events like those that befell Becca can awaken more than mere memories." I glanced around and saw a number of nods. "Because Becca was forced to face her abuse and deal with the associated feelings, she was jettisoned forward developmentally at warp speed. Intense stress can act upon the psyche in a manner similar to raising the temperature in an oven. The higher the heat, the quicker the change. By the time Becca left therapy, she was a strong, loving woman who could take care of herself and be present for others."

A tall, thin woman with dark hair pulled back into a bun stood. "How can you account for Becca's inability to identify the real perpetrator when he was literally under her nose?"

"I was going to address that topic. Beside the fact he was disguised at the time of the abuse, trauma has a tendency to distort memory. Emotional shock can camouflage details that would normally be evident to the alert mind. This is especially true in children because they lack the capacity of adults to process information. But that doesn't mean the data isn't stored in the unconscious. It is our job as therapists to find a way to excavate these buried treasures so that they become useful tools for healing.

"Add to this the fact that memory and perception are always subjective. What one person recalls about an event may be a far cry from what another remembers. Think about Faulkner's *The Sound and the Fury*. His characters all experience the same situation, but recollect it in disparate ways. I think it's best said in *A Course in Miracles*." I glanced down at my notes for the quote. "'Perception selects and makes the world you see. It literally picks it out as the mind directs... For what you look for you are far more likely to discover than what you would prefer to overlook.'

"It goes on to say, 'Memory is as selective as perception, being it's past tense.'"

A burly man in the back row with his tie undone and his top shirt button opened raised his hand. "Dr. Abrams, did Becca ever complete treatment?"

I squinted at him under the fluorescent glare. "Please bear with me. I know it's been a long two days, but I'm about to tie up loose ends. What I have to say should answer your question."

While I addressed him, I noticed Adrian half-hidden behind the social workers and was suddenly distracted. What power did this man have over me that one look rattles me this way? Scary to think what an evening with him might do. "Any other questions?"

Since there were none, I continued.

"Shortly after the incident with Drew, Becca called and requested an emergency therapy session. Since she was now convinced he was the one who molested her, she wanted to go back in time to see if her memory fit her newfound knowledge. I arranged an appointment with her for the following day.

While still shaken, the woman who entered my office the following afternoon was a far cry from the woman I first met six months earlier. She arrived wearing a pair of conservative black slacks with a black jacket and low-slung black leather pumps. When she led the way into the inner office, her posture matched her mood. While somber, her stride expressed both resolve and readiness to do the work.

She spread out on the sofa without my even asking. "Okay, Doc. I'm ready to return to that bedroom."

Before I had a chance to reclaim my seat, she had closed her eyes and taken a couple of audible breaths. I readied my pad and pen. "I want you to go back to the time of the molestation in your parents' bedroom. Envision your molester by your side and watch what he does."

After a couple of silent minutes, she suddenly shouted, "No! Don't do that. Stop it. That hurts."

"What is he doing to you?"

"He's touching me and putting his fingers up me. It's hurting me."

Since she was so young, how frightening and painful this must have been for her. I tell her this, then ask her to let me know who was doing this to her.

"Drew..." she muttered, "I knew it was you. It was you who did all those awful things to me. How could you have been so mean? I hate you, you asshole. You're a horrible perverted person!" She balled her fist by her side, and shouted out the last words. Her face had taken on a deep scarlet hue.

"Why?" she asked. "Why? Why? Why? I was so young. Why did you do that to me? You stole my innocence and I'll never, ever, ever get it back."

Since Becca had taken the initiative, I sat back and allowed her the space she needed to vent all her myriad emotions; one minute yelling out her rage at Drew in a fitful burst of fury, the next wailing in pain and shame. One instant threatening to shoot him in the groin. The next begging for his understanding. She ping-ponged back and forth like this repeatedly before finally quieting to a whimper.

By the time Becca had calmed enough to sit up, tears had dried in flesh-colored streaks that etched their way down her rouged cheeks. "I'm not surprised by what I saw. The nutty part is that he came back for more. I'll never understand what sort of craziness compelled him to seek me out again after all those years, but I don't think he'll stop now."

The thought sickened me. "Let's hope you're wrong, but if you're not, what do you plan to do to protect yourself?"

"I'm going to lay low at your friend's apartment until I feel safe. You'll be the first to know when I'm ready to move on."

"No problem. I've cleared it with her. She said you can stay as long as you like."

"Thanks, I appreciate that."

"But there's one other thing you might want to consider, a restraining order to keep him away from you. The police or your lawyer can help you with that." I waited for her to blow her nose. "Please be careful. You know what you're up against. And, whatever happens, wherever you go, whatever you do, please stay in contact with me. I want to know you're safe and sound."

She hugged me one last time. Then she left. I only met with her once more when she came by to return the key. That was the last time I saw her.

"Fini. I'm sure you'll all be happy to hear Becca only returned once to her apartment with movers. The following summer she married Evan, and they moved away from Philadelphia for good, leaving only a forwarding address with family and a couple of carefully chosen close confidantes. With Evan, a new name and a career in alternative medicine, she started her life over in another state.

Every once in a while Becca writes to catch me up on her life. She and Evan have been in couples counseling in their new city and have worked diligently together to overcome Becca's sexual anxiety and develop a warm and loving relationship. Recently, she wrote to tell me she's pregnant with their first child and her dream of becoming a parent is finally going to come true. Even though thrilled about the pregnancy, Becca has matured enough over the past couple of years to realize a baby won't be the solution to all her problems; that as a parent, she will be asked to give more than she receives. This has been one of the great lessons for her.

The other lesson is that the past imprints an indelible blueprint on our central nervous system, which shapes our perception of the world and defines how we act and react within it. While we can never erase or alter our memories, we can overwrite them through conscious choice and experience. Armed with awareness and a willingness to change, we become master over our beliefs and behaviors instead of slave to them. Becca is a beautiful example of how that lesson can be put to work. She has grown into the self-possessed, competent and dignified woman she always dreamed of being.

I hope my lecture has adequately demonstrated the benefit of psychotherapy and hypnotherapy in the successful treatment of Repressed Memory Syndrome and you will be able to apply my ideas in working with your own RMS patients. Thank you for joining me this weekend. You were a wonderful and attentive audience."

A round of applause filled the room and I watched as participants stood, stretched and meandered toward the exit doors. After answering questions from a couple of hanger-ons, I scanned the room for Adrian, anticipating my encore performance with him. The thought of our rendezvous caused my throat to tighten. While facing a full house of professionals was intimidating enough, it paled in comparison to facing Adrian alone.

A couple more people approached the podium with questions and comments, but even after they had departed, I failed to spot Adrian. Deeply discouraged, I wondered if he was the one who had cold feet. I considered gathering up my paper and leaving before he could catch up with me, but I had made a commitment to myself as well as to him. And, petrified or not, I planned to keep my end of the bargain.

Ten minutes later, Adrian was still nowhere to be seen, and I was about to give up on him. With disappointment overshadowing any relief, I packed away notes in my briefcase and prepared to take my leave of the hotel. Perhaps my date with Adrian wasn't meant to be. He had come on so strong, it might be for the best.

I rifled through my purse for my car key when a baritone voice boomed behind me. "Sorry, I'm late, Sarah. I had to change out of that monkey suit. Now I'm ready to rock. Are you ready to roll?"

Against my better judgment my spirits surged. With a nervous laugh, I glanced up into the deep blues of Adrian Farley. He wore a boyish grin on his clean-shaven face and his eyes sparkled mischievously. He had changed from a pale blue shirt to a red polo and from his suit jacket to an *Izod* windbreaker and he still looked spectacular. My breath hitched.

"I thought you ducked out on me."

"Never," he said and his eyes darkened to a navy blue. "I'm been looking forward to this all weekend."

I felt as giddy as an adolescent at a school dance. "Where to from here?"

"I thought we'd take my wheels and head into center city to that restaurant I mentioned earlier. After we eat, I can drive you back here to pick up your car. How's that for a plan?"

"Sounds like music to my stomach. I'm famished."

"Let's go then." From the conference room ,we took the elevator to the parking garage and he helped me into his yellow Mercedes convertible.

"Nice," I said once he was seated. "Your practice must be flourishing."

"That and the book I've written on the Borderline Personality Disorder. It's sold well."

"I'd love to read it."

He started the car with a roar and peeled out of the lot and onto City Avenue. "I don't have any copies with me, but I'll bring a signed one the next time we get together."

I liked the sound of 'next time.' It warmed me all over to think there might be a future with this man.

Instead of taking the Schuylkill Expressway into town, he chose the East River Drive, saying it was more scenic. We drove past hovering oaks and thickly needled pines. Sculling teams navigated the river practicing for their competition. Cars whizzed by. I leaned my head back against the seat enjoying the scenery and the company as we made small talk. About a mile or two down the road, Adrian mentioned a picturesque overview of Center City and made a sharp turn onto a side road. While we traveled up a steep hill, I reached into my purse to touch up my lipstick when a whiff of the same cologne I inhaled earlier, so subtle yet so spicy, piqued my interest. "What's that wonderful scent?"

Adrian turned to stare at me. His eyes had changed from bright blue to steely gray. All at once, my lust mutated into fear. I clutched the purse closer. I knew what he was going to say before he said it.

"*Aramis.*"

Instantly struck scared and mute, I had to keep my wits about me if I hoped to get out of this in one piece. With his attention back on the road, I surreptitiously palmed the container of pepper spray I've kept in my purse ever since my mugging.

Gone was the suave, exciting hero of my dreams. Replaced by a reprehensible sociopathic chameleon. He may have played his role to perfection, but I was the one who overlooked clues to his true nature because I wanted to believe in him.

At the top of the hill, he pulled the car to a halt, reached across me and opened my door. "Get out."

By the time I stumbled from the car, he stood at my side, grasping my arm and jerking me toward the edge of the hill. I squirmed, attempting to loosen his grip, but the more I struggled, the tighter he clutched my arm. He dragged me to the rim, overlooking the road below. "Nice view, no?" he hissed through clenched teeth.

I glanced down at the steep drop and went rigid. It didn't look too lovely from my vantage point. "Drew," I croaked. "Don't do this."

He watched me through hooded eyes. "There's only one way you can stop me. Tell me where Rebecca, or should I say Rachel, lives or you're taking the direct route down."

"What if I don't know?"

His sharp laugh sounded ominous. Petrifying. "Don't lie to me, Sarah. You said she's been in contact with you. You know where she's at. I don't want to hurt you, but I will if you don't cooperate with me."

"Like you did Angela?"

"Angela should have left me alone. I wouldn't have harmed her either, but she wouldn't let go. I was afraid she'd expose me to Rachel; get in the way of my plans."

"How about Rachel's husband?"

His sinister stare hardened as did my heart. "Rachel didn't need a husband. She has me. She's been mine since we were kids. I'll never let her go."

"I see. Even if you have to kill me to get to her. And how about the *Aramis* you gave to her uncle at the party? What purpose did that serve?"

"It kept her off my trail for awhile, didn't it? It gave me time to get to know her."

"And that explains why you encouraged her suspiciousness toward Evan, I mean Ethan. You had it all figured out, didn't you? And you still do, even though you're not a doctor, a lawyer, or a chief of Psychology. Are you?"

"No, I'm not."

Curiosity emboldened her. "So how do you finance your activities?"

"Let's just say I've had a couple of benefactors."

"And are any of these benefactors still breathing?"

He wore a stony expression. "What do you think?"

My throat constricted, but I had to stall for time and managed to mutter, "How did you find me anyway?"

His face became a grotesque mask. "Rachel's card file made that easy. And you were kind enough to list the weekend seminar on your website, paving the way for me to meet you. All I had to do was sign up and show up."

He pinched my arm. The face looming above mine flushed fire-engine red with rage. He scared the hell out of me. "Ouch. You're hurting me." He eased a little, just enough to allow me to think, but not enough to allow me to escape. "Tell me something. What would stop you from killing me even if I give you her information? If I were alive, I could warn her before you had a chance to find her. As far as I can see, I'm doomed either way. I might as well die without bringing anyone else along."

"You don't understand. If you say anything to anyone, including Rachel, or the police, I'll hunt you down like an animal and finish you off in the slowest, most painful way possible."

I shivered at the thought, as though I'd suddenly spiked a fever. This man had no conscience. He was more than capable of doing what he said. I had to think fast. "Okay, I'll tell you what you want to know if you promise to spare me."

"You have my word."

"How do I know your word is good?"

He jerked his head toward the hill's rim. "What choice do you have?"

I looked over the precipice at the stunning drop-off. No one could survive the fall. "She's in Baltimore, but I don't know her address. I have it in an office file." I hoped this maneuver would help me stall for time.

"Is she using Ethan's last name?"

"I don't know."

"It would make sense." He scrutinized me. "Are you telling me the truth about Baltimore?"

"Do you think I'd lie when my life depended on it?"

A sneer crossed his lips. "I guess I can check it out, but it doesn't matter one way or the other for you." His fingers gouged my arm and he shoved me closer to the edge.

"What are you doing? You said you'd spare me if I told you Rachel's whereabouts. I have her address at my office. Why do this now?"

He laughed heartily. "And you believed me? I thought you were a highly educated professional. For a doctor you're none too swift."

A further push. The descent loomed long and steep before me. I could picture myself falling, the sensation of weightlessness, the ground telescoping up to meet me. I could feel the wind rushing at me. The velocity increasing, nothing to arrest my fall...until impact. The image knocked the breath out of me. I could barely squeak out, "Don't do this. People must have seen us together at the conference. They can identify you."

"No one saw us leave together. I made sure of that."

I had to stall him off, or I was a dead woman. "Please," I pleaded. "I'll do whatever I can to help you find Rachel."

"You've done enough. I know how to find your office. I can take it from here."

My chest clenched; I couldn't catch my breath. Only one step stood between me and eternity. One more shove and I would somersault over the edge. I raised my hand to my face as though to protect it and pressed on the cylinder's lever, releasing a steady stream of pepper spray into his eyes.

Adrian shouted loud enough to drown out the rush hour traffic. He released my arm to rub his eyes. The shock sent him stumbling sideways. With only a small shove, he lost his balance and slid over the side of the hill in a spray of dirt and debris.

To my surprise, the yelling continued way past the point it should have according to physics. With hammering heart, I peered over the rim and saw him dangling below by the nape of his jacket caught on a tree branch.

Spotting me, he stopped screaming and began to beg. "I need you to help me, Sarah. You know you can't leave me like this. It's not in your nature. I promise if you help me out, I'll never hurt you..."

I began to back away and, as I did, he implored louder and more aggressively. His tone turned belligerent. "Don't leave me. You can't do this. You'll never be able to live with yourself. Help me..."

I spun around to leave, and his words became arrows piercing me.

"Come back here you bitch...don't you dare

leave me hanging here...if I get my hands on you you're a dead cunt..."

I hustled to the car as quickly as my feet would carry me. Once inside, I silently thanked Drew for one thing, leaving the keys in the ignition. Retracing our earlier trip, I pulled onto the East River Drive and headed straight into Center City Philadelphia. The setting sun to the west illuminated the skyline with a supernatural glow. Buildings looked iridescent; their reflections shimmering in the Schuylkill River below. Beyond them skyscrapers reached up to touch the heavens.

I rolled down the window and breathed in the cool evening air. When far enough from Adrian, I'd call the police and direct them to him. In the meantime, I reveled in my newfound power. My sense of mastery. Since Ken left, or maybe long before that, I've felt as if I was at the mercy of men who didn't give a hoot about me. Today I experienced a new freedom and a new happiness.

If I could handle Drew, I could certainly depend on myself to deal with whatever a saner man would send my way. With my foot on the accelerator, I sped up. No one could stop me now.

For once in my life, I didn't feel like a man had the upper hand. I knew I could leave him hanging. And that's exactly what I did.

The End

About the Author

J S Winn earned graduate degrees from the University of Pennsylvania and the University of Metaphysical Sciences. She has one prior novel published in genre, and one play produced by the Actor's Alliance Festival in San Diego. Her poetry has been anthologized in, For the Love of Writing, by the San Diego Writer's Workshop in 2011. Her play, Gotcha!, was selected for a reading at the Village Arts Theater in Carlsbad, California, May 2012.

She presently lives by the beach in San Diego County, California.

Made in the USA
San Bernardino, CA
12 February 2014